I'd like to dedicate this work to Jean, with all of my thanks and love for her continued support and belief in me and my writing. Without you, where would it all be?

Author's note

'The Accursed Dawn' is the prequel to 'The Well of Constant Despair' and sets the scene for all that is to follow. It is not necessary, however, to read this story before 'The Well...' as both can be enjoyed in their own right.

Certain scenes within this tale are particularly gruesome and may not be deemed suitable for younger readers, or those of a nervous disposition.

PART ONE

ONE

When we moved in, I was struck by how high the ceilings were, but nothing more. Not at first. The rooms were big. So were the windows. And it was unbelievably cold at night...but nothing else, nothing that you would say was unusual. Not really.

But then, after a week or so, I heard the voices and from that moment everything began to change.

I'm looking back to a time when life was simple. Now I'm older, with my life so complicated, I can see that now. But at the time...well, you never do really appreciate things when you're younger. What happened to me all those years ago certainly changed my life, changed who I was. It's coloured the way I deal with situations, people, places. How could it not? No one could experience those things and come away unscathed. On balance, I'm hoping I've turned into a better person because of it, certainly a wiser one. I'm more open-minded, have a greater ability to see the other side of things. I'm glad about that. But deep down, if I think about it hard enough, if none of it had happened, perhaps I would be happier, certainly safer. I still have nightmares you see, that's the *real* problem. So, although I've learned a lot about the world and how people's minds work, I've caught glimpses of a darker side that is unsavoury and disturbing. And that frightens me. Even now. This retelling is going to be a form of catharsis for me, a way of dispelling the demons that come and visit me in my dreams. We all have those, I suppose. In the dead of night, as we lie alone in our beds, with only the dark to keep us company. The difference with me is, they're real. Not illusions. As real as the world, the air, the sky. Demons. And soon I'll

1

have to face them again. So, given all of that, let me take you back to when I was younger to a time when I didn't know about such things and I was happy in my ignorance. A time, however, that was still fraught with uncertainty and tinged with sadness. And touched by death.

About three months before my fifteenth birthday my entire family had packed up and moved. It had happened incredibly quickly. One day I was in my old school, with my old friends, doing all the normal stuff I'd always done; the next thing I knew I was sitting at the kitchen table listening to Mum and Dad telling Christy and me how 'great' it was going to be. I didn't quite get that. How was it going to be 'great' if it meant leaving all my friends? And why hadn't my parents told me before, given me some sort of warning? I mean, didn't I have any *rights*? Why was it that I'm always the last to hear anything?"

"Because you're an insignificant little squirt," said Christy in that superior voice of hers. I just looked at her. Life was pretty cool for Christy and was about to get even cooler. She'd finished with school, having completed her 'A' levels and done really well. She was off to university...but me, I still had years and years and years of studying left to do! How was I going to cope?

But none of that mattered, of course. The decision had been made – we were going and that was that!

My good friend Russell came to see me on the day we were due to leave. We didn't really say very much. I suppose we both felt we had so much to say and so little time to say it... but neither of us knew how to start. So we ended up saying hardly anything. We just sat in

2

my empty room, the room where we had played so many times in the past. Scalextric, toy soldiers, Action Men. Fun times. Times which, I dare say, neither of us ever thought would end. Now we gazed blankly at the bare carpet. So many memories, so many happy moments. We exchanged a knowing glance and, although neither of us did, we both felt like crying. When it was time, silently we got up and went downstairs. I stood at the front door and said goodbye, then on impulse I threw my arms around him and gave him the biggest hug in the world. My best friend. My only *true* friend.

Later, when he'd gone, I sat in my old room again, alone, and did quietly cry. It was the worst day of my life.

We loaded up the car and as I sat in the back seat, waiting for Dad to give the house a quick 'once over' as he called it, I looked up and down my old street. Over there was the bus stop where Nan used to stand, waiting for the Number 9. It was always the same ritual from Mum, 'Have you got your purse, your hanky, your glasses case?' Nan was eighty years of age, but she still used to go off to work every Saturday morning. She'd been doing that forever. Then one Saturday she couldn't get up out of bed. No one could get her up. She'd died.

I missed Nan. I missed that ritual. And now I was going to miss that bus stop.

Further down was the little chip-shop, the one we always went to on Friday nights. Friday night was fish and chip night. Another ritual, but what a lovely one! We'd always had a chippy in our road. It had closed down for a short while for 'redecorating', but it soon reopened. My favourite was the liver and onion dinner. I can taste it now! Then, without any warning, the place had closed down completely. Dad told us it was because the owners had gone bankrupt. The shop was still empty. No more Friday night ritual. No more liver and onion dinners. There were other chip-shops, only a few minutes away, but none of them were as good.

Across the road was where Mr and Mrs Gill used to live. Mr Gill was a wonderful old bloke! He had the best laughing face I'd ever seen! All lined and chiselled, his face was a museum of emotions, but the deepest cuts had been made from sheer fun. I loved him. He used to tell me stories about the War. Thrilling stories; he'd been at D-Day, seen some of his mates being blown up by booby-trapped trees and bushes. When he talked about those things his voice would drop to a low whisper. But then, almost instantly, he'd bring his face up and his eyes would be sparkling again. Dad always said he was just a silly little man who had all his brains jumbled up, but I think that Dad was secretly jealous of him. Dad hadn't done any of the things Mr Gill had. And Dad didn't have the same sort of face. Dad's was a serious face, probably due to his job. *Bank manager.* God, how dull is that? Anyway, I thought Mr Gill was great. He was only a little man, but *so* funny. He taught me loads of different card games. Then his wife suddenly became very ill. I remember the ambulance taking her away; then, the next day, Mr Gill coming home on his own. I wanted to go and ask him how everything was, but Mum said that I shouldn't. So Nan went to see him. Mrs Gill had died. It was all very sad, all very shocking. I was told that I should stay away for a while. So I did. Two weeks later, Mr Gill also passed away.

I suddenly realized, sitting in that seat, that actually I was surrounded by the most awful collection of memories you could imagine. Everywhere I looked there was sadness, despair, loss. And here I was feeling depressed! I should have felt elated that I was leaving it all behind. What an opportunity this was – putting the past inside a dark cupboard and throwing away the key.

Nevertheless, despite it all, I had a fondness for the place that went deep. I'd grown up in this street, walked the pavements everyday, watched it as it changed. Even in my short life, I'd seen so many things. Clearly, I felt I was going to miss it, but this may have been because I didn't know anything else. It's strange that, isn't it, how you become comfortable with what you know, how you accept everything that's thrown at you without question? If it had been up to me, I would probably never have even thought about leaving. Now that I was, it was becoming clear to me that I should be looking forward, not back. There was one big thing, though. Most of all, I'd miss our house. Our small, friendly, warm house. Home. A friend. And in the back seat of our car, like some sad, sick pathetic little wimp, I began to cry again.

"Oh for goodness sake!" spat Christy, elbowing me in the ribs. "Just grow up and get over it."

I glared at her through red, swollen eyes, "But I'm going to miss so much." I dragged the back of my hand across my nose. "Aren't you going to miss anything? What about your friends?"

"Not really. I hate this town, it's so dull. Anyway, Angie's going to Lancaster Uni with me, remember?"

I hadn't remembered, and the news only caused me greater anguish. It was *so* unfair. I'd have to face all of it alone. New street, new house, new school. It was going to be hell on earth and life wouldn't be the same for months...perhaps even years! Bitter, angry, sad, all of those emotions bubbling up together inside me. Regardless of what Christy or anyone thought, I couldn't hold it in any longer. I put my head in my hands and cried and cried and cried.

TWO

It was a strange looking place. When we pulled up in the car I first of all thought that Dad had taken a wrong turning, or perhaps had just stopped for a rest. But no, this was it. Faceless, characterless, a white building, with black windows and green doors. If I had to think of one word to describe it, I'd use clinical. Like a hospital.

How right I was!

We unloaded the car and as we struggled with the biggest cases, a man stepped out from the building. I took to him immediately. He was a big man with a happy grin in a happy face and he waddled like a duck. He had a mop of tight, curly hair, but it was that face that I took to straight away. It was a really interesting face, as if someone had popped it in their mouth, chewed it up, then spat it out again, all crumpled and misshapen! He was all red and blotchy, chubby cheeked and deep dimpled. His name, when he introduced himself, was Stan Hedges and he was the caretaker of the little block of flats into which we were moving.

He showed us to our flat. It was spacious, and all the furniture was modern and brand-spanking new. Provided by the bank, so Dad explained. My room was vast. As I stood in the doorway and looked around, I wondered how I could fill it with all my stuff. The floor space was almost as big as our entire house back in my home town!

I went over to the window and looked out. From here, at the back of the block, I could see that there was a whole range of similar blocks all assembled around an inner courtyard. This was where most people parked their cars. There weren't that many cars there when I first looked, so I guessed that perhaps there weren't that many people living in the complex.

Christy walked in and tutted loudly.

"This is much bigger than my room, you squirt."

I gave a patient little sigh. "That's because you're going off in a few weeks – to your precious university."

"Oh yeah...I forgot. Free at last...well, free from you anyway."

"Thanks Christy. So nice to know you care."

"What you looking at?" She came over and peered out into the courtyard. She shivered slightly. "I don't like this place."

"You don't? Why not?"

"Dunno...it has a nasty *atmosphere*. Haven't you picked up on it?"

I thought for a moment. The place was certainly different. It was...*odd*, but I wouldn't have said 'nasty'. But then Christy thought 'Bill and Ben' was nasty.

I shook my head. "No. It's just a bit strange, like it used to be something else."

"Yeah, that's what I mean. It's full of ghosts!" And with that she breezed out, tossing her hair as she went.

I frowned at what she'd said. Funny word to use, 'ghosts'. I was soon to discover how prophetic that word was to be.

Mum made us chip butties and we all sat round the big kitchen table and munched our way through them. Delicious! Someone, probably from the bank, had provided some basic food stuffs for our arrival – bread, butter, jam, tea and coffee. Down by the fridge was a rack with some vegetables. But Mum didn't feel much like cooking lots, so she just did the chips. We could have gone somewhere to eat, but we didn't know our way around and Stan had wandered off somewhere. As it was, the chip butties were fine – better than fine, they were great!

8

Later I started to unpack some of my things. The removal van was supposed to have followed us, but there had been a problem with the crossing from the mainland and it was delayed for twenty-four hours. I still had a lot of my personal things with me, so I wasn't too worried. I had my comics and my annuals. I'd also managed to stash a bag of soldiers in the bottom of one of my cases, so that was okay. Dad had bought a huge Vauxhall estate car, so there had been plenty of room for our cases, which was just as well really.

It was beginning to get dark when I flopped down on my bed. It was hard that bed, and I could feel the springs in the mattress. It was the first little negative thing I'd found. But I soon forgot it as I flipped through my copy of *The Hotspur.* I loved that comic, it was my absolute favourite. Before long I was lost in a wonderful tale of red-skins battling with trappers in the frozen wastes of the far north of America.

I must have drifted off to sleep because when I heard something, I sat up with a start, and found myself all tucked in under the bedclothes. That would have been Mum, bless her. A real fusspot, just like any mum the world over. Not my real mum, but nevertheless where would I be without her?

Reaching out, I remembered where the light switch was, but as my fingers crawled along the wall searching for it, I froze.

There was something in my room, something moving.

It was this noise that had woken me.

The tiniest of footfalls, almost as if something, or someone, was creeping across the floor. I sat there, poised in the act of switching on the light, and waited. My mouth fell open, allowing me to hear a little more clearly and I tried to slow my breathing right down. But it was difficult. A feeling of unease grew inside me. There *was* a presence in the room, I could feel it. Over in the far corner. I forced myself to look in that direction, but I couldn't make anything out in the gloom. As I said, the room was big and that far corner was as black as...I regretted using the word almost as soon as it popped into my head...*hell.*

There was a breath then.

A single, rattling sigh, full of despair and woe. Very low but very clear. It was terrifying.

By now I was rigid with fear, clinging on to my bedclothes, pushing myself back against the headboard, hardly able to think straight. Panic was beginning to overwhelm me. I wanted to shout out, but I couldn't. My voice was gripped with icy, steel fingers, my entire body unable to react. Terror had mastered me.

Sitting there, in that dark room, unable to do anything but stare wide-eyed towards that corner, I wondered what would happen next. Whatever it was, this presence, I had a feeling that it did not mean me harm. And yet, because it *was* a presence, something unknown, I felt terribly afraid. I couldn't come to terms with these conflicting emotions, so slowly, painfully slowly, I slipped down beneath the covers and pulled them up over my head and lay there, as still as I could, trembling.

The minutes passed. There was no repeat of the sigh, no further sounds of movement. Only that feeling that there was something there, watching me, perhaps waiting. But waiting for what, I had no idea. So I closed my eyes and tried to think more rationally.

Rational thought did not come easily, only a swirl of imagined horrors. Most of these had to do with bug-eyed monsters, fat, slobbering things, lurking in corners, slavering through wet, slack lips, drooling and moaning constantly. When I snapped open my eyes, light filtered in through the curtains. It was morning and I had been dreaming.

Amazing how normal that room appeared in daylight. I sat up, rubbing my eyes and stretching. I peered into the corner. Had that been a dream also? Had I imagined that sigh, that dreadful, woeful sigh?

Swinging my legs out from under the bedclothes, I stood up, crossed over to the curtains and pulled them back. I didn't know what time it was, but when I saw someone, a blonde-haired woman, getting into her car and driving away, I guessed it must have been somewhere around eight. People were getting up and going off to work. Another day. Nothing unusual.

I padded over to my door and opened it, about to go down to the bathroom for a wash and scrub. Then I heard it and I stopped.

I turned my head back into my room. Over on the far wall was my chest of drawers. I hadn't begun to put anything in them yet, I had the whole day after all. But as I looked I saw something which I knew couldn't be happening.

The drawer, third from the top, opened on its own. Something unseen, invisible, had slowly pulled it out and it sat there, waiting.

But waiting for what?

I gave a cry and ran, like a whippet, to the bathroom, slamming the door shut behind me, pushing across the little bolt. I stepped back into the room, facing the door, not daring to believe what had happened, my breath coming in great gulps.

I didn't move from that room until Dad came along and began to hammer on the door. It was only seven in the morning, *what the hell was all this noise about?*

If only I'd had an answer for him, I would have told him.

THREE

I drifted through those first few days of school. We'd only been in the house for a short while, the weekend going far too quickly. The last weekend of the summer holidays. Monday came and flashed by. I got up extra early to try and make it last as long as I could, but nothing would stop those clock hands from moving around.

Of course, I lived in dread of something else happening. Voices, sounds, movements. Fortunately, nothing did. What had happened that first night was not repeated and the drawers remained closed. As time passed I began to suspect that it really had all been in my mind. Probably because I was tired after all the travelling. My imagination was always 'over-active'. That's what Mum used to think. 'Too many comic books,' she'd say, 'Too much time spent in make-believe!' Perhaps she was right.

Tuesday was fairly dull. I hadn't slept much the night before; worried sick. But as the day arrived and dragged by I asked myself what I'd actually been worried about. School was school, whether it was in a city, or here, on a little island stuck in the middle of the English Channel.

I came home, loaded down with homework, to find that the removal van had at last shown up, the men busy unloading our personal effects. They were a rough looking lot, those men, hardly saying a word.

They were putting some boxes in my room when I staggered in. A big man was standing there, hands on hips, looking out of the window towards the courtyard. He started when I came in, a guilty look on his face. But I mustered up a smile, then a shrug. "Funny place," I said.

He looked at me for a long time, probably trying to sum me up. Most people couldn't. I keep myself to myself most of the time. I try not to let much slip.

"Yeah," he grumbled, "but not funny ha-ha. You know about this place then?"

I shook my head, frowning a little. Perhaps here was an answer to what I'd seen, and heard – if, indeed, I'd seen or heard anything!

"Well...perhaps you should."

He nudged past me without another word, and I was left wondering what he was getting at.

After tea – mince and onions – I settled back into my bedroom and began to unpack some of the boxes. I was mostly interested in becoming reacquainted with some of my toys, but Mum had ordered me to start filling my drawers with clothes. It was something to which I hadn't been looking forward, mostly because of what had happened. Now, filling the first and second with socks and underwear, I came to the third one down. The one that had mysteriously opened of its own accord. Or, possibly, the one I had *imagined* had done that.

I pulled it open.

It was almost the same as the others. I say 'almost' because it was lined with an old, worn piece of wallpaper. Floral designed, very heavy. Flock I think it's called. Once it was probably perfumed. I began to wonder where all this stuff had come from, who had chosen it, supplied it. Someone from Dad's bank no doubt. I had supposed everything would have been new, but I had been wrong in that assumption. Someone had owned these drawers before. And I didn't really want drawer-liners, so I pulled it out without a second thought.

14

Lying there, hidden for goodness knows how long, was a single piece of paper. It looked like a letter, or more accurately a note. Hand written in a small, neat hand. I picked it up and began to read it. As I did, my blood began to run cold.

'My good friend,
Now that I have your attention, perhaps you would be so good as to lend me your services.
We have much to do; do not waver.
As you discover the truth, do not dismiss, do not shirk. The truth will out.
Find the cellar, my good friend, and begin to put right the wrongs that have been done.'

I flopped down on the edge of the bed and read through the curious words again. Was I the 'good friend'? Whoever had written this, and there was no indication on the paper who had, they were trying to guide me into discovering something. Something, but what? Dangerous? Wrong? *...begin to put right the wrongs that have been done.* I looked into the distance, gazing out through the window. I couldn't see anything from where I sat, but I knew what was out there nonetheless. The courtyard and other flats just like ours. What was this place, what did this message mean...and where was the cellar?

Whilst thinking all of this through, I'd screwed up the paper in my hand. I now put it on top of the chest of drawers and smoothed it out again. Then I went to the bathroom and threw water over my face. A dread fear was making itself felt. The pushing out of that drawer by an unseen hand had not been my imagination after all. Someone, or something, had been trying to tell me to look inside. And now, I had. That letter could only be the beginning.

I returned to my room, still rubbing my face with a towel. The cellar? What had the letter said...I had to find it? Where was I supposed to start? Perhaps the note would give me some sort of a clue, a starting place.

But when I went over to the chest of drawers to read through it once more, it had gone.

As if it had never existed.

FOUR

It was close to four thirty when I got home and saw her for the first time. The rain had come down in sheets throughout the day, but now the sun was out, warm and still surprisingly strong. There was a heat haze in the courtyard and when she walked across the gravel towards her parents' car she looked for all the world like she was stepping out of a television advert. She was stunning, tall and blonde, the kind of girl who turned heads. She certainly turned mine. But it wasn't her good looks that had caught my attention. It was the fact that she was carrying a tennis racquet.

Mum was a member of a tennis club back home. I'd gone down to watch her in a tournament and caught the bug myself. It was that simple. I'd played as much as I could since, trying my best to emulate Rod Lever, not succeeding obviously, but doing reasonably okay.

So, the fact that I had a neighbour who played, one who just happened to be good looking, well, it set me to thinking of how I could fashion together some sort of 'accidental' meeting.

Later on, as we sat around for tea, I seized an appropriate moment to announce to everyone what I'd experienced with the sounds and the note. I finished with the letter's mysterious disappearance.

"It...*disappeared*?" Dad paused in his munching of a lamb chop, his fork poised just inches from his mouth. He raised an eyebrow and looked at me. I knew that look all too well.

As if to confirm my worst fears, Christy chimed in, "What an idiot you are Max! At least if you're going to make up some wild story, make it half-believable."

"You have a great imagination," said Mum. "You really should write these stories down."

"Yeah, but not very *exciting*, is it?" Christy was laughing now.

Dad joined in, "Why not add a monster or two, or a ghoul climbing through your window."

That was it. Everyone was laughing. So I sat there, finished my tea and decided to stay quiet.

I would have to find someone else in whom to confide.

Of course, this was easier said than done. I've always been naturally shy. My mum would have said 'painfully', and that could be a better description, because I always felt as if I were in pain whenever I spoke to someone new. Usually, I would become terribly self-conscious, as if I were imposing myself on someone else and that they would very soon tire of me, resenting my intrusion into their lives. People rarely listened to me and this only conspired to cement my own feelings of inadequacy still deeper. I could be sitting in a room, together with some others, and during a lull in a conversation I might utter an observation or a remark and nobody would register it. Or, perhaps much more infuriating, someone would ask me a question and, as I began to give my answer, they would look away and talk about something else! I could never understand that. So, consequently I retreated into my shell. That 'over-productive' imagination became my true friend.

So, when I stumbled up to Stan as he stooped down to clear out some fallen leaves from one of the drains, I had to stand there for a long time before he noticed me. I'd rehearsed my opening line. I always did that, it gave me more confidence. "Hello, Stan. I wonder if you could help me."

But Stan then did something quite unexpected. It completely threw me, when he said,
"Of course I can Max – what's the problem?"

He stared at me, his big cheery face cracked into a wide grin. Was he serious, did he actually mean what he'd said? I blinked. He laughed. "Yes?"

Shaking my head quickly, I managed to stutter my first few words before I became slightly more confident, "I-er-had a favour, sort of, to ask you, if that's okay. I mean...if that's okay."

He stood there, looking at me. Then threw out his arms. "Well? What is it?"

"Cellar, Stan. Do you know if there's a cellar?"

All of a sudden, he stopped smiling.

FIVE

A few years earlier, Aunty Peg had arrived from Ireland. I'd never met her before. I knew about her, but I'd never seen her in the flesh, so to speak. She was my Nan's sister and had come over for the funeral. She'd flown into Speke Airport (it's not called that now, of course, John Lennon Airport is its current name) and had made a fairly slow journey to our house. But when she arrived she was like a breath of fresh air. Everyone was feeling pretty miserable at that time. Nan had gone downhill very rapidly, within just a few days and we were all still suffering from the shock of it all. When Aunty Peg came through the door, all of that negativity and depression was almost instantly replaced by a sense of optimism and hope.

Aunty Peg was a clairvoyant.

I'd never thought about such things before then. Once, some years back, Nan had told me about her, but I could hardly remember anything that was said, except for that one word *clairvoyant.* It stuck in my head. At that time I had absolutely no idea what it was, but then in school one day we were having a discussion with Mr Clarke, the English teacher. Mr Clarke always liked having discussions and debates. It was all so he didn't have to mark our work, but none of us complained. Talking about anything was much better than answering questions in an English comprehension test!

Clarkey, as we called him, had had some experience of 'spiritualists', or so he said, and wanted to know what we thought. We had to get in little groups, come up with some good arguments, then present our case to the rest of the class. All I could think about was Aunty Peg. We had two days to get it sorted. When I got home and spoke to Nan, she'd been a little reluctant to say anything. But when she did, the flood gates opened.

"When we were very little, growing up in Limerick with my father and mother, we had no idea. No idea at all. When the War came and my brothers went off to fight, that was when it all started. Nineteen seventeen. That was when my first brother, Michael, was killed. He'd always been my father's favourite. He was a sergeant-major in the army, my father was. I can still hear him now, barking out his orders on the parade ground...Well, he was never the same again after Michael. Then, a few months later, Valentine was killed. Reggie came home in early nineteen eighteen. He'd been shot in the face. Dreadful he was."

I remember her sitting there, in her little room surrounded by all the memories of her past life, staring at the photographs she kept on the sideboard. Her eyes were wet. It was strange, but her brothers had died in order. First Michael, the eldest, then Valentine the middle one. Reggie, the youngest, horribly disfigured. He had to go into a nursing home, didn't come out until the nineteen-twenties. He'd been affected by it, "terribly affected," Nan had said. Well, who wouldn't! Being shot in the face...

After a short while, her memories faded away and she returned to her story, "My father came home from the Front. He'd seen Michael laid-out, dressed in what he said were *long johns.* He'd become angry, apparently. Insisted that he be dressed in his uniform before they put him in the ground. Which they did, of course. Nobody ever argued with my father.

"It was sometime later, maybe six months, just after Valentine was killed, that Peggy went into some sort of fit. I remember it really well. I'd just got home from my job at the solicitors – I was a clerk then – and we were

21

sitting down for our evening meal, mother ladling out the potatoes and father cutting the joint...Suddenly, Peggy jumps up in her chair, stiff as a rod, and her eyes rolled up at the back of her head. We thought she was having a fit. Epilepsy or something. Father ran to her side when she started shaking. Mother was crying, it was awful. We'd suffered so much, you see. My brothers...all gone. So, naturally, we were all a little afraid. Fourteen she was. Barely out of braids!"

"What happened, Nan?"

"That was it – nothing! After a few minutes, she returned to her old self. She didn't seem to know what had happened, got a little angry when Mother kept quizzing her about it. The next day Mother took her to the doctor, but he could find nothing wrong. How could he? There *was* nothing wrong.

"A few days later, a Saturday it was, we were sitting in the parlour. It was early evening and the sun had just gone down. Father was looking through the newspaper. By then, he rarely spent any time at the barracks. I think he'd been given compassionate leave, but I can't be sure."

"What's that?"

"Time off, simplest said. When things get too much. Father had always been a very strong man, very correct and strict. But after the boys had been killed," she shook her head sadly, another memory washing over her, "He was never the same. Became very quiet, very withdrawn. He found it difficult to drill the new recruits, all so young and fresh-faced. I found him crying once...my father!" She sat in her chair, her liver-spotted hands drumming out an indistinct tune on the arms.

"So, what happened that Saturday night?"

"Eh? Oh...yes...We were all sitting in the parlour, when Peggy goes into another fit. That's the only word I can use to describe it. We were all scared. Mother crying again, Father kneeling down next to her, stroking her head, trying to calm her down. Then, she shoots out her arm and pushes father away. He almost fell onto his back. Then it started. My God, looking back..." Her eyes filled up with tears. I should have told her to stop then, the memories were obviously too painful. But I didn't. I was so intent on hearing her story. I just sat and waited, leaning forward in my chair, hardly daring to breathe. "She spoke. But...this is so *strange*...she spoke, but it wasn't her voice. It was Michael's."

"*Michael's*? Your brother?"

A single nod. "We were all struck dumb at that point. I felt like I'd been punched. I couldn't move. Mother put both her hands over her mouth and began to rock backwards and forwards. And father...he sat there, on the carpet, his eyes wide. 'You mustn't worry,' the voice said, 'I know you're sad, but you mustn't worry. We're fine. Val and me. Fine. You mustn't worry. We love you all.' And slowly, very slowly, Peggy began to recover, her eyes blinking crazily, and she looked around, startled to find us all like that, craning forward, mouths opened, stunned."

"Did she say anything?"

"No. not a word. She had no memory of any of it. Well, from that moment, these 'visits' became more and more. But not from my brothers. They never returned. Almost as if they'd done what they had to do, I suppose. No, other people came through. Word got round the town and fairly soon she was doing regular meetings. Séances they were called. We had to make the parlour into a sort of meeting room, putting the big dining table in there, covered with Mother's best linen.

"Father was furious, of course, but couldn't do anything to stop it. He'd go down to the army bar on

Saturdays, something he'd never done before. Never drank to excess, but he did drink. And Mother, she seemed so much brighter. As if the words that had come through had given her hope. She was like that up to the day she died. In fact, I remember her saying to me, about two or three days before she passed, 'I'll be seeing my boys again soon!' Excited, she was. Can you believe that? Excited about dying..."

"And Aunty Peggy? What did she do?"

"Carried on. When we finally came over here, to Liverpool, she stayed on in Ireland. She'd met some chap. That was...ooh, *years* later. Anyway, she's still there. Married. No children of her own, though. Funny that. She'd always loved children. Always playing with her dollies, pushing prams, all of that. But never had one of her own."

And so it was that when Aunty Peg came over for the funeral, as soon as she saw me, she came straight over to me and put her hand on my head and looked at me as if I was something from outer-space. "Oh my God," she muttered, "You've got the gift."

She came over all pale and had to sit down. Mum gave her a sherry.

Me. I had the gift.

The gift being, I could talk to the dead.

SIX

Around two or three days after I'd spoken ... the cellar, he came up to me and took me int... looking furtive as if he didn't want to be seen ta...., me. I felt a little nervous, not knowing what he wa... but then he smiled and those feelings went. "I've bee... thinking. About what you asked. I might be able to help. But, you need to know something."

I frowned. "What is it, Stan?"

He shook his head, "Not from me. I've got a name for you. You need to talk to him. About this place. He's very good. Local historian. Written a book all about it – well, about most of the stuff that went on, not just here." He pressed a piece of paper in my hand. "But not a word to Mum and Dad, eh?"

I wondered about that. Why didn't he want me to talk to them? I shrugged, nodded my head, and took the paper. When he hurried off, I unfolded it. There was a single name and an address scrawled over it. That evening, I went down into the town centre and knocked on the door.

Peter Mumford was a very learned looking man. By that, I mean he always wore a suit, with a waistcoat, and his glasses were suspended by a cord which he had looped around his neck. His ties were always bright and colourful and looked totally out of place against his dark jacket. When I first called, it was his housemaid who answered, and she didn't look too pleased to be answering the door to me! She told me that I should ask for a meeting in writing. I let my chin drop onto my chest and, groaning inside, I went to walk away. If it hadn't been for Stan, I would never have called and now

...ing made to feel like some sort of lesser person, *of the earth* as most people would say.

However, as I turned to go, a new voice called me back. I turned to see, for the first time, Peter Mumford. 'It's all right, Mrs Jenkins! This is the *new boy*, lives up at the hospital."

She looked at me with a new understanding. "Oh. Really?" She didn't seem too impressed, all the same.

Mr Mumford came out onto the doorstep and placed a reassuring hand on my shoulder. "Hedges put you on to me? He told me he was going to."

"Stan? The caretaker. Yes, yes he did."

Mrs Jenkins huffed, as if the mention of Stan's name was an even worse offence than my being there!

"Well, I'm rather busy right now, but you're more than willing to call around mid-week. Same time?"

"Wednesday?"

"Wednesday is perfect."

But Wednesday was *ages* away! As I tramped back home, feeling more than a little deflated, I didn't know then that something was about to happen that would cheer me up no end.

SEVEN

Her smile was pearly-white and I couldn't take eyes away from her mouth as she spoke. "You must the family that's just moved in," she said.

"Part of them."

"Huh?" She frowned for a second, then smiled, "Oh, I see. Yeah. But you are, aren't you?"

"Yes."

I've never been particularly good at talking to girls. Always becoming very self-conscious, I usually dry up after the first 'hello'. It was the same this time. I kept running my hand over my chin and nose, thinking that perhaps I had a spot there, or something. She didn't seem to notice, but I felt sure I had, so I kept rubbing.

"I'm off to tennis. Do you play tennis?"

These were the words I was longing to hear! She had a big holdall with her and sticking out of it were two handles. I nodded enthusiastically. "Yes."

She laughed. "Not very talkative are you. What's your name?"

"Max. Maximilian, but I'm known as Max."

"*Maximilian?* Wow, what a great name!" She was the only person who had ever said that. Most simply broke up in fits of laughter. "I'm Clarissa, but you can call me Clari." She put out her hand and I shook it. It was warm and dry, with a fair bit of strength behind it. That would have come from her tennis. "So, you pla ~"

I nodded, trying to think of something to Finally, I managed to dredge up, "My Mum's qu player. I think she's going to join the club." I s again. "Me too."

"Wow. Well that's great. We'll have to ha game." She thought for a moment and was abo speak again when her mother — I assumed it wa

r – came out from her house and crossed the
yard. She grinned when she saw me. "Hello. Who's
, Clarissa?"

"His name is Max, and he plays tennis."

"Really? That's good – we could do with some
males down at the club. Are you any good, Max?"

"Not bad."

"Well, 'not bad' is pretty good in our circles! Why
don't you come along and watch us. See how useless we
are."

I gaped at her, then turned to Clari, who was
nodding her head enthusiastically.

"I'll just go and tell my mum," I gushed, and ran
off to do just that.

As it turned out, Clari was excellent at tennis, making
shots and running returns that the everyday club-player
wouldn't even have dreamt of attempting. I was
impressed. Too shy to go into details all I managed was
a somewhat unimaginative, "You're good." Pathetic
really. Nevertheless, it received a smile and that made it
worthwhile.

Later, as we rode home in the back of her mother's
Riley Kestrel, her mum asked me how long I'd been
staying at the flat.

"Just over a week," I said.

"You like it?"

"It's okay. Much the same as anywhere else, I
suppose."

"Really? I've never heard anyone say that before.
You'll soon grow to love it. Everyone does."

Clari shot me a glance, and I could tell by that
simple look that she, for one, didn't entirely agree with
her mother's sentiments.

We turned into the courtyard and when we got out, Clari said, "You must come and meet Aneeka. Do you like horses?"

"Yes." She was making a real effort with me. I couldn't understand why, but I was emotionally mature enough to realize that if I didn't start reciprocating she would probably give up on me. So, I pulled in a breath and plunged straight in. "I used to ride – pony-trekking I think it's called – most weeks during the summer."

Clari raised her eyebrows, "Wow...me too! Max, we have *so* much in common!"

"I haven't been for ages, though. It was getting too expensive – tennis sort of took over."

She shook her head, still smiling. "I don't believe this...that is *exactly* why I gave it up!"

I pressed my lips together, feeling terribly self-conscious. I could feel my cheeks beginning to glow bright red. This was more than I'd ever said to any girl, ever!

"Do you want to come in for some tea?" It was her mum, slamming the boot of her car, laden down with sports bags.

I looked from Clari and back to her mum. I could feel the sweat breaking out on my brow. "I-er-think I should be getting back. Thanks anyway."

"That's okay. Why don't you come round next weekend? We could make a day of it. You have your own racquet?"

"Yes. Dunlop."

She seemed impressed. "Well, that's it then. Next weekend it is." She gathered up her various bags and began to move away. Clari stood looking at me for a moment longer, then she smiled, raised her hand in a little wave, and she ran off to join her mother.

I stood watching them as they crunched over the gravel towards the door of their house. At the door, she turned and waved.

I hadn't felt so happy for a long time.

Later on, Mum seemed to notice my mood. "You're cheerful," she said. She was right, I was. Sitting at the dining room table, just finishing off my homework, grinning like an ape and feeling on top of the world! Who cares about homework? Like everybody, I never did my homework until last thing Sunday night. I'd had my bath and *Sunday Night At The London Palladium* was on the television. My stomach was already churning at the thought of school the next day. I hated Sundays with a passion, but I had the beginning of a new hope – perhaps if playing tennis with Clari was to become a regular thing, then Sundays wouldn't be so bad!

"Max!" I looked up. My mum was laughing. "You're miles away."

"Can't be your school work, can it Max?" Dad was sitting, his legs stretched out, watching Norman Vaughan putting his thumb up. He laughed out loud when the comedian cracked a joke.

"No...just thinking."

"What about?"

"Things. Mum...do you think it's possible for me to take up riding again?"

"Riding? What, here?"

"Yeah...not like before, not every week, just now and again."

"I suppose so. Is there someone who does it here?"

"I think so. Clari told me about—"

"Eh!" spouted Dad, "There's that name again – you'll be getting all cosy with that girl soon."

"*Da-d*!"

"Leave him alone, Jeff. He's only been to watch her play tennis. It's nice," she turned to me and smiled. "It's nice, Max."

Dad smirked. "Yeah. You'd know." There was an edge to his voice that I'd never heard before. I didn't understand why, not then.

At the thought of Clari, I felt my cheeks glowing again, so I buried my head in my maths book and tried for about the hundredth time to work out how to draw a straight line graph using a mind-boggling equation to discover the co-ordinates.

I lay in bed, gazing up at the ceiling, trying to draw faces in the cracked design. As I tried, one face really began to take place. It was a girl's face, longhaired, full mouth, a little like Clari. I turned over. This was beginning to get silly. I was becoming obsessive! Even so, after about thirty seconds, I turned over and searched out the face gain. There it was. But as I looked, I realized it wasn't Clari. The hair was a little too long. Same age, possibly...then as I looked more closely, unbelievably the mouth turned upwards into a smile.

EIGHT

The days dragged, as they always do during the week, but then Wednesday finally came and I found myself outside Peter Mumford's door again. This time, the housekeeper let me in without a word. I stood in the darkened hallway, looking at the framed pictures that ran along the opposite wall. Hunting scenes, mostly. But there was one which held my attention. A simple landscape, no doubt of where we lived, the sea a huge expanse of unbroken blue. A few birds flew across the sky, and a little boat was in the harbour. I stepped closer. There was something else. The more I looked, the more clear it became. On top of the main rise, a hump, like a tiny little hillock. But not natural. Man-made.

"Mass grave."

I turned, startled. Peter Mumford smiled down at me. "Sorry, I was..." I shrugged, a little embarrassed.

"No problem...Max, is it?"

"Yes, how—"

"Stan, don't you remember? He told me you'd been asking him some questions about where you're staying."

"Of course."

"Come into the parlour. Mrs Jenkins is making us some tea. Do you like tea-cakes? She makes the most delicious tea-cakes you could imagine..."

After I'd set my empty tea-cup down on the little table, Mr Mumford sat back, hands intertwined over his ample stomach. He was smiling. "So, Max. You want to know about the hospital?"

"Hospital? No, it wasn't the hospital I was asking about, it was—"

He held up his hand, "Sorry. My fau... should explain. The flat you're staying in – the who... complex in fact, used to be a hospital. Around ten ye... no it was all converted into flats. One or two of the... rds haven't been finished yet, but they will be. One day.

"I see. I had no idea."

"No reason why you should – the builders have done an excellent job."

" A *hospital*? But...what sort of hospital was it?"

"Ah...well, that's the whole point of the story, you see. History. We've got lots of history in this place. Like that painting you were looking at."

"Mass grave, you said."

"Yes. Well it was. All the bodies have been laid to rest elsewhere, most of them back in their homeland."

"Homeland? I don't understand."

"During the War, Max. During the War, foreign prisoners were brought here to work. Forced-labour. The term *slave-labour* is a very emotive one, but that essentially is what they were. Nothing new in that, of course. Prisoners taken in war have always been put to work by the victors. But this, this was something more. It was their treatment, you see, which made it so terrible in many eyes. So *unforgivable.* Essentially, they were starved to death, forced to work until they dropped. There were always plenty more to replace them, you see. Plenty more. The Germans were running riot across the Eastern Front. Thousands, *hundreds* of thousands of prisoners. A natural resource, you could say. Never mind that it was totally against the Geneva Convention, but then, what did the Germans care about any of that. Thousands were put to work, building autobahns in Germany mostly, but some came here. To build the bunkers and other fortifications."

"So, the hospital was for them?"

...ot quite. German soldiers who became ill, had ...dents, wounded, that sort of thing. They came to the ...spital and were treated there. And sometimes, they were treated by the prisoners - some of them were nurses you see."

"What? Girls?"

"Girls isn't quite the word I'd use – you can't remain a *girl* after being involved in war, Max. Young they certainly were, some only fifteen. The Soviets had no qualms about using females in frontline operations."

"So...these prisoners, some of them were nurses, and the Germans forced them to work in the hospital...And that hospital...."

"Yes. That's it, Max. That hospital is now your home. Well, part of it at least. The whole complex was taken over for the treating of wounded and sick Germans...but there was something else. Something a lot more sinister."

I looked at him. His face grew grave and for a moment I thought he wasn't going to finish the story there and then. But, fortunately, that was not the case; he managed to take in a ragged breath, then sighed long and slow. "Some of the wards were used for medical experiments. Medical experiments of the most repulsive and ghastly kind. And a lot of them were carried out in the wing that, part of which at least, has now become your home."

ΠIΠE

On my way back, I wandered up to the cricket ground and found a bench that looked out across the bay. It was still and quiet there. A few people could be seen walking around the harbour, but it felt as if, at that particular moment, I was the only person in the whole world. Mr Mumford had given me some notes he'd made for another book he was researching, together with the paperback edition of the first he had had published a couple of years previously. It was only a slim volume but, so he'd told me, there were some details in there about what had happened in the hospital. I wondered then, and not for the first time, that when I had pieced together the whole grizzly story would Mum and Dad continue to stay there, in the hospital-cum-flat? And, more to the point, why hadn't anybody mentioned anything before now? If I hadn't been so nosey, if I hadn't experienced that voice, that letter...I hated myself for who I was and what I could do. Psychic, Aunty Peg had said. Cursed, I would say!

I started reading the book later on. Most of it was fairly dull, lots of information about all sorts of different things, but as I skimmed through I began to pick up little shreds of evidence relating to the hospital. I read these more closely and learned a little about what was done there. It wasn't all that graphic, but it was detailed enough to form some gruesome conclusions.

Many of the prisoners died from malnutrition, whilst being kept in the most awful conditions. They were given only the bare minimum of sustenance. It seemed that the Germans didn't want to spend any money on them at all, so they received things like nettle soup, boiled potato skins, but very little else. Naturally, most couldn't last for more than a few weeks. When they became too weak to work, they weren't fed at all. This led to slow, agonising deaths. It was just barbarous.

But that wasn't all. Experiments were conducted on them. How fast could they recover from physical exertions when given only the meagre amount of food, or water. How did their capacity for work and physical exercise diminish, and how quickly, if they were only fed on dry bread. How did this compare to someone who was given meat? Did the amount of meat change the results? What about fish? And so it went on, all conducted in a seemingly-scientific way but no matter how you dressed it up, it all came out as the same thing – torture.

The worst part was the sleep depravation. They conducted two 'experiments', one on men, the other on women. The idea was to discover if there was any difference between how long a man and woman could go without sleep. So, they were woken up every time they closed their eyes, either with bright lights, loud music or, the worst thing of all, a bucket of cold water thrown over their faces. Locked in tiny cells, they would have to endure this torture until they became so exhausted no amount of hitting, screaming or dragging them around would waken them.

I tried to imagine what it must have been like for those poor people, but no matter how hard I tried, it was impossible. I'd lived a nice, clean, simple life with everything provided for me. I was a million miles from what these people had experienced. But it made me sad and angry nevertheless.

The notes that had been added by Mr Mumford hinted at most of the story being hidden away; barely any of the inmates had survived the War. Those who had were too traumatised by their experience to find the

"I'll get it!" I stood up and went to the bench. The sugar bowl was there, but with only a few chunks of congealed sugar clinging desperately in the bottom. I managed to chip away a few pieces and dropped them into my tea. Then I sat down again. "You've been here a while, Stan. All of this," I swept my arm around the shed.

"No, most of it belonged to the man who was here before me. Don't know who he was. German. You-er-you've heard the story from Mr Mumford, then?"

"About this place being a hospital?" I nodded. "Yeah. He gave me a book. It's pretty grim."

"Mmm...well, the guy who had this shed, he was tried. Hanged."

"Really?"

"Seems like he assisted in some of the...you know. *Experiments.*"

"So he confessed?"

"Must have done. There were no witnesses. With the Germans retreating at the end of the War, they tried to destroy all the evidence relating to this place – including most of the prisoners."

"What, you mean they killed them?"

"Most of 'em. Shot them in the back of the head then dumped them in a mass grave over on the far side. One or two of the more *valuable* ones they took with 'em."

"Valuable? What does that mean?"

"Rich. Jews I think. Apparently, there were three or four really important Jewish people here. Well, important before Hitler came along, of course. They had been very rich, had lots of money secured in Swiss bank accounts. I think some sort of deal had been done with the Nazis, but I couldn't be sure."

"What? They'd bribed the Germans to keep them alive?"

"Think so...Mr Mumford might know more than me."

"I'll have to go and see him again."

"How come you're so interested in all of this? No one else has ever seemed bothered."

I shrugged. He was looking straight at me, perhaps a little suspicious of my motives. "Just curious."

"There's more to it than that, I think."

I took a sip of my tea, trying to divert his attention a little, but also to give me a moment to think. I was concerned that if I told him he might take me for some sort of crank, dismiss me as a daydreamer, just like most other people did. But then there was an honesty about Stan, an openness that made me believe that I could trust him, so I settled my mug down on the ground next to my chair and sat back, smiling. "I heard voices."

He perked up at that, raising one of his eyebrows. "Voices? What sort of *voices.*"

"Don't know. Not long after we arrived. There was something in my room."

The silence lay heavy between us. His reaction, or should I say *none*-reaction gave me the courage to relate the whole story. When I got to the part about the note and what it said regarding the cellar, he put up his hand.

"So, that's where you got that idea from? I was wondering about that."

"You believe me then?"

I held my breath. Slowly he nodded. "I think...it could have happened...but why did the note disappear?"

"I don't know. Perhaps it wasn't real."

"But you just said..."

"No, I mean, it was real to me...it was *meant* for me...a sign, if you like."

"But you could read it. You could read the words."

"Yes, I told you."

"But no one who stayed here was English, Max. They were either German or Russian. Maybe a couple of Poles. But definitely no English."

I shrugged, "Well, whatever, I could read it and it told me about a cellar."

He put his head back and finished off his tea. Cradling the empty mug on his lap he stared at the ceiling of the shed. "I can only think..." He sat forward again. "I'm going to look around, Max. See if I can find this cellar of yours. But I haven't got a clue where to start, and this is a big site."

"You *do* believe me...most people think I'm a nutcase. Especially my family."

"So, this sort of thing has happened before?"

"Yes. Quite a few times. My Aunty Peggy says I'm clairvoyant. I can see things, hear things, from the other-side."

Stan was nodding his head very slowly, thinking things through, making his decisions. "I see...Because I heard something once. A few years back."

"You did? What was it?"

"Someone crying. I was in one of the other rooms, on the far side. No one is living there at this moment, but about three years ago a family moved in. They didn't stay long. After they'd moved out, I had to clear up the place and it was then that I heard it. I thought at first it was coming from outside, but it wasn't. It was in the room, with me! I left pretty sharpish, I can tell you."

"Have you ever heard anything else?"

41

"No. Not a thing. Although...this sounds stupid...I did *see* something. A shadow, that was all. Perhaps that's what it was."

"A shadow? What sort of shadow?"

"Well...perhaps shadow is the wrong word. It was misty, indistinct. It was in the shape of a nurse."

TEN

Later that night I was woken by the sound of something being moved in my room. At first, just like Stan, I thought it was coming from outside. It sounded distant, far away. But the more I listened, the more I realized that it only *seemed* far away. It was a small sound. Squeaking. A mouse. Relaxing, I drifted back to sleep.

The images came to me then. It was like watching an old film, black and white, flickering and jumping from scene to scene. The squeaking wasn't a mouse. I could see that now. It was the movement of the small castor-wheels of a trolley, being pushed by a large man, a porter. On the trolley, strapped down, was another man, but very different from the first. Shaven-haired, ashen grey, his eyes bulging in his skull-like face. A man close to death.

There was a room then, its details becoming clearer. Like an operating theatre, only bleaker. The walls were chipped and dirty-looking, the lights weak, almost the colour of lemon juice. Colour. I was beginning to see colours, washed out, diluted. The patient, the one on the trolley, had a hideous yellow sheen to his skin, skin stretched thin over protruding bone. A third man, dressed in white, instruments in his hand which glinted evilly, and his face, a mask of glee. Was it glee? I couldn't make out his features, only his mouth, those teeth, grimacing like a maniac. Someone else flittered by then, a woman. A nurse, also dressed in white, long thin hands reaching out, holding the hypodermic needle which she slowly began to push into the patient's scrawny neck.

He screamed.

I sat bolt upright, my face covered in sweat, heart pounding so hard I thought it would burst through my chest. Swinging my legs out from under the covers, I sat forward, my face in my hands, trying to calm myself down.

It came again then. The squeak of the castors. Coming closer, growing louder. I slowly drew my hands away from my face and looked around. It was early morning, watery light seeping in between the cracks in my curtains. It was light enough to see.

The trolley was there, at the foot of my bed. Only it was empty, the straps dangling limply from the sides. As I gazed at it, the shadow fell over me and she was there.

The nurse.

"Hello Max," she said softly.

She was beautiful. Her eyes like liquid blue, strands of blonde hair peaking out from under her cap. Full, red lips which shimmered with lipstick. Lipstick. Why would a nurse wear lipstick? Then I realized, and I dragged myself carefully back into my bed, beginning to whimper as the full horror took hold of me, seizing me by the throat, squeezing. Squeezing hard.

It wasn't lipstick. It was blood. I screamed, like the man on the trolley, a single piercing cry of sheer, total fear.

The door flew open, the electric light flooding the room so brightly I had to bring up my hand to shield myself from the sudden glare.

"Max!"

It was Dad. He was suddenly next to me, holding me. He hadn't done that since I was a small child. But I didn't care. He was there, and the images had gone, and he held me tightly to him and I cried into his shoulder, not caring what he thought, or how shameful it was for me to do that. The relief was overwhelming. I was safe, and that was all that mattered.

*****

I stayed off school that day. Dad was adamant about that, despite Mum's objections. "It's only one day," he said before she could say another word. "Max, you try and take it easy." He looked at Mum, who was standing there, bristling. "I'll talk to you when I get in." Then he was gone and I was left to sit at the table, stirring my cereal, watching the milk slowly drizzle from the spoon, with no intention of taking a single mouthful.

ELEVEN

Nothing happened for the next few nights, and for that I was grateful. My sleep did not go untroubled, however. I still had faint, flickering images invading my dreams. But they were not as obvious as last time, nor did I experience the sound of that damned patient trolley.

The days went and at last it was Saturday morning. It had been overcast for most of the week, but as I woke up and went to my window, my mood instantly lifted. It was sunny and my heart sang at the thought of seeing Clari again.

My breakfast was thrown down and as I packed my bag, Mum was there, leaning against the door frame, that look on her face, the look of displeasure.

"So, well enough to go and play tennis?"

"Mum. Please."

"You can't fool me, Max. I went through all of this with Christy."

"Went through all of what?"

"Skiving off school. She did it, as soon as she was fourteen. Refused to get out bed. It was a nightmare. Had the school board come round and everything."

"I don't remember any of that."

"You wouldn't." Her voice sounded bitter, resentful. No doubt she and Dad had been having words about what happened to me a few nights before. Dad had nearly always taken my side on things. Mum hardly ever did, always favouring Christy. At least, that's how it seemed to me. "She soon snapped out of it. Look how well she's done since."

I forged on, trying my best to ignore Mum's accusing stare. "I'm feeling better, thanks. I'll be back in school on Monday."

"Miraculous recovery." Thick with sarcasm now!

I pushed passed her, feeling angry. Sometimes, living with Mum was too stressful.

The warm air instantly made me feel better, but not as good as I felt when I saw Clari coming towards me. Dressed all in white, she was a perfect picture. What was waiting for me was a perfect day.

As it turned out, it *was* a perfect day. We played three sets of tennis. The first, she breezed passed me, chalking up a score of six-two. I don't think I'd ever been so soundly thrashed since I'd started playing! I had to really knuckle down and concentrate for the second set, but I managed to hold my serve, even breaking hers to win six-four. We broke off then, slurping down masses of orange-squash.

"You're good," she said, not sounding in the least bit patronising.

"Thanks. You're not so bad yourself!"

She smiled. "You're coming to tea tonight, don't forget."

"I haven't."

"Then Aneeka's tomorrow. You can still do that?"

"Yes. No problem."

"You've done your homework?"

"Homework?" I shook my head, barely able to contain my glee, "I haven't got any homework!"

"Your school is soft," she said, tossing her hair over her shoulder. "Wish I went there." Christy was in the upper school of the private institution on the other side of the island. The fees there were astronomical, so Dad said. The main reason why I didn't go there.

"Me too," I mumbled. She frowned. "I mean...I wish you went to my school, too."

"Euk, no thanks! All those spotty-Herberts with their bad breath and stinky armpits? You must be joking."

"Like me, you mean?"

"No, not like you!" She took a slurp of squash, "So, why no homework?"

"I've been off sick."

"What? Why didn't you say? What's wrong?"

"Just a tummy bug," I lied. I regretted it, but I didn't think it was the time or the place to go into details of what had happened. I shrugged, "I'm much better now though."

"So, I don't need to go easy on you, like I did in the last set?"

I gasped. "You never did!"

"Want to bet?" She brought out a tennis ball and began to bounce it, "Let's see, shall we."

We certainly did see.

She destroyed me, six-nil!

Her mum ladled salad onto my plate to accompany the piece of cheese flan that was already sitting there. "Hope you like all of this, Max," she said. "Clari tells me you haven't been well, so I've kept it fairly bland and simple."

"No, it's lovely."

"Tummy bug going round, is it?"

"I-er-think so." Did she catch my tentativeness? Could she read through my lie? If she could, she didn't say anything. She sat down opposite me and smiled. I began to eat and it was delicious, the best I'd tasted. Home-made. Perfect cook. Perfect daughter.

At the door, Clari touched my arm and I felt the blood rushing to my cheeks. "It wasn't a tummy bug," she said softly. I looked into her eyes briefly, but soon I had to look away. "It's all right, if you don't want to tell me. But I'm right, aren't I?" I gave a feeble nod. "Thought so."

48

She squeezed my arm. "If you need to talk, Max, I'm here…"

I wish I could have told her, knowing intuitively that I could trust her. But I hesitated, probably because I didn't really believe any of it myself. If my so-called *gift* was allowing me access to a secret, dark realm, I'd prefer my gift to go away. I was frightened and I was trying hard to suppress my feelings.

"You mustn't worry, Max. I won't judge you. I won't laugh at you. I'll just listen."

"Thanks," I mumbled. Then she did the thing that I expected least of all. She gently pulled her hand from my arm and moved it to my face and stroked my cheek, ever so softly with the back of her fingers. I was mesmerised.

"I wish you'd trust me." Her hand dropped away.

"I do!" I blurted out breathlessly, and a little too urgently. I must have sounded stupid as I continued, "It's not that…it's…oh God, I don't know! Look, I'll talk to you tomorrow, try and get my thoughts straight. If that's okay?"

"Of course. Whatever you say. Call round at ten, yeah?"

I nodded and began to walk away, in a sort of a dream-like state. The sky was already streaked with grey and soon it would be nighttime. I knew I wouldn't get much sleep, but it wouldn't have anything to do with nightmares!

TWELVE

Of course, preferring to keep my head well and truly buried in the sand, I hadn't thought about how to broach the subject of my visitations. When I called round at Clari's the following morning I simply hadn't given any time to what I would tell her. So, when she put her head to one side and gave me that look, I panicked. It just came out, in an unrehearsed rush, "I'm having nightmares. No, more than that. Real things. People. Pictures. I can see them, most nights. I can do that, you see. I can see the dead."

Her eyes were wide and wet. Shocked, she sort of shied away from me, shaking her head.

"I knew you'd think I was crazy."

Bringing her head up, her mouth was slack, her complexion drained of colour. Frightened. "No, no it's not that...Max...I've had visions too."

We walked up over the hills that surrounded the hospital complex and reached a point where we could look out across the sea. On a clear day, France was clearly visible and sometimes I thought I could hear trains; but that was fanciful. A little like what was happening to me perhaps? I'd always thought there was something a little unhinged about me...but now Clari was telling me she'd experienced something similar, so perhaps there *was* something to my visions after all? There was only one way to find out. I asked her what she'd seen.

"Nurses," she said simply. "Two of them, dressed in white. They had surgical instruments...... knives....... sharpening them and laughing."

I frowned. These were not the same as my own experiences. True, I'd had the nurse, but only one and

50

nothing to do with surgical knives! And Stan too had seen a nurse. What did it mean?

"They don't speak, they just stand there, in my room, sharpening. I can hear it clearly, the quick scratching sound as the blade is dragged over the steel. Like a butcher getting ready to carve up meat."

"That's pretty descriptive, Clari."

"True though, don't you think?"

"Carving up meat? I don't know. I've not seen anything like that. One nurse, with a hypodermic, that's all. Vague figures strapped to trolleys, being wheeled into what seems to be an operating theatre. Men in coats."

She shivered. "Max, although they're different, they're also the same – what you and I are experiencing. There must be a link, but what is it?"

"I don't know, not yet. Stan put me on to a local historian, a man called Mumford. He gave me a book and some notes of his own. I'll let you read them, then things might be a little clearer." I breathed a sigh and looked out across the sea. It was calm and flat, the merest ripple percolating across the surface. Such an enticing sea, the Channel. At times like this, when it was friendly, inviting almost. But I knew it could turn, such were the vagaries of its mood. One moment still, then suddenly a raging torrent. A little like my life at that point.

Without a word, she slipped her hand in mine. I shot her a glance, but she was looking out to sea. I couldn't read anything on her expression, so I stood there, her hand in mine, feeling wonderful.

Aneeka was a serious looking woman, blonde hair scraped back from her head and gathered in a bun, piercing ice-blue eyes, bare arms tanned to a deep nutmeg colour. She spoke with a slight accent. Claris had said she was Scandinavian, but from which part I had no idea. She was friendly enough, however, and after she'd taken us into her house, she offered us some orange juice and biscuits. "Clari has told me much about you. Maximilian, isn't it?"

"Max. most people call me Max."

"Ah. You hate Maximilian, yes? German name. Are you German?"

"My grandparents were German, I think. But they died years and years ago, before I was born."

"Ah. But you never go back? To Germany?"

"No, I've never been. We have no other family there."

"It is the same with me. No family. Only my friends. You have come to see my friends, Max? My horses?"

I nodded.

We were sitting in a small room, piled up high with books and papers and all sorts of discarded junk. The rest of the house wasn't much better, but for the most part it was tack and other related bits and pieces to do with horses. There was a strong smell of hay as well, and as she led us outside I saw the reason why. Next to the kitchen, door wide open, was an adjoining garage, and it was full of hay bales and straw. It wasn't a bad smell, just overpowering. Aneeka probably didn't even notice it.

She was already dressed in skin-tight black jodhpurs and riding boots. She was slim and wiry, her body honed hard from a life spent mostly in the saddle. I wondered why she lived such an isolated existence. Her house was stuck out on a limb from the rest of the hospital-cum-apartment complex and it looked dishevelled and lonely. I doubted that Stan's duties extended to looking after

52

Aneeka's place, which was a pity, because I felt an overwhelming sense of woe at every turn.

Often I'm not aware of atmospheres and feelings. Sometimes I can go weeks, months without experiencing anything at all. Then, out of the blue, a sudden smell or strange sound can trigger my visions. Apart from the dreams I'd been having, and the disappearing note of course, I hadn't really sensed much. But here it was different. It was becoming oppressive and I could feel the despair seeping out from the very walls. Aneeka caught my change of mood and she came over to me. "Max. You are feeling unwell?"

"Eh? No, I-er-I'm fine...honestly."

"Max sees things, Aneeka."

The woman narrowed her eyes at Clari's revelation. "*Sees things*...What sort of things do you see, Max?"

I shrugged, not sure how much I should say. "Oh, you know...stuff."

"No, I don't know, Max. You can feel something here, in this house?"

"Well..." I looked uncertainly towards Clari. She gave me a little encouraging nod. "Yes. There is something here." I scanned the walls of the kitchen. "Not so much here, but back in the other room...sadness. Overwhelming....I can't..."

"Regret? Regret at something that was once done, something that was bad? Terrible even?"

"Yes! That's it...regret. Despair."

"Remorse too, maybe? You know what remorse is, Max?"

"Of course. Yes...remorse. Something terrible did happen here. Not violent, or anything like that...I don't know. It's weird."

She reached out and placed her hand on my shoulder. "I sometimes have felt this. My dogs, they

53

won't come inside, no matter what I do. When I first came here, I could feel it very strongly. Now, only now and again. Some days are worse than others. Perhaps it is the same with you?"

Nodding my head, I turned to Clari again. I forced a smile, although I didn't much like doing so. "Let's go and see the horses."

Aneeka, who still hadn't taken her hand away, remained still. "Max. Do you know what happened here?"

"A little. Stan told me some of it, but mostly Mr Mumford."

"All they know is what the German guards confessed to. Max, far worse things happened here. Dreadful things. And this house...this was where the commandant lived."

"The commandant?"

"The officer in charge of the hospital. This was his home, and it was here that he made the orders. Orders that sealed the doom for almost every single person held here." She stepped away, and a single tear rolled down her cheek. "And he signed those papers, those death warrants, in the room in which you have just sat."

THIRTEEN

I pottered around whilst the other two brushed and swept out the horses. The stables were at the far end of the garden. Garden is a bit of an understatement. It was a paddock, half an acre of good ground, approached through a tiny lynch gate which was hidden amongst a jumble of ornamental shrubs and bushes. It was the sort of place you could lose yourself in. Perhaps that's what the commandant did, to keep himself sane?

Later Clari and I wandered home. She was anxious to take a bath, so I left her with the promise I would meet up with her in midweek, and hopeful that she would have no further visits from things unexplained.

Crossing the courtyard, which had taken on a honey-coloured glow as the sun began to set, a voice called out to me. It was Stan. He was standing at the entrance to his workshop, waving me over.

"I didn't think you'd work on a Sunday, Stan."

"I don't usually. But I've been thinking, racking my brains over that cellar of yours."

"Not to worry, it probably doesn't mean anything. I doubt it's even real."

"Oh no, that's just it – I've found it!"

Across the worktop he'd laid out an old plan of the original hospital, drawn up, so the date said, in the spring of nineteen forty-two. Everything was there: wards, storerooms, operating theatres, cellars.

"Where did you find this, Stan?"

"In a box, stuffed under a pile of old yacht sails."

"Yacht sails? What made you look there?"

"Well, that's just it. I was having a nap after my dinner, and it came to me – just like that." He snapped his fingers together to accentuate the point.

55

"As a picture, or...?"

"Exactly like a picture. I could see it, clear as day. So, when I woke up, I came over and there it was – just as in my dream. It's the strangest thing, don't you think?"

"Oh yes, Stan...I do."

We stood outside the door to the cellar, securely padlocked as it was, both of us rubbing our chins, wondering what to do next. The door was metal, painted dark green, almost black. Solid and heavy, it seemed to be in remarkably good condition, although the lock and chain that was wrapped tightly around the lever-like handle were both well rusted. The sea-air had not been kind.

"It hasn't been opened for a good while," mumbled Stan.

"What are we going to do?"

"We've come this far," declared Stan, clapping his hands together. "I'll be right back."

He scurried off.

I stood there and pressed my palm against the cold, hard metal. It seemed thick. Probably a blast door. We'd found it in a half-buried bunker up on the hill, some fifty yards or so from the far end of the hospital. Overgrown and forgotten, it had taken us a little while to find the steps. But the plan was perfectly accurate, and it didn't take long before the bracken was pulled back to reveal the door. There were many such bunkers. Few of them, however, had doors.

Stan returned, a little out of breath, puffing hard. He had in his hands a pair of long-handled heavy-duty bolt cutters, and across his shoulders a small canvas bag. He carefully fitted the jaws of the cutters around the metal loop of the padlock and grinned towards me, "Four thousand pounds of cutting pressure. Perfect!" He now applied this pressure on the tubular steel handles and the padlock parted as if it were made from soft plastic. I was amazed at how easy it had been.

Quickly Stan unthreaded the chain and threw it on the ground. Then he gripped the lever and pushed down.

Nothing happened.

"Must be rusted. Thought it would be." He reached into the little bag and pulled out an oil can and began to apply the lubricant liberally all around the handles, moving it up and down as the oil got to work.

I waited with baited breath. The handle gradually became easier to move, then, with a final push, it was released. The heavy bolts inside slid back with a clunking sound and Stan put his shoulder against the metal door and began to force it inwards. But only by the tiniest of amounts. "Give us a hand," he grunted.

Joining him, together we both strained to get the thing moving. Inch by painful inch, the door crept open, the great hinges screaming their defiance as we struggled to maintain momentum.

At last, the gap was sufficient for me to squeeze through. Stan looked at me, wiping his hand across his brow. "God, that's heavy! Here," he brought out from the bag a large torch. "Use this. Be careful. I'll carry on trying to open the door a bit more."

Nodding, I took the torch and managed to squirm through the gap.

The air was musty and thick with the smell of stale sweat, the tang of salt hitting the back of my throat and stinging my eyes. Ignoring this, as best I could, I switched the torch on and gasped. Everywhere I looked, the light picked out filing cabinets, shelves, desks. It was all very neat and tidy. The floor was strewn with dust, but other than that it was all in a remarkable state of repair.

The door gave an almighty groan as Stan mustered up one, last, forceful shove and the light from outside streamed in, and he had succeeded. He came up next to me, breathing harder than ever.

"My God," he said, shocked, "it's like it's only just been closed up."

"It's amazing. What do you think is in those cabinets?"

He shrugged. "I guess there's only one way to find out, isn't there."

Almost every single cabinet was empty, as were the drawers in the desks. The whole lot had been cleared out. I felt such a sense of anti-climax that I flopped down on one of the old chairs, which creaked alarmingly. I sulked for a moment or two, but then pushed these feelings away and stood up again.

"There's got to be something here," I muttered. "Why else would I get that message?" I looked up at Stan. "Why else would you have that dream?" The beam of the torch, combined with the natural light flooding in from outside, gave a curious sort of sepia effect to the room, and the deep shadows created around Stan's face made him appear almost like a gargoyle, his features were so distorted. "Unless, of course, I imagined it all."

"No. I don't think you did, Max." He surveyed the room, hands on hips, sighing deeply. "This place has been swept clean, everything taken away. So why padlock it up? If there's nothing to hide..." His voice trailed away.

He had spoken perfect sense. Why indeed lock it up?

He span round and grinned apishly. "Out the way, Max. I've got an idea."

With a sudden determination, he went over to one of the desks and began to push it to one side. It grated across the floor, but otherwise it moved fairly freely. There was nothing. He looked up, and nodded towards the other one. "Come on!"

This time we both put our shoulders to it. This desk was bigger and more substantial than the first. An officer's desk, perhaps? We strained again but slowly the thing began to slide.

And there it was.

I could hardly believe it.

A hatchway, in the floor.

"I knew it," cried Stan and got down on his haunches, took hold of the handle and pulled it back.

The hatchway opened and revealed a set of steps disappearing into the blackness. Stan grinned again. "Are we intrepid explorers, or what?"

I clutched at his shoulder. A sudden fear had taken hold of me, something I couldn't explain, but real nevertheless. "Stan. Whatever's down there..."

"Whatever's down there, Max, it's going to solve this mystery!"

FIFTEEN

We brought the small wooden crate back out into the dying sunlight, having managed to haul it up from the hidden room we had discovered underneath the hatchway.

Stan sat down on the ground after pulling the metal door shut and pushing the handle back into place. "I think..." he pulled out a handkerchief and wiped his face. "I think, they forgot about that room."

"Why would they do that?"

"Just a hunch. Why else leave this?" He tapped the lid of the crate. It was about the size of an average suitcase, only deeper. It too was sealed with a padlock. Much smaller this time, it easily came apart as Stan applied the pressure of the bolt cutters. He smiled at me. "Shall we?"

Before I could answer, a shadow fell over us. Both of us started in surprise and Stan scrambled to his feet. I had to bring up my hand to shield my eyes. The figure had the setting sun behind him, and it was difficult to make out his features. But I knew it was a man. A very big man, wide shouldered and heavy set. He wore a hat, which made him seem even bigger.

"I am sorry," he began, his voice heavily accented. "I am looking for someone. I saw you here and wondered if you could help me."

Stan reached down to take me by the hand, pulling me to my feet. Now, level with his chest, I could see what the stranger was like. A hard, impassive face, small, piggish eyes, heavy jowls. A man used to being obeyed.

Then he did the strangest thing. He pushed the crate with his toe. "What have you there?"

Something settled down between us all then. A sense of danger. I could feel it strongly and I turned my worried features towards Stan. Even he looked uncertain, licking his lips. "Who is it you're looking for?"

The man shrugged, then doffed his hat before swinging around, "No matter. Thank you for your time."

Then he went, his heavy footfall slowly diminishing as he marched off into the sunset. His exit was as mystifying as his arrival and I was left feeling positively uneasy.

We decided to open up the crate in Stan's workshop. It was now distinctly gloomy and Stan flicked the switch, the naked bulb hanging from the ceiling giving off a sickly, but adequate light as we peered at the lid.

I looked at him, hardly able to contain my excitement. "Well? What are you waiting for?"

He shrugged. "Just preparing myself...it might be empty."

"It didn't feel empty."

"No...but maybe there's nothing of any value inside."

"So why hide it?"

"Like I said, perhaps it was forgotten, left down there by accident."

"Stan," I said, "just open it."

He nodded and brought out a flat-headed screwdriver, pressed the point under the lip of the lid and eased it open.

It wasn't empty, not by any means. But I didn't know then the true value of its contents. Or the dangers that lurked within.

There was a thick stash of card folders, tied together loosely with coarse string. There was no label on them, but each folder was stuffed with papers, records of the people who had been kept in the hospital. I leafed through them quickly, then placed them aside for further study later. For underneath was something that held my attention far more than mere printed words. Photographs. Dozens of them.

I laid them out across Stan's worktop, dealing them out one by one like playing cards. They ranged from simple, frontal portraits, to family gatherings. Some were obviously holiday shots, pictures of parents and children on bicycles or skis, enjoying visits to the Alps. A few showed pets, some were of houses and places of interest. Some were profile shots, with numbers scratched beneath them. Like the photographs police take of suspects or arrested criminals. Records of lives long gone.

Both of us stood there for a long time, simply gazing down at the faces of people we didn't know.

But then...

There was one photograph which seemed different from the others. Professionally taken, it was of a girl. Very pretty, with perfectly coiffed black hair, huge eyes, smiling confidently back towards the photographer. The shadows subtlety picked out the fine features of her face; perhaps she was a model, or an actress. Perhaps even someone famous.

Stan delved inside the crate again whilst I picked up that one photograph and went over to the window to look at it more closely. Definitely a film star, I thought. This was the photograph of a person well used to publicity, of showing off her considerable charms. She had an amazing face, one that drew you in, preventing any notions of escape because that was something you simply didn't want to do. Captivating.

"Max!"

I blinked, and turned. "What?"

"Have a look at these."

He'd found more photographs, but these were very different. They were the photographs of soldiers, all head and shoulder shots, all in uniform. Some were of officers, their peaked caps sporting the famous skull badge of the SS.

Stan looked at me, his face serious. "Max. These are the guards." He picked up one photograph, a hawkish looking man, an officer, his eyes piercing, the sense of hardness, cruelty almost, glaring back out from that black and white image with such intensity that it was as if he were alive in the room with us. Stan began to chew his bottom lip thoughtfully. "This is the commandant," he grunted.

"How do you know?"

He flipped it over, and there, scrawled across the reverse side was the name: *Paul Heinlein, Kommandant.*

"The really scary thing is," said Stan, ignoring my question for a moment and carefully placing the photograph down on the worktop, face up..."I think I know him."

SIXTEEN

At the very bottom of the crate were some bundles of letters, postcards with faded writing on the reverse and a notebook. It was late and knowing that Mum would be angry because of the time, I gathered up what I could and told Stan that I'd see him some time in the week.

"You won't be able to read any of that," he said pointing at the notebook. "It'll be in Russian or Polish or something like that."

"You never know, I might get given a translation."

Stan stiffened at that. "Don't joke about it."

"I'm not, Stan. That's the point."

Mum *was* angry and told me to get upstairs straight away for a bath. "Your tea's all but ruined," she added as I bounded up to my room. But I couldn't care less about tea. All I wanted to know was what the letters and notebook said. And to do that, I'd need Aneeka.

I sat up in bed later, thumbing through the notebook. Although I couldn't read the words there were sufficient clues to make me realize that what I held in my hands was a form of journal. Each entry began with a date. The passages which followed were sometimes short, others quite long. Often there were gaps between the dates and, at the March seventh entry for nineteen forty-four, they stopped. I counted them up until that point and there were thirty-two separate pieces of writing. I was desperate to know what they said and after I leaned over to switch off my bedside lamp, I spent a restless night pondering over the meaning of those strange, indecipherable words.

***

As usual, school dragged and the day hung heavy around my neck like a dead weight. No matter what I did, I couldn't speed it up. By lunchtime I was frantic. How I contained my impatience throughout that afternoon, I have no idea. Lessons blurred, exercises became meaningless. All that mattered was the home-time bell. But every time I glanced up to the classroom clock, the hand had hardly moved at all.

At last the moment came and I raced out of the door faster than anyone. I didn't stop running until I got to Aneeka's door. I'd taken the notebook with me to school, so I had no need to stop off home on the way. If Mum was going to be angry again, well it was a risk worth taking. I had to know what those words meant!

Thankfully, Aneeka was home and when she came to the door, blonde hair hanging down in ringlets, she looked tired and drawn. Her eyes lit up momentarily when she saw me. "Why, Max! What a surprise. Come on in, I've nearly finished."

What she'd nearly finished was the mowing of the lawn in the back. She poured me a glass of lemonade – homemade, I might add – whilst she quickly finished off the few last edges. I felt that she was grateful for my interruption because when she came back into the kitchen she was grinning broadly. She helped herself to some lemonade and gulped it down in one.

"So, Max," she said, smacking her lips and sitting down, "what brings you here?"

"A favour, Aneeka. I hope it's not too big."

"Sounds intriguing. What do you want me to do?"

I fished inside my school bag and brought out the notebook. "This," I said. "I haven't a clue what language it's in, but I thought..."

She took it from me and very gingerly opened it up. Within a few seconds, she looked up. "It's Russian. My Russian is not so good. I haven't spoken it for a very long time...and as for reading it...Where did you get this, Max?"

I hesitated for a moment, not knowing how much to reveal. I decided on a middle-course, halfway between truth and lies. "Stan found it, in one of the rooms. He gave it to me, but he didn't have a clue what it was. It seems old. I managed to read some of the dates."

"Yes. Nineteen forties. During the War. It's a journal, written by a girl called Alana..."

"Alana? I didn't see that."

"No, she doesn't mention it all that often. It's written like letters, to someone that perhaps she knew back home..." She screwed her eyes up as she scanned the words. "This will take me a day or two, Max. But I will do my best."

"Are you sure? I'd really appreciate it, Aneeka."

"No problem. Perhaps you could come and clean out my horses at the weekend? Repay the favour?"

"Absolutely! Thanks, Aneeka." I finished off my lemonade and stood up. She was still reading and she was now frowning heavily, immersed in the words. I quietly made my way out, closing the front door softly behind me, and looked skywards and breathed out a long sigh. At last, I was beginning to get somewhere.

SEVENTEEN

The sound of the castors came to me again that night.

I rolled over in my bed, pressing my hands against my ears, but nothing would shut out the noise. I sat up, and through terrified eyes, I watched as the nurse pushed the trolley into the centre of the room. It was dimly lit by a single bulb, suspended from the ceiling, which swung alarmingly, creating weird, distorted shadows. A man came out of the darkness, very tall, dressed all in white, a surgical mask across his face, and in both hands he held up instruments. Scalpels, their blades overly large, glinting wickedly. The nurse laughed and pulled back the cover from the trolley to reveal a young boy, strapped down. He was gagged but already he was writhing in the bed, his eyes wild with fear.

The man with the knives bent over the boy and peered down at him before he stepped back again and readied the blades.

I shouted out then. From somewhere I managed to drag up enough courage to try and halt what I knew was going to happen. Throwing back the covers of my bed, I was already standing up when I called out, "No!"

They looked at me. All three of them. But it was the boy who looked the most surprised and, dare I say it, angry. His straps fell away and he sat up, pulling down the gag. "You fool, Max!" He swung his legs around and stood up. As tall as me, his eyes bored into mine. "You fool!" Then he hit me, back-handed, right across my mouth. It stung, bringing tears to my eyes, and I fell back towards my bed. Except that my bed wasn't there any more and I fell down into a great gaping hole that seemed to have simply appeared from nowhere.

I hit the ground hard, and for a moment I was stunned, my breath coming out of me in a loud gasp. It was dark in that hole. Dark and thick with menace. For I was not alone.

Rolling over I got up onto my knees and waited, trying to peer through the blackness. This was no dream, I could sense that at least. In a way that I didn't understand, I had been transported out of my bedroom into another part of the old hospital complex.

The floor was slippery, the tiles well worn and I could see, even in the gloom, that they were covered by a thick layer of filth. I slowly moved on. I had to grope my way up, hands spread outwards against the side of the wall in order to stop myself from slipping down again. Managing in this way to climb to my feet, I stood, trying to find my bearings. But that was impossible, it was too dark. So very tentatively I began to stumble forward.

From far off in the distance a light appeared as a door was opened momentarily, then closed again. Slowly I moved towards that light, keeping myself close to the wall, creeping forward. At last, I came to the door, the light appearing like a thin line along the bottom. I found the handle and pushed the door open.

There was a body suspended from the ceiling, held by thin wire. It – for I could not tell whether it was male or female – had been gutted like a pig, a mere shell of a body, all of the inner organs removed, the carcass empty and cleaned.

It had no head.

I screamed then and whirled round.

But I couldn't take a single step forward.

A man – could it have been the same man I had seen before? I couldn't tell – was standing baring my way. Tall and dressed in white, wearing a surgical mask. He put his on one side, "Come to join us, Max?" With a flurry, he brought out a long bladed scalpel. Too big.

Too vicious looking. Then I realized that it wasn't a scalpel – it was a butcher's knife. Its blade was curved slightly and looked impossibly sharp.

Not able to find my voice now, my muscles also seemed to be frozen with fear. I couldn't move, there was no feeling in my legs. My mouth was dry and constricted and all I could do was watch helplessly as the man with the surgical mask stepped to one side and beckoned for others to come into the room. And there were many. A long line of bedraggled souls, shuffling forward, men and women, heads down, moaning slightly. They moved past me so close I could smell their stench. The stench of fear. As each one moved by, they would look up and with pleading eyes, they implored me to help. But what could I do? I was alone and terrified and simply didn't have the courage, or the means, to aid these poor unfortunates.

As they went further into the room, other masked and white-garbed men appeared, some checking off names in a register, others barking out orders, none of which I understood but which I took to be instructions to keep moving. The moaning of those who shuffled past became louder and more melancholy. So loud that I had to cover my ears and I fell to my knees, trying to make myself as small as I could, desperate to shut out the noise which was now beginning to fill the room with the intensity of some powerful piece of machinery. An engine of death, great cogs whirring, grinding relentlessly on, until at last it was so clamouring, so painful that I had to get out of that place, knowing that if I lingered a moment longer my eardrums would burst.

As I lurched forward like a drunkard, the tall man in the mask caught me, swung me round, his mouth pressing close to the side of my face so that I could hear his words, spoken with sneering, wicked humour, "Your time will come, Max. Your time will come!"

Blackness.

The sounds, the light, the room, all gone.

I was sitting in bed, holding my head, rocking myself backwards and forwards, mouth agog.

Had it been a dream? I dare not believe it had been real.

And yet, it *was* so real, so intense...

I looked down to my feet. I knew then. I was sitting on my bed, on top of my sheets, and my feet were filthy, stained black by the unwashed tiles that I had walked along.

I had been allowed a glimpse of what had gone on in that place. A glimpse, and a promise. A promise that I too would join those souls that had been tortured there. A promise that I would die.

EIGHTEEN

I kept what I'd seen to myself. No one would understand and, even if they did, their solution would be a visit to the doctor. So, as I sat at the breakfast table, with Mum humming an unknown tune, and Dad trying desperately, and without much success, to sponge off a blob of margarine from his tie, I kept silent. Christy came in. She had two more days left before she got onboard a plane and headed off to the big adventure of university education. As she sat down I wondered if I'd miss her. She'd barely spoken to me since we'd arrived, no doubt too wrapped up in the preparations for the next important stage of her ever-so important life. When she kicked me under the table and snapped, "Pass the toast, dog breath," I knew that actually I'd hardly miss her at all.

Dad stood up and left without a word. Mum threw down a tea-towel and glared at his retreating back. Then she turned those eyes on me. "Will you be coming *straight* home tonight, after school? Or will it be another visit to the horse lady?"

"Do you mean Aneeka?"

"Is she the good looking one with blonde hair?" piped up Christy.

I hadn't thought of Aneeka in those terms, but now Christy's words made me realize that yes, Aneeka was very good looking. But that held no interest for me.

I must have blushed because Christy leaned forward, beginning to mock me, "Ah yes, but you've got that other little sparrow fluttering around you, haven't you." I didn't want to talk to my sister about Clari, or anyone come to that matter.

Closing my eyes I went to stand up. Mum barked, "Well? Will you be home after school?"

Suddenly I felt angry. It was like being interrogated. Perhaps a little like those poor people who had been held in that very place not so very long ago. "I don't know!" I snapped back, venting my rage. "What does it matter? What do you care?"

I could see her bristling. Christy turned away, content that she had achieved a reaction and caused a row. "For your information, I *do care* ! I don't like you going round there all the time."

"I don't *go round there all the time.* What's it to you, anyway?"

"In case you've forgotten, I'm your mother."

I could have said something then. Something barbed and pitiless. But I didn't. I also caught a look from Christy. A wide-eyed warning. So I let it go and contented myself with a growling sigh.

"A man called here last night," she continued, "whilst you were out."

I frowned then, feeling a tiny tingle of something playing inside my stomach. "A man? What sort of man?"

Mum leaned back against the sink, folding her arms. "Foreign. He said he wanted to speak to Stan Hedges. Said he'd seen you and him earlier on and that he wanted to ask you something."

"What?"

"He didn't say. Who is he?"

"I don't know. Just some bloke, I suppose...Did he say anything else?"

"No. But he said he worked for the police and that he'd call around again tonight, after school. Which is why I want to know what you're doing."

"Mum, why don't you just tell him to come home straight away?"

I shot a glare at Christy. "Why don't you just keep your fat nose out of my business?"

72

She stood up and faced me. I'd never seen such a looked of controlled fury as the one that crossed her face at that moment. When she struck me across the face the force of the blow knocked me sideways and I fell against the breakfast table, my arms trying to break my fall. Instead all I managed to do was flail away at the assorted teacups and plates, knocking them to the ground as I completely lost my balance and fell down next to them.

Mum was on me like a hound, gripping me by the shoulder and lifting me to my feet. She was shaking me, ramming her face into mine. A woman possessed by something far more intense than mere anger.

"You get home! Straight away!" she yelled. I winced, turning my head away sharply, desperately pushing myself from her. I didn't want to be anywhere near that face.

They stood there, the two of them, dishevelled, breathing hard, sinister vipers ready to strike. I stepped back, dabbing at my lip with the back of my hand, watching them, not recognising them. They'd been transformed into something I didn't know.

I turned and ran, tearing through the door and out into the sunlight at a sprint. I didn't care that I was early for the bus, or that I'd left my school bag behind. I only had one thought – to flee.

NINETEEN

The meeting I had with Stan that night after school was a curious one. He seemed distracted, unable to focus very much on what I was telling him. He kept getting up and looking out of the shed window. When I asked him what the matter was, he mumbled, 'nothing', but kept looking anyway. It was obvious he was worried.

I knew it was the stranger, the man who had come up to us when we'd come out of the cellar, the same man who'd called at my house. What sinister power did he possess to change people so? First my mother and sister, transformed into maniacal harridans, now Stan. Distracted, confused, worried.

When I asked him if I could take the photographs, he simply tossed them over to me without a word. Then he peered outside again.

I said I'd call round the following evening, or perhaps one day after school next week. Soon it would be half term, I'd be free during the day then. Perhaps we could uncover some more details about the place, study the plan in more detail.

"Plan?" he said, looking at me confused.

"The plan you found, of the hospital."

"Oh, that! You can take that as well. I don't want that any more."

I was puzzled by all of this, but gathered up the drawing anyway. My idea was to take the photographs and the plan to Mr Mumford. I was sure he would be interested and may well have been able to use them to shed some more light on who the people in the photographs were. "Are you sure you're all right, Stan?" I asked the question to his back. He shrugged. There was no other answer. "Okay. Well, I'll get off then. See you, Stan."

I stood there waiting for a reply. Something. Anything.

But it was as if I wasn't there.

I slowly went outside and looked around the courtyard. I stood there for a long time, an awful sensation coursing through me. I felt I was being watched.

And I knew who it was.

TWENTY

The day dawned bright and clear, another beautiful day. I wondered how long it would last. I doubted it would continue on into half-term – it never did!

Thankfully, there had been no repeat of the previous night's experiences. No sounds, no images. Just a deep, impenetrable sleep. When I'd got home after seeing Stan, Mum acted as if nothing had happened that morning. She was her usual, cheerful self. And, there was no mention of the stranger. I ate my tea, watched some television, then went up to my room and pored over the photographs. Nothing else had happened.

Until later that morning.

I went downstairs and there they all were again, sitting around, munching on toast, slurping down coffee. Dad looked up as I came in. "Max! I didn't get chance to tell you. Sorry, work and that. It's about next week."

I frowned, looking at him as if he had grown a new head, "Dad...what about next week?"

"It's all been taken care of," said Mum, "so you don't have to worry. Your school has been told."

I swallowed. Had this something to do with the cellar, what Stan and I had discovered? But how did they know, how had they found out? "Am I in trouble?" I asked hesitantly, dreading the answer.

Dad laughed. "No, it's not that. Silly! No, we-er-have to go back. Just for a few days."

"Back? You mean, back home?"

"Well, yes...if you want to call it that. Yes. Home. It's the house. It's been sold. We have to clear it of the last few bits and pieces."

I slumped down on a chair and groaned, "Do I have to come?"

"Of course you do!" snapped Mum. "Christy leaves for University next week, so it'll be a perfect chance for us all to go over together."

I looked up sharply, half-expecting to see her face transforming again. Thankfully it didn't. "Why 'of course'? Can't I just stay here?"

"Who with, Clari?" That was Christy. I forced myself not to rise to her bait. "Or Aneeka? Which one do you fancy the most, Maximus?"

"That's enough Christy!" I silently thanked Dad for his intervention. I may have said something I'd regret, or that would have turned Christy into the snarling banshee that she had been the previous day. "Max, you *have* to come. It'll only be for a few days. It's all happened rather quickly, so you'll have to pack your bags fairly pronto. We're catching the twelve o'clock flight on Saturday."

Saturday? I groaned inwardly. That would mean missing tennis with Clari and letting Aneeka down over the clearing out of the horses. I'd have to go and make my excuses. I said this to Dad, who seemed fine. Mum was a little vexed and Christy just grinned. The thought of being with them all, for a whole week, with no hope of escape...then I remembered. It would give me a chance to catch up with Russell! Suddenly, the proposition didn't seem quite as bad as it had.

Clari was upset. I went round to see her after school. I told her as soon as I got back that we'd play more tennis, but that only made a partial difference.

"I was hoping we could play every day after school, Max! There's a club tournament coming up in a few weeks during half-term. We could have played together, doubles."

Just another reason for me to feel depressed.

I didn't catch sight of Stan. Tomorrow was Friday, I could try and meet up with him then, tell him that we'd all be away for most of the week. Just in case I didn't see him, I scribbled him a note and slipped it under the door of his workshop. Then I went home and began to sort out some things. I picked up the photographs again, a sudden thought coming to me.

Running down the stairs I called out to Mum that I was going into town. My push-bike was standing outside, as it always was, and soon I was shaking my way down the rutted track that led to the road and then to town.

Mr Mumford wasn't home. I spoke to his housemaid who had opened the door, asking her if I could call around the following evening. I had something of importance for him to look at. Photographs. She said she would make sure that he got the message and I cycled back home.

It was harder peddling back up that track. The road had been fairly easy, but not the track. The ruts were too deep and the incline was proving dangerous, so I climbed down and began to push the bicycle up the slope.

From nowhere, the big stranger stepped out in front of me, hand outstretched as if he were a traffic policeman. I yelped and almost dropped the bike in shock.

I stood there, panting, staring at him. He very slowly lowered his hand and came closer.

"It is Max, isn't it? Yes. I know it is Max. Forgive me," he smiled and took another step closer. I could smell his after-shave. It was very distinctive, very strong. "We need to talk you and I, Max. About photographs and things. I will call again, Max." He smiled, put his hands into the pockets of his long, brown overcoat and took a few steps past me.

"Who are you?" I managed to ask, my voice sounding quite frail. My throat was tight and dry. He frightened me.

He paused and turned, looking at me from beneath the rim of his large hat. "Just an interested party, Max. Nothing more."

I watched him as he walked away and wondered how he knew about the photographs. No one did, except Stan and Mr Mumford. But Mr Mumford hadn't even seen them yet. That was to be tomorrow. I had a terrible sensation growing inside me that soon, perhaps very soon, I would meet that man again.

As it turned out, Mr Mumford had telephoned the house. When I came through the front door, Mum was just finishing writing me a note. She handed it over without a word. There was something different about Mum, something I couldn't quite come to terms with. But then I read the note and I forgot all about Mum.

'Mr Mumford rang. He said, *Come to my house immediately.*'

I sighed. That would mean another bike ride down into town. But I didn't want to do that, not just yet. That man would still be around, so I went into the kitchen, poured myself a long glass of dandelion and burdock and sipped at it slowly. When I estimated enough time had passed, I left. Mum didn't say a word.

Mr Mumford met me at the front door of his house. Immediately he took me into his study and told me to spread out the photographs. He looked at them for a long time, chewing his lip. He didn't speak, but I could see he was troubled.

79

Now, why would he be troubled?

I didn't think I should ask him. He'd changed too. He was not as relaxed as he had been during our previous meeting. He was tense, his brow shiny from a thin film of sweat.

He picked up one particular photograph and waved it at me. "Do you know this man?"

I blinked. How would I know anyone in those pictures? "No," I said softly.

He frowned, almost as if he didn't believe me. He looked at the picture again and shook his head. "I didn't think these existed," he said, almost to himself.

"I have a plan too," I said. "Of the hospital. Stan found it."

"Stan? Where did Stan find it?"

"He said it was in a box, under some old sails in his workshop."

"His workshop? No, that can't be...No, he must be mistaken." He picked up another photograph. "He found these in the same box?"

"No. In the cellar." Mr Mumford gave me a sharp look. "We-er-found an old room, hidden I think. Maybe not deliberately...anyway, these were all in another old box. There were..." I bit my tongue. Mumford's expression had taken on a wild, almost haunted look. I had a sudden stab of uncertainty; perhaps I had said too much.

"There were what? More photographs? Like these?"

I nodded once. "Yes." I'd lied, and I didn't understand why. The letters and the notebook, the one I'd given Aneeka to translate. I felt that perhaps Mr Mumford didn't need to know about them.

He told me he'd need to keep hold of the photographs and then showed me to the door. I left with a distinctly different feeling about Mr Mumford, about who he was and what he was. I was relieved I hadn't told him about the other material. I was also relieved I'd kept back the one photograph that had affected me and Stan more than all the others put together.

Saturday came and we all squeezed into the car, ready for our trip back home. Clari was there to wave me off. That was kind of her. Christy was giggling, but I didn't care.

"Hurry back, Max," said Clari. "We need to practise."

Then she reached through the open window and gave me a tiny hug, barely able to take hold of me, but it felt like the most wonderful thing in the world. On the way to the airport I couldn't help smiling. We would only be gone four days. Two days off school to miss. A sort of bonus holiday in a way.

I had turned around when we pulled off and I had waved to Clari. She'd waved back.

I wasn't going to share such a moment with her again.

When I returned, the world had become a very dreadful place indeed.

PART TWO•

TWENTY-ONE

By the time I'd arrived on the island the story, which had warranted no more than two column inches in the local press, was all but finished. Hardly a mention was made of it in the subsequent weeks. Despite this I had a start, a lead. Max. He'd been comparatively easy to find, thanks chiefly to his name – Maximilian Schelenberg is not the most common of handles! It was my hope he could give me some answers.

The unexplained death of a local man wouldn't usually have grabbed my attention the way it did, but that was all due to the circumstances and, of course, who it was.

He'd died, the report had said, in his garage and his body had remained undetected for three days until Max discovered him.

No suspicious circumstances, the police had said.

Suicide, the newspaper had reported.

But I knew that couldn't be the case. You see, I knew he simply wouldn't have done something like that.

Stan Hedges, the dead man, was my brother.

Max was very subdued when I first met him. It had been around ten days since he had stepped into that garage; the memory was still fresh and very raw.

His parents were warm and welcoming and didn't seem as concerned as they should have been over Max's depressed mood. Perhaps he hadn't told them the whole story.

Our first interview took place in his lounge, in the converted apartment that was once the old hospital. Very little of the original building remained to give any clue as to its past, everything was clean and new. His mother was present. I didn't object, but I did wonder how much the boy would open up in such company.

After I'd introduced myself and Max had gotten over the shock, I asked him if he knew of anything that might have been troubling my brother, causing him sufficient heartache to take his own life.

Max's eyes betrayed what I myself had suspected from the moment we'd met. He was uncertain, doubting the pointed conclusions that had appeared in the press.

"I don't think so," his voice was low.

"It's all been a bit of a shock," put in his mother.

"I'm sure. Max, did he say anything to you, anything that would make you think—"

"No. nothing. I think he was perfectly happy."

"Happy? Are you sure?"

"Well, he didn't know him that well," continued the mother, "I think, all things being even—"

"Mum. I knew him *very* well. We talked." He turned to me and there was something hidden behind his eyes. A message perhaps? "We talked a lot."

"I didn't know that?" His mother's voice sounded strained.

"Mum. There's lots you don't know." He looked at me, a sudden resolve in his expression. "Stan was my friend. One of the few people who actually took the trouble to make me feel welcome. Clari was the other one."

"Clari?"

"A girlfriend." The mother again, a thin smile on her face.

"She wasn't my *girlfriend,* Mum!"

"Sorry." She smiled at me, a touch embarrassed. "They were close."

"Were?" I frowned. "What happened? Did she move away?"

"No. Killed. Car crash. Her and another woman. Aneeka Kriltski. Dreadful accident."

"It was no accident."

I snapped my head round towards Max at that. His face was set hard and his eyes slowly narrowed. "And Stan didn't hang himself."

His mother showed me to the door. "He's a bit distraught."

"I can see that."

"You shouldn't put too much credence on what he says. He's upset, confused. All those deaths. They all happened whilst we were away, you see. To come back and find out that your friends…well, it was a terrible time for him. The funerals were only the other day. He's very upset still. But I don't think there's any great mystery – the police were very thorough."

"I'm sure. Was it the same investigating officer in both cases, do you know?"

"I couldn't be sure. They often bring someone over for a case like Mr Hedges', but I don't know about Clari. That was all very straightforward so I would think that would probably be local."

"Well, you've been most kind. Thank you for your time." I handed over my card. "I've scribbled the name and number of the hotel where I'm staying on the back. Just in case you think of something."

"Mmm…well, I'm not sure I will, but…" She took the card, then put out her hand and shook mine with surprising strength. "Nice to have met you, mister…?"

"Hedges. John Hedges."

"Of course. Stan's brother. Well, goodbye then."

As she closed the door and I turned to say goodnight, I caught a glimpse of Max, standing in the hallway. There was something he wanted to say, I was sure. But then the door was pressed shut and I was left pondering on what exactly Max knew about what had happened to his young girlfriend and Stan.

TWEПTY-TWO

It was late by the time I reached the town centre. I'd already checked into my hotel, but finding it again was a little difficult. At last, I parked the car in a car park close to the cricket pitch and wandered over towards the hotel. It might have been my imagination, but I was certain there was a figure over by the cricket pavilion, lost in the shadows, watching me. I stopped and strained to see. Definitely something. But it probably wasn't anything sinister, just someone waiting for a friend. I dismissed it and went inside the hotel lobby.

Alone in my room I flipped open my notebook and jotted down, as best I could, my thoughts from the meeting with Max and his mother. This wasn't my usual way of working. Normally I'd make notes throughout the interview. But this was different. Max was only young and was obviously still grieving. I knew I'd have to go back and talk to him again, get a few names from him, try and find out if there was anything that might give me a clue as to why my brother should have done such a dreadful thing.

The other case wasn't as baffling. I still had the newspaper report. The two women – well, one of them being a young girl – had been travelling home late at night. The car had left the road and careered down the side of a cliff. It had been found the following morning, on its roof, the two females inside, dead. It was a horrific, tragic accident. The woman – Aneeka Strilski – had no relatives on the island, but Clarisa, the girl, had a mother. Interestingly, she lived in the same complex as Max. I decided to visit her the following day. I didn't believe there was a link to what had happened to Stan, but all the same the coincidence that all of them lived in the same old hospital building was enough to put just a tiny question mark into my brain. I was a journalist after all, and even a grain of intrigue was all I needed.

The following morning, as I clambered behind the wheel of the little motorcar, I spotted a slip of paper under the windscreen wiper. I got out and read it. It was handwritten and said simply, *'I need to speak to you. P Mumford.'*

Not having any idea, at that stage, who *P Mumford* was, I gunned the engine and trundled down to the old hospital. It was early, not yet nine o'clock and my hope was that I would catch Clarisa's mother before she went out for the day, possibly to work.

As I pulled into the courtyard, it had started to rain. I cursed because I hadn't brought a coat. That was foolish. It was late September and the weather was changing, summer becoming a memory. Although the season was longer here, there was a distinct chill in the air. All I had was my sports jacket, which I now pulled tightly around me and ran over to the front door.

She opened the door almost immediately, almost as if she were expecting me. She was a stunningly attractive woman, despite the black rings around her eyes and the drawn, ashen grey hue of her skin.

"I thought you'd call," she said. I frowned. "Max told me. He came round. He comes round most nights." She smiled, but it was only a ghost of one, flitting across her lips briefly. She stepped aside. "You'd better come in."

The house was Spartan, minimalist and furnished in a modern style. All black and white flooring and plastic tables and chairs. She had some music playing on the turntable and she now flicked the switch and we were plunged into an awkward silence. I stood in the doorway to the lounge whilst she carefully put the long-playing record away in its sleeve. I caught sight of the picture on the front. It was Beethoven's face. The record was his Sixth Symphony.

"This was Clari's favourite." She turned and looked at me. "Come and sit down. I'll make us some tea."

She went out and I crossed to the mantelpiece and gazed at the many photographs there, all in frames. They were all of the same girl, some together with her mother. Clarisa.

I felt a sudden twinge of grief. We'd both suffered loss. But I hadn't spoken to Stan for...well, months. We were never particularly close, keeping in touch only spasmodically. But this, this was different. A mother, torn from her daughter in such a tragic, terrible way. Could there be anything worse?

Suddenly she was standing next to me. I gave a little jump; lost in my own thoughts I hadn't noticed her approach. "Sorry," I said.

"It's all right. I understand Stan was your brother?"

"Yes. Older, by about five years."

"Terrible thing."

I shrugged and nodded to the photographs. "So was this. She looks like a lovely girl."

"She was."

I went over to a nearby armchair and sank down into it whilst she began to pour the tea. She passed it over without proffering any sugar, but I drank it nevertheless.

"Max tells me you're a journalist?"

"That's right. Don't know whether that's a good thing or not in the present circumstances."

"Oh? Why not?"

"Bit too close for comfort...I don't know." I settled my teacup back down on the little table that separated us. "Did you know Stan?"

"Not really. Only to say 'hello' to. Max liked him, would spend a lot of time in his workshop."

"Workshop?"

"Yes. That's where...you know."

I didn't and I started shaking my head slightly, confused. "I thought he was found in his garage?"

"No, that's what the paper said, but that was wrong. He was in his workshop. Sorry, I thought..."

"No, that's okay. I didn't...So...whereabouts is this workshop?"

She stood up and crossed to the window. I followed her and she pointed across the courtyard to a small blockhouse-type building at the far end of the opposite wing. "There it is. I don't think anyone has been in there since...Not even Max. I dare say he wouldn't want to."

"No. He was the one who found Stan?"

She nodded, returning to her seat. I stood for a moment longer, looking across to the other apartments that ran around the courtyard. It was so quiet, hardly even a bird to be heard.

"Yes," she said, pouring out more tea. "Poor Max. He was in a terrible state. But then, he would be...He'd been away, you see. The family had gone back to England, something to do with their house. To come back to..." She sat back, gazing into space. I stood with my back to the window watching her carefully. It was going to be a lifetime before she could come to terms with what had happened. Maybe she never would.

I came back to my own seat and decided to change tack. "Do you know a man called Mumford?"

"Peter Mumford? Well, I know *of* him. He's a local historian, art dealer and socialite. Has a house in the town, very grand. Absolutely filthy rich."

"But you're not what you'd call friends?"

90

"Good God no! We're from different worlds, Mr Hedges. The closest I get to the upper echelons of the middle classes is through my tennis club. Why do you ask?"

"I received a note from him. He wants to meet me."

"Well, he probably has some information for you. Clari told me that Max and Stan had found something. Letters and the like."

"Letters? What kind of letters?"

"She didn't say. I don't think she knew. But Aneeka did. Max had given her a notebook, a journal to translate. Aneeka was Polish, you see. I think the journal had been written in her language. But I couldn't be sure."

I rubbed my chin. This was an interesting development. No doubt Mumford would be able to fill in the gaps. For him to have taken the trouble to seek me out and invite me to visit him was a very gracious act.

Finishing off my second cup of tea and struggling to keep the grimace from my face, I stood up. "You've been very kind. I apologise for intruding on your grief." I handed her my card. "Perhaps, if I think of anything else I could call again?"

She got to her feet and forced a smile. "That would be nice. No one calls, except Max. I think people feel awkward. Don't know what to say." She was looking down at my card, rubbing it with her thumbs as she held it in both her hands. "But there's nothing awkward about any of it." She looked at me and I could see the tears welling up in her eyes. "It's just all so...you know...unfair. You must feel the same?"

"Yes. Yes I do. But..." Now it had become awkward. Both of us were consumed with our relative grief, but only for a moment. She seemed to gather herself and she led me to the door.

91

"Please," she said, her eyes holding mine, "you will call again? Soon?"

I smiled and nodded, then, without another word, I went back to my car.

I heard the door close but didn't look round. I debated whether or not I should go and have a look at Stan's old workshop. Curious that the newspaper had got the detail wrong. Why wouldn't they report the correct details? It was only a tiny error, but an error nonetheless.

As I stood there, mulling this over, I caught a movement over to my right and looked around to see a large man dressed in a long, brown overcoat and trilby hat standing near the alleyway that led to the other side of the apartments. He was staring straight at me. I matched his gaze, feeling my heartbeat beginning to rise. I wasn't normally the kind of person who scared easily; in my job I'd come across many unsavoury characters. But this guy was different. And it wasn't just his size. Perhaps it was his brazen, almost contemptuous way in which he stared. He didn't look away. That unnerved me somewhat. So I called out to him, "Can I help you in any way?"

But he didn't answer, just very slowly turned and disappeared down the alleyway.

Something told me that I would see him again.

TWENTY-THREE

"I'm more interested in what you know about the journals."

I was sitting in Mumford's study. A curious room, locked in the past, it had the feel of a scene from Dickens. The walls were lined with bookcases, right up to the ceiling, filled with more books than I think I'd ever seen outside a major library, the perfect soundproofing, making the room seem very intimate, quiet. As a study no doubt should be. A clock ticked sonorously, the minutes seeming to hang in the air, making slow progress, helping to create a relaxed, stress-free atmosphere. A pleasant room, a room where you would like to spend a lot of time, leafing through various volumes, immersing oneself in learning. If it hadn't been for Mumford, it would have been perfect. But Mumford was there, lending the room, and everything within it, an icy edge.

Mumford himself seemed amicable enough, at least on the outside. But I was acutely aware of the way he sat, bolt upright, loaded like a coiled spring, alert and tense. He didn't appear to be in the mood to share very much and he was no more forthcoming about Stan than he would be about the president of Mozambique.

"Stan and I were not particularly close. I only knew him in passing."

He recharged my glass. Luscious, full-bodied red wine. He'd opened up a bottle almost as I'd arrived and now I was about to start my third glass. I noticed, with a slight feeling of unease, that Mumford had barely taken a sip from his first.

He settled back in his armchair, palms together, fingertips tapping against his lips, and he surveyed me like a hawk, preparing to swoop on its prey. He wasted no more time in bringing the conversation round to the point where he wanted it to be. "So, Mr Hedges. The journals?"

I spread out my hands, "I don't know anything about them, Mr Mumford. All I'm really trying to do is get to the bottom of why Stan would take his own life."

"Depression I shouldn't wonder. Stan was very up and down."

"I thought you said you hardly knew him."

Mumford paused, interlocking his fingers together now in an attitude of prayer. "Mr Hedges, all I do know about Stan was that he was a very solitary man. Could always be found pottering about up at that damned hospital, putting in far more hours than were required. A heart of gold. But a lonely man, I think. Lonely and..." he looked at me, the pause lending weight to his next word, "sad."

"How could you possibly know that?"

"Just a hunch. I'm a historian, Mr Hedges. Sometimes I have to make informed guesses. Most of my work is to do with evidence and reaching conclusions from that evidence. Whenever I would meet Stan he seemed...distant. As if he had many problems. Of course, I could be wrong...but I don't think I am."

"So, Stan was lonely...and depressed. Depressed enough to kill himself."

"Tragically, it would seem so."

I wasn't convinced, and there was nothing in what Mumford was telling me that was going to change my mind. If Mumford didn't know my brother all that well, how could he pass judgement on something that was so relevant, so central to what had happened? Not for the first time, I changed the course of the conversation, "Why the interest in the journals, Mr Mumford?"

"I thought that would have been obvious." He smiled. "I wrote a history of that place not so many years ago. Lent a copy to young Max. But with this new evidence, I could write a revised edition. First-hand, primary evidence, Mr Hedges. You can't get better than that."

"I'd be correct in saying that your book was based almost entirely on the statements of the men who worked there."

"And women. But yes, that would be correct. There were no survivors, you see. So, anything that could corroborate what the German soldiers said would be very useful indeed."

"Or perhaps shed a whole new light on what went on?"

"Hardly that, I'd say. The men made full confessions, Mr Hedges. Many of them paid for those revelations with their lives. The hangman's noose was tied very tight."

"But can you be sure that what they said was the whole truth?"

"Exactly! Which is why I need those journals." He smiled again, that sickly sweet smile that I was learning to loathe. "Where are they?"

"I thought I'd answered that question."

It was his turn to look sceptical. "Max brought me some photographs. Very interesting. But the journals I have yet to read."

"Have you asked him?"

"Who, Max? Well, I wouldn't – not at this moment in time. I think he is suffering, Mr Hedges. A little like yourself."

The note of total indifference in his voice irked me. It was just something for him to say. I was growing to dislike the man more and more. "Well, perhaps I should ask him."

"If you think it will help. I will be very grateful. And..." he smiled again, "I'll make it worth your while."

I nodded and stood up. "The wine was delicious, but I couldn't quite finish the last glass. Sorry."

"Don't apologise, Mr Hedges." He stood up next to me, "You will be in touch?"

"As soon as I've found something, yes."

"Excellent."

Out in the street I sauntered down towards the ornamental garden and found a bench on which to sit. Two people had now been desperate for me to contact them again. Mumford and Clarisa's mother. Given a choice, I knew which one I'd rather see.

I put my hands behind my head and stretched my legs, looking up at the sky. It was early evening and the air was humid. A pleasant place to live, unhurried, almost sedate. If I'd had the means, I'd consider moving there myself. But I didn't have the means. All I was allowed was a brief visit. Tony Andrews, my editor back home, had given me a week's 'compassionate leave'. Perhaps it would be enough, perhaps not. But the thought of returning to the mayhem that was my workplace was not one that I wished to dwell upon. I remembered when I was much younger. Whenever I stumbled across somewhere new, that really affected me, somewhere like a pine woods, or a meandering river in early summer, I often used to think that I'd like to stay there forever. Forget about the world, immerse myself in the solitude. Perhaps if I stayed there and was happy, the rest of the world would forget about me and I could leave everything behind. I'd be free. Free of school, everyday existence. If only I had the courage, outstay my time. Who would know, who would care? This place was a little like that. I could simply not go back. What would be the worst that could happen? Get the sack? I laughed.

If only I had the courage...

"Mr Hedges?"

I sat upright at the sound of the voice, startled that someone could approach me so quietly.

The man sat down next to me. Slim, athletic build. The kind of middle-aged man who spent more time in the gym than he did in front of the television. He was nervous looking, eyes darting around as if he were half-expecting someone to suddenly spring out. A little like he had to me. "My name is Peter Phelps. I was Aneeka's fiancé."

I gaped at him. "Aneeka being...the woman who was killed in the car crash?"

A sudden steely glance. "Not killed. Murdered."

We found a bar and sat down with our drinks. His was non-alcoholic, which I could have predicted. He was tense, anxious and insisted we find a table which faced the entrance. As we talked he would constantly glance up towards the door, that same hunted looked on his face that he'd shown when he first spoke to me in the ornamental gardens. I had to admit he made me feel nervous too.

"Aneeka telephoned me the day before it happened. I live in Manchester. I don't often get the chance to come over here. Maybe once or twice a month if I'm lucky. We usually talk on the 'phone, but nothing like this. She was frightened, you see. Said she'd been given a journal by a young boy, Max I think she said his name was. Anyway, it was in Russian and she'd started to translate it. But she said it was terrible. *Full of nightmares.* Those were her very words. *Full of nightmares.* As she spoke she began to get hysterical, saying that there was a man hanging around and that she was hearing things, in her house. Strange things. *Supernatural* things." He drank his drink down in one, smacking his lips, then dragging the back of his hand across his mouth. "I couldn't calm her down. I told her I'd come over, get a few days off work, but she insisted I didn't do anything of the sort. Instead, she said she'd post everything to me. The journal and her translations."

"And she did?"

"Oh yes. She did that all right."

The door opened and Phelps jumped up. But he soon relaxed as two young men came in, obviously out for a good time, laughing out loud.

"You need to relax," I said as he flopped back down in his seat.

"Relax? You don't know what's going on here, Hedges. You've got no idea."

"Then why don't you tell me."

"You're a journalist, right? You could report all of this, couldn't you? Your paper could publish the whole lot."

"If I knew what *the whole lot* was, then yes."

"Once I tell you, then they'll come looking for you too. That's what they did to Aneeka, see. Her and that poor girl."

"Clarisa?" I shook my head. "Clarisa didn't know anything. I've been to see her mum. She was just a little girl, a friend of Max's."

"Yeah, a little girl who just happened to be a friend of Aneeka's. They probably thought that boy Max had told her everything. He's the key to all of this, I'm sure."

I sat back, raising a cynical eyebrow. "I think you're just distraught, looking for something that isn't there. A reason why your girlfriend died that night."

98

"Don't patronise me, Hedges. I don't need your contempt."

"I'm not being patronising or contemptuous! You're upset, overwrought ...who wouldn't be? But the sad truth is, it was an accident."

"You're wrong." He reached inside his jacket and brought out an envelope. He quickly opened it and laid out the handwritten note that was inside. He passed it over to me. "That was what Aneeka wrote to me, when she sent me the journal. Read it. Read it and then tell me it was an accident."

I quickly did as he asked. It was only short, but in those few lines the dreadful state Aneeka was in soon became apparent. "All right," I said, folding up the letter again and sticking it back in the envelope, "but this doesn't *prove* she was murdered...just that she was terrified."

"I think that's enough. Strange she should write that, then within a day she was dead."

"Coincidence."

"For pity's sake, why are you being like this? I thought journalists were supposed to sniff out stories, make headlines, stick their noses in? It's almost like you've accepted what's happened. Even what happened to your own brother."

"What do you know about that?"

"Nothing. It was only once I got here that I found out he'd died too. Still a coincidence? The three people who knew Max, all dead within the space of a day of each other?"

I drained my glass and stood up. "Okay, I'll give you that. But up to now no one is giving me very much, Only hearsay, opinion, conjecture. I agree that Max is the key. But I can't speak to him, not yet. He's overwhelmed by what has happened. I'm going to give it another two

99

days, then I'll go and see him again. Then you and I will meet. Hopefully, I'll have some answers, something concrete. Deal?"

He put his face in his hands. "Two days...I hope I'm still here, Hedges, I really do."

"You will be. Drink?" I raised my glass, but he didn't acknowledge my invitation, so I went over to the bar and ordered him another anyway.

I stood there, foot on the rail, elbows propped up on the counter. I hadn't given much away. I didn't want him to think that I agreed with almost everything he had said. There was too much coincidence to all of this. Stan wouldn't have killed himself, not for anything. And Aneeka, from what I understood, was a strong and resourceful woman. Perhaps too strong. Perhaps she had stood up to whoever was trying to intimidate her. Because I felt sure that whoever was behind all of this knew that she had the journal. How they knew that was another matter. But that journal was worth killing for. I was convinced of that now. The only question that remained was why.

The barman placed the two glasses in front of me. I paid the money, picked them up and turned. I didn't take another step.

Peter Phelps had disappeared.

TWENTY-FOUR

I woke up the following morning, head banging, and a feeling like I'd stuffed my mouth full of cotton wool. My tongue was thick and fur-covered and I brushed it with my toothbrush and gradually began to feel a little better. Too much drink. All of that wine from Mumford, then beer at the bar. How did the old saying go, *beer before wine is fine.* Well, I'd done it the other way round and I was suffering because of it.

Breakfast was not something I was looking forward to, but I struggled down to the restaurant anyway for some coffee. About a gallon would do, make me feel a little more human again. As I sat down at my table, the manager came up, smiling broadly. He had a package in his hand. "Morning, Mr Hedges. Sleep well?" I peered up at him through blood-shot eyes and sighed heavily. How could anyone be so damned cheerful so early? He laughed. "Well, you've every right to try and enjoy yourself. This was left for you at the bar this morning."

"This morning?" I glanced at my watch. It wasn't yet nine.

"Yes. Early."

He handed it over and as he waltzed off I ripped open the seal and pulled out a thin, tattered exercise book together with some type-written notes. The journal and Aneeka's translation. There was also a note, from Phelps.

'Read this. Then tell me you don't believe what I said.'

The coffee came and I poured myself a cup. Black, with four sugars. I gulped it down, then made a decision. I had planned on going up to see Clarisa's mum again but that would have to wait. Right now I had something else to do. Read the journal.

I went back to my room and spread myself out on the bed, pulling out the journal and the notes. I could tell straight away that Aneeka had made only partial translations, but as I read them a picture began to emerge of what went on in that hospital, revelations that were to change my life forever.

'February 1943
Dear Lulu,
I should be grateful. I no longer have to live amongst the snow and ice. But they have brought us to this place and I can see that it is as much a part of Hell as the frozen steppe. I shall not bore you with the details of the journey, only to say I have never endured such thirst and hunger. The cattle trucks we came in were crammed with men. Many died. When we reached France they brought us here on ship. Of the two hundred men that left that shore, maybe half survived.'

'February 22nd 1943
Dear Lulu,
Ten days, I think, I have been here. I have managed to steal this notebook. If they find it they will punish me, so I must be quick. I write from memory. Sometimes it is hard to remember. I wrote about many of us dying. More have died. But more have come here. They keep maybe two hundred of us together at any one time. Soon, they have said, we will start work. But on what, I do not know.'

'February 25th 1943
Dear Lulu,
We began to work today. Digging holes. We did this all day. My hands are bleeding. My shoulders are in so much pain I can hardly walk straight. I saw one man fall

down and one of the soldiers shot him in the back of the head. No one falls down now. Only two days and already I feel that I cannot last another.'

'March 1943
Dear Lulu,
The officers came yesterday. They picked out four or five of us. Myself and one other girl and three men. All young. They took us to the hospital. They gave us food. Real food, not like the filth they have been giving us in the camp. This was meat. We ate and ate. It was horrible when I think how much we forgot about our compatriots, and so quickly. All I could think about was getting the food into my belly. I think if someone had tried to stop me, or had taken my food away, I would have killed them.'

'March 7 1943,
Dear Lulu,
We sleep in a long room. Very bright, very clean. In the morning they took us to a piece of ground and made us run. We had to run all the time. If we stopped, they hit us. When one of the boys stumbled, they kicked him. But at least we weren't shot. We had to run until we could not run any more. Then they took us back to the hospital and made us write down what we had done. No water. Nothing to drink. Then they made us walk up and down stairs. I don't know why they do this. There are three men, all officers, all the time watching us and they keep writing things down. The soldiers, they kick us when we stop. Always, up and down. No water. One of our boys fell down, unconscious. His face was so swollen, his lips so dry. They took him outside and they shot him. I think I will die soon.'

March 9 1943,
Dear Lulu,
Yesterday they let us rest. We could drink as much as we liked. They brought in another boy. Very young. Sixteen maybe. He was very frightened. Today they took us to the beach. It was very cold. They took off our clothes and forced us into the water. I think I was the only one who could swim. We had to swim against the waves and it was very difficult. When we tried to come back, the soldiers shot at us with their rifles. The officers made notes. The young boy, he could not swim and they kept shooting at him, forcing him to go further out. The waves were very big and he disappeared. Two more disappeared. A boy and the other girl. I do not know their names. All I know is that they are dead.'

March 10 1943,
Lulu,
Last night they put us in bed and the nurses came. They were very brutal to us. They stuck needles in my arms. Many times. I felt like I was in a nightmare, lots of horrible faces and sounds of people screaming. I saw them take another boy out of his bed and they put him against the wall. He was like a rag doll, no strength left in him. Then the officer came in, the commandant. He is very cruel and he struck the boy across the face, shouting at him in words I did not understand. Then the others, they lifted him up and they put hooks in his shoulders. Meat hooks and they left him there and he screamed all through the night. I could not do anything. They tied me to the bed and they stuck more needles in my arms. No sleep. Just the sound of him screaming. When the morning came he gave his last cry. They came in again. The commandant and two more men. Big men. They took the boy down. There was no weight in him.

104

They let him drop to the ground. Then the commandant looked at me and smiled a terrible smile. I will never forget that smile. Keeping his eyes on me, he brought out his gun and shot the boy in the head. I screamed and they all laughed. Then they went out, leaving him there, on the ground, the mess, the blood. My God, it was like nothing I had ever seen. He died without a word, without a sound. I knew I would be next.'

I rolled onto my back and gazed at the ceiling. So this was what had happened at the hospital. Experiments in how much the human body could withstand before it gave out? It was barbarous, inhuman, insane. Why subject people to such torture? To what end? What possible good could it do anyone to carry out such murderous deeds? Was it simply dressed up as science, a disguise to mask what in actual fact it really was – sadism? I glanced at the notes again. There was more, but not much. She described how the men had subjected her to the most unspeakable things. Then, the sleep depravation. Every time she closed her eyes, they woke her, with ice-cold water, glaring lights, beatings. She endured it for days. Her last entry was March 22, 1943. It simply read, *'They will come for me again soon. My life is at its end. How I hate them and curse them for what they have done to my compatriots and me. They have selected more of us from the camp. This will not stop. Cruel, evil, they revel in our suffering, they laugh as we die. I cannot write more.'*

Carefully, I put the papers back in the package and looked around for somewhere to put it. I could have kept it with me, and for a moment I did think about doing that. But something was nagging me at the back of my mind, telling me I had to be cautious. So, where to leave it?

The obvious place was my suitcase. But that was too obvious. I considered putting it under my mattress, between the spare blankets in the wardrobe, underneath the bedside rug. In the end I opted for what I believed to be the most unsuspecting of places. It took a bit of careful positioning but in the end, I was satisfied. I couldn't imagine anyone would look there.

I felt as if I had entered a spy-movie. What would I do next, I wondered, place one of my hairs across the catch of my suitcase? That way I'd know if anyone had been inside my room. Laughing at my own wild imagination, I went out to call on Clarisa's mother. I needed to find out exactly what Clarisa had found out about all of this. That would clarify Peter Phelps' suspicions that Clarisa had been killed, along with Aneeka, because of what she knew.

TWENTY-FIVE

Driving up the winding hill that led to the old hospital complex, I had an idea that there was one person who hadn't really figured very much in any of this. Max's father. A respected man in the community, a bank manager, if anyone could put a more measured and considered spin on all of this, it was him. No fanciful explanations, no bizarre stories of murder and ghostly visitations. A man with his feet placed squarely on the ground. I decided to give him a call as soon as I left Clarisa's mother.

I turned the last sharp bend before the hospital loomed into view. It was a clear day, a gentle breeze rustling through the trees. I wasn't going fast and the windows were down. It was a perfect day.

From nowhere, I saw too late the body burst from out of the bushes that ran along the side of the road. All I knew was that it was a man. He hit the car with a loud, dull thud, his body arcing up into the air, flipping over in a somersault before coming down again to land heavily across the bonnet.

I'd jammed on the brakes, but too late to prevent my car hitting him. Now, as I sat there, pressed up against the steering wheel, I was staring straight into the open, lifeless eyes of Peter Phelps.

It was a little like a circus, policemen and plain clothes investigators milling around, using measuring tapes, taking photographs, scribbling down copious notes. A policewoman was sitting with me, on the verge, some twenty or so feet away from the scene. Clarisa's mum was also there, chewing her nails, looking shocked. I'd ran up to her house and pounded on the door. I couldn't think of anyone else to tell. Within ten minutes her telephone call had brought down a swarm of emergency people. Peter Phelps still lay on the bonnet. I still sat on the verge.

"Hedges is it?" The voice belonged to a small wiry man with a moustache. He was smoking and looked rather stern. "My name's Mitchell. Detective Sergeant Mitchell. I understand you were out drinking with the deceased last night?"

That was quick! I was impressed, but a little disturbed. "Yes."

"Barman said you were arguing."

"*What?*" I looked around and found Clarisa's mum looking straight at me. She raised her eyebrows but didn't say a word.

"Raised voices. Agitated. What were you talking about?"

"Nothing much. Just some information he was giving me."

"Information? What sort of information would that be?"

"Just some bits and pieces, about my brother." I was still in shock, but I had enough wits about me not to divulge the actual contents of our conversation. I was very quickly beginning to doubt every single person with whom I was coming into contact.

"So, was that why you were shouting at him? Thought he had something to do with your brother's death, is that it?"

"I...Look, what is this? What exactly are you accusing me of?"

"I'm not accusing you of anything, Mr Hedges. What would make you think that...unless, there *is* something about your argument with Mr Phelps that you'd like to tell us?"

"But it wasn't an argument!"

"That's not what the barman says. Often lose your temper do you?"

"Now look here, sergeant—" I stopped, glaring at the policeman and annoyed at myself for falling into his trap. I let my shoulders slump and blew out a long sigh. I kept my voice controlled now. "Are you going to arrest me?"

"Now why would I do that?" A leering smile. Match-point to him! He nodded towards the police woman. "Get him something, will you? He looks like he needs it." He threw away his cigarette and turned towards Clarisa's mother. "Can we have a little chat, please?"

I watched them both as they wandered out of earshot. Suddenly my world was caving in and I didn't have a clue what to do about it.

TWENTY-SIX

"My name's Samantha. I wish you'd use it, not this silly formal stuff."

Forcing a little laugh, I tried to relax. But it was difficult. Images of Phelps hitting my car kept looming up in front of me. I couldn't shake them. I couldn't shake that look on his face, those lifeless, doll's eyes staring sightlessly at me. I shivered.

The breakdown truck had finally taken my car away and although the entire area was cordoned off, it was still a public highway and bollards had been placed all around the accident scene. Cars couldn't get through and signs directed any drivers to park their cars on the waste ground further down the hill. Only those on foot could continue up to the hospital. Mitchell had told me he'd be in touch and then I'd come here, to speak to Clarisa's mum. Samantha.

I sipped the brandy she'd poured me.

"This has been quite a morning," she said quietly. "It brings it all back. The police. The questions."

"I'm sorry."

"It's not your fault." I appreciated that little sign of support. With all the police questions I was beginning to have doubts. "What do you think he was doing up here?"

"I don't know. Perhaps he was just looking around. After all, he must have been as desperate as we both are, to get to the truth."

"It's just all so...horrible. Four people dead in the space of a fortnight." She leaned forward, elbow on her knee, fingers in her mouth, chewing at her nails. "I'm not sure how much more I can take...doctor's given me pills. Tranquillisers. They don't work. Every time I close my eyes I see Clari's face. And now this..."

110

She broke down then, burying her face in her hands, sobbing uncontrollably. I suspected it was the first time she'd actually let go. Hesitantly, I slipped down next to her and put my arms around her shoulders.

We sat like that for a long time.

She took me down to the beach later, when both of us were feeling slightly better. It was a glorious afternoon, the sun warm, the water inviting. We sat on the dunes and looked out to sea. She'd made some sandwiches and we ate them in silence, trying in our own individual ways to come to terms with everything that had happened.

Something like this had happened to me before. Years ago. I was in the Gulf of Eilat, reporting on one of the many communes that had begun to spring up around that part of the world during that time. Hippy culture had reached the Middle East. I'd clambered out of the jeep I'd parked up on the roadside and a man came running towards me. He was waving his arms in the air, white eyes bulging out of a black face, bearded, wild looking. I didn't know who he was or what he wanted, or even if he was actually running towards me. He didn't get more than ten feet away from me before he was shot. He staggered forward and fell into my arms. Soldiers came up to me then and rammed their rifles in my face. Screaming something about gunmen and terrorists, they told me to get out and never return. I didn't need much persuading.

I held him as he died.

Then I left that place. A few weeks later, war broke out between Israel and her neighbours. The so-called Six-Day War.

Memories.

Death.

The two seemed to go together.

And now here I was again, trying to come to terms with what had happened to Peter Phelps. A man I hardly knew, a man who had been so terrified that he didn't know what he was doing. At least, that's how I saw it. I might have been wrong. Perhaps it was all deliberate. All I knew was that he was dead and I was inextricably involved.

"Clari told me a little about what Max had seen." Samantha had her knees drawn up to her chest and was rocking herself backwards and forwards ever so gently. "I didn't believe it, of course. Thought it was just the product of an over-ripe imagination. But, now that he comes and visits me, I can see that it isn't anything of the kind. What he sees is real."

"What he sees? I don't understand."

"Visions, John. Visions of things that used to go in that place. The hospital. Max can see what they did to those poor people. The Germans. Nazis. Their experiments, torture, vile, despicable games. It's getting too much for him."

"Have you told him to talk to someone?"

"Who? A doctor? A psychiatrist?" Her voice sounded sharp, close to the edge of anger. I'd touched a nerve. "That's what his mother told me. I met her. We were going to play tennis together, then all of this...Well, it sort of put paid to anything remotely enjoyable. It's all so trivial, isn't it."

"I didn't mean to suggest he was—"

"I know, but you're a journalist. You deal in facts, not superstition. But when you talk to Max, you'll understand."

"I read the journal. The one Max found." She looked at me, a deep frown creasing her forehead. "The one

Aneeka translated for him. Peter Phelps had it. Aneeka had posted it to him, the day before..."

She held my eyes. "Before the car-crash? Just say it, John. I'm not a little girl."

"I know...I'm sorry, I don't mean to sound...Oh God, I don't know what I mean! I thought I could come over here, find out why Stan did what he did and then that would be the end of it. Back to London and my job. Back to reality, all the ends neatly tied off."

"You really thought that would happen?" The scepticism in her voice was ladled on thick. "I don't think so. You never actually *believed* Stan killed himself, did you?"

"No. And what with everything that's happened since...I'm even more convinced of it. Phelps was convinced too. And now he's dead. It's just too...*neat.* Everyone who has had anything to do with that damned hospital, its secrets, has ended up..." I bit my tongue again. I could sense her eyes boring into me but I kept my gaze on the sea. "Except for Max."

"You think he's in danger?"

"I hope not. But this mystery is deeper and more complicated than any of us, certainly me, could have possibly imagined."

"You're best talking to Max, don't you think? He's the one person who can make sense of this, I'm sure."

"I'm worried about his state of mind, though. If I start pitching in with questions..." Despair was beginning to gather in all around me.

She seemed to sense my mood. "I'll come with you. He trusts me. I'll go and speak with him this afternoon, suggest that you and he get together. In the meantime, you get back to your hotel, try and relax, then call back at mine round-about six." She touched my arm, "John, you're suffering too. What happened...you're coping with it, but I'm worried that it's just a front. First your brother, now this...You need time to come to terms with what's happened. To gather your thoughts."

No one had ever spoken to me like that before, not since I was a little boy. She was so kind, so understanding. She had been through so much and yet she still found a way to give me some words of comfort. Our mutual grief had brought us close.

TWENTY-SEVEN

The alarm woke me and for a moment I panicked, not sure of where I was. I'd been driving, in my dream, whistling. Whistling? I never whistled. Then the body came through the windscreen, its face looming up right in front of me, its eyes so close I could feel the eyelashes as they blinked. It was Peter Phelps. And he was laughing. Laughing at me, mocking me. And the emergency vehicles, speeding up behind my car, their bells clanging. Like a scene from *Gideon of the Yard*, those bells filled my world. It was this sound that had woken me and now, slowly, my mind brought everything back into sharp focus and I sat up, went over to the washbasin and swilled my face with cold water. I looked at my reflection and the face that stared back at me was grim and drawn. I ran a hand over my chin and felt how rough it was with stubble. I looked a mess and was in desperate need of a bath.

Later, lying in the warm water, letting it soak away the stiffness of my joints, I tried to calm myself. I'd begun to shake almost as soon as I got back to the hotel. The walk from Samantha's had been invigorating. I'd followed the coastal path and hadn't come across another human being. Something I was grateful for. I tried to keep my mind off the details of the day and had almost succeeded until I came into the town centre. There were people gathered outside the newsagents and they were in a tight gaggle, all jabbering away excitedly and when they spotted me, they stopped abruptly and just stared. It was then it came back. The picture of Phelps, lying there on the bonnet, his eyes…Then the dream. Or should that be nightmare? I didn't know and I was trying not to care as I slid back in the soapy water, warm and relaxing. If I could just let it all just soak away...

It all happened very fast then. The door burst open. I couldn't see the face, just the hat and the big hands. They seized my throat and I was being pushed down beneath the water. "Where is the journal?" he demanded, in that guttural, heavily accented voice of his. So that was it, that was what he wanted. Was he prepared to kill me for it? Did I really have to ask that question as he continued to press me down? He was immensely strong, too strong for me to be able to stop him from the position I was in, certainly. I clawed at his hands, but it was useless. Panic ensnared me and I began to thrash out with my legs, trying to get some leverage. I couldn't think straight. I'd been in the army, spent two years national service tramping through the stinking jungles of Malaya, involving myself heavily in counter-insurgency operations. I'd never seen a single enemy soldier, or bandit as they were known, let alone killed any. Not a one. So I never had any need for all the tricks they'd taught us. But I had need of them now and from somewhere I managed to haul up the memory.

I gripped his hands, twisting them, putting pressure against his thumbs, and swung myself around. I had the tiny advantage of lying face up. If he managed to get me head first into the water, I'd be doomed.

His hold was momentarily broken and I jammed up with my elbow. I struck him somewhere in the face and he gasped and staggered back. Now all I had to was get to my feet. I was still on my side, trying to gather my knees under me in order to get myself into a standing position. But it was too slippery, and I was trying to move too quickly.

He hit me, hard, across the back of the neck. I shot forward, then he was pushing me down again, towards the water. But I was still on my knees, which probably saved my life. He simply couldn't manage to push my head beneath the water. I threw my elbow backwards again, trusting in mere hope rather than technique, and I connected with some part of him. I'd been given a moment's reprieve, and I managed to get up as he staggered back, his grip on me broken.

I whirled round, hands coming up, ready to ward off another attack, but I needn't have bothered.

He'd gone.

Gasping and spluttering, I stepped over the rim of the bath and took a few moments to gather myself. Breathing hard, I reached out and grabbed for a towel, pressing it against my face. It had all happened too fast, not giving me any chance to take any of it in. But one thing was certain.

I knew exactly who it was.

His hat was lying there, at my feet.

TWENTY-EIGHT

My room was not how I'd left it. There had not been a lot of consideration given to my personal belongings, most of which were strewn across the floor. The bed had been rifled through, together with the wardrobe. And I hadn't needed the hair across the lock of my suitcase for me to see that it had been opened and gone through. With my heart in my mouth I very gently eased forward the painting on the wall. There was the journal, undisturbed. A small victory, I mused. Without any further hesitation I quickly got dressed.

Downstairs the bar was quiet but I still managed to catch the eye of the manager as I came down, having pulled myself together sufficiently enough to button up my shirt correctly.

"Are you all right?" he asked, pausing in the act of polishing a pint glass.

It must have been the dishevelled state I was in that had caused him to make the comment. I shrugged and moved closer. "You didn't see anyone running through here? Heavy-set guy, raincoat?"

"No. I've been down in the cellar for the best part of the last hour. Friend of yours was he?"

"Er – not exactly, no. If you see him again, tell him I've got his hat, will you?"

I left him looking suitably bemused.

Samantha was shocked when I told her what had happened. I whispered the events to her in the hallway, not wishing to frighten Max any more than was necessary. "Shouldn't you 'phone the police?"

"I don't think so. Something tells me that all is not as it should be with our local constabulary."

"Pardon?"

"Nothing. Just a hunch. Let's go and talk to Max."

He was sitting in the lounge, looking relaxed and not at all as I expected to find him. Then again, kids always surprised me with their powers of recovery. If anything, I probably felt more nervous than him.

"How are you, Max?"

"I'm okay. You?"

I shrugged and sat down. Samantha brought in the tea. "I need to tell you something, Max. Have you heard of a man called Peter Phelps?"

Samantha paused in the act of pouring a cup of tea. "Sorry. I told Max what happened this morning."

"I see. Well, so did you know of him, Max? Who he was?"

"Only what Sam's told me."

"He was Aneeka's fiancé. She sent him the journals."

Max's jaw slackened a little as the news bit home. "Okay," he said slowly. "So, she translated it. All of it?"

"Not all of it, but enough to give us...a flavour of what went on here. Phelps gave it to me for safekeeping. I read it." I looked at Samantha for support. She smiled her encouragement. "Max, what went on here was nothing short of ritualistic torture."

"I know," he said quietly but with no trace of nervousness, "I've seen it."

I pulled myself upright. "Sam has told me that you have had visions, Max. Can you try and tell me some of the things you've seen?"

"I've seen what they did. Wheeling prisoners into rooms, jabbing them with needles, putting them through hell. I've heard the guards laughing while they did it. Officers. Nurses. The commandant."

"The commandant? Can you be sure?"

"Oh yes. I've seen his photograph. Stan and I found it all down in the cellar. Hidden inside an old, forgotten crate. Photographs, letters, the journal, and official documents."

"Official...you saw those? You know what they contained?"

"No. Stan kept them. I gave the photographs to Mr Mumford. Except one. I kept that back."

"Which one?"

He reached inside his coat and pulled out a creased black and white portrait of a young girl, a stunningly gorgeous face beaming back out at me as I held it in my hands and looked at it, transfixed. "I wonder who she was..."

"I know who she was," said Max. "Her name is Alena and she wrote the journal."

I gawped at him. "My God." I returned to the face. So this was she, the girl that had endured so much. Now I knew who she was it made her words even more immediate, real and personal. I felt my stomach begin to knot and I had to look away for a moment, desperately fighting off the urge to cry. "Are you sure?" I managed to ask.

"Yes. I've seen her too. Mr Hedges, I'm a clairvoyant. I can talk to those who have crossed-over."

The silence was palpable. It took a long time for me to react.

I'd come across this sort of thing before, obviously. Both professionally and personally. I'd always dismissed it, either as an elaborate hoax or tricks of the imagination. But there was something about Max, an honesty and a directness that made me begin to feel that perhaps there was an awful lot of truth in what he said after all. How else could he know so much? Unless the journals had merely served to fuel his dreams.

But there was a problem with that, of course. The journal was written in Russian. And, as if sensing my line of thinking, Max then brought up the second problem with my hypothesis. "I began seeing things before I knew about the journal. In fact, it was a dream that told me about the cellar."

I ran my tongue across my teeth. "All right," I said slowly, "so, let's consider that what you say is true…why do you think all of this is happening?"

"I think I know." Max turned from me to Samantha. "I never meant to involve others in this. I had no way of knowing what would happen."

"I know that, Max." She smiled reassuringly towards him. "We've spoken about this before."

"I know. I just…I just wanted you to understand. I never meant for any of this to happen."

She smiled again and sat down next to him. She squeezed his arm. "I don't blame you, Max."

"Stan told me he recognised the commandant. As soon as he saw the photograph."

Surprised I raised an eyebrow. "How could he know him? That couldn't be."

"But it was. Stan knew him because Stan had met him. Many times. He lives here, on the island. A new name, a new identity, but the same man. They say the criminal always returns to the scene of his crimes. It seems like that old saying is true."

At that point everything fell into place. If what Max was saying was fact, then it was clear why Stan and the others had been killed. And why I had been attacked. The commandant would be a wanted war-criminal. If his identity was revealed, then he would have no place to hide. The evidence that Max and Stan had found was clearly explosive.

The problem remained – who was this man? The one person who knew him, Stan, was no longer around to identify him.

"You think we can find him?" I asked at last.

"After what happened this morning," cut in Samantha, "I think he has already found you. The man goes to extreme lengths to protect himself."

"So, there can only be one conclusion to draw from that – he must be immensely important in this community. He's built up a base of trust and friendship that he wishes to guard very jealously. He's probably successful, rich and powerful. The one place the authorities wouldn't look for him is here, living right under the shadow of the crimes he perpetrated. That's clever...and brave."

"Perhaps foolhardy."

"He probably never even thought that his real identity would be revealed, simply because nobody knew about that crate."

"And nobody would have known about it if it hadn't been for Max."

I went over to the window and looked out across the courtyard towards Stan's workshop. "It's only a matter of time before he tries to strike again." I turned and looked at the others. "He'll know we've met. He seems to know everything. Which is why I'm suspicious of the police. There's something going on here which is far more than just a war criminal hiding out, no matter how important that is. I think we're on the brink of uncovering something. What, I don't know. But it must be extremely important if whoever is behind all of this is willing to kill. Repeatedly. So we have to assume we're all in danger. And that means you two are going to have to leave."

TWENTY-NINE

With one firm squeeze, the heavy-duty bolt-cutters sliced through the padlock that held Stan's workshop door closed. Without a moment's pause, I slipped inside and waited whilst my eyes grew accustomed to the gloom.

It was a ramshackle sort of place, just like Stan would have preferred it. He hated order and tidiness. I had to smile as I went over to the worktop and picked up the crumpled pack of dog-eared playing cards that were sitting there. Stan would use any excuse for a quick game of patience, anything to put off what had to be done. He was a good worker once he got started, but it was getting him started that was the problem.

I didn't know what I was looking for, just a sense of him, perhaps. A memory. An item, something belonging to him, something to prove that he had once been alive. I sank down on an old, threadbare chair and I knew I couldn't hold back the tears any longer.

I must have sat there for a good hour, drinking in the atmosphere, the smell. It was hopeless, of course. There wouldn't be anything there. It was just an opportunity to try and regain something of my brother. I stood up, scanning the worktops for anything I might have missed, delving through heaps of old screws and nails, moving rusted tools, old broken bits of tile. A note, a pocketbook, any sort of clue.

My eyes alighted on the wall calendar. It had pictures of old motorcars and the page was turned to July. July. It was almost October. And motorcars. For as long as I could remember, Stan had no interest in motorcars. Football, yes. Cricket in the summer. But cars...

The various drawers didn't hold anything of any interest either. More nails, screws of various sizes, bunches of rusted keys, a few foreign coins. I blew out a sigh and leaned back on the worktop. They'd found the body here. Or, at least Max had. I hadn't asked him about that, there was no real need. It was all in the papers. He'd come in, expecting to see his old friend sitting down working and instead...I looked at the heavy beams that ran across the ceiling. The hooks.

I closed my eyes.

Why in here? What a way to end a life, strung up in such a lonely, cold and dark place. And surely...

That was it. My eyes sprang open.

If Stan *had* committed suicide, he would never have chosen this place, for the simple reason that Max would have come inside. Stan could never have wished such a terrible discovery on his friend. Max was only a boy, but the two had grown close. Stan had few friends. He'd always been a loner. To have become this friendly with someone was rare for my brother. Then, to have put his newfound friend through such a harrowing ordeal...No, it just wasn't right. They'd murdered Stan and trussed him up in here for exactly that reason – to frighten Max, put him off the scent, perhaps even force him to run away.

And there was something else. There *was* a clue and I knew exactly what it was. Stan was cleverer than I could have ever believed.

THIRTY

I had the copy of the coroner's report in my hand. Having read it through, at least twice, I could no longer agree with any of the findings. '*A lonely man, deeply troubled and depressed, had come to the end of his tether. Witnesses have given testimony which clearly leads me to conclude that Stanley Hedges took his own life whilst in a disturbed state of mind.*'

The first witness was Roger Styles, a man Stan had known vaguely through the sailing club. Wealthy, tanned and fit, Styles met me at the club, bought me a gin and tonic, and seemed amicable enough. "It was a shock," he began, sipping at his drink, "but I should have been able to notice the signs. He came round here on the Saturday night. Distraught. In a sort of panic, but really very, very low as well. As if he were lost. Yes, that's the word, lost. I'd never seen him like that. Hardly ever saw him at all, to be perfectly honest."

"Did he say anything? Give any clues as to why he was so *distraught?*"

"Nothing. Just stood at the bar, head in his hands most of the time, had a drink, then left. Without a word or a by-your-leave. The next thing I knew was that he'd been found...well, you know the rest."

Marjory Poole was the editor of the local news-magazine. She'd run a tiny piece on Stan, most of it taken from one of the main newspapers, which was printed on the larger islands. I was interested to know why the newspaper had reported Stan having been found in a garage.

"Well, he was, wasn't he?"

"No. He was in his workshop."

"Oh. Well, isn't that a *sort* of garage?"

"Not really. It wasn't built for a car."

125

"Yes, but I know plenty of people who don't put their cars in their garage. I don't see that it's of any great importance."

"Well, it might not be, but it is a curious mistake to have made."

She snorted and turned to the latest edition of her magazine. "I hope I have the reporting of our latest tragedy correct." She found the page and showed it to me. There it was. Peter Phelps. 'Another dreadful road accident claims yet more lives.'

I frowned. "*Life,* surely?"

She snorted again and I knew I'd out-stayed my welcome.

The last person on my list was Bramwell Stoates. A local plumber, Bramwell had been a good amateur boxer and he still looked useful when I arrived at his house that afternoon. He took my hand in a big, beefy paw and shook it briskly.

"Glad you came. I've got something that might interest you."

He showed me into his dining room. Darkly furnished and heavily curtained, it seemed that Bramwell preferred to keep the daylight out.

"How did you know who I was?"

"I didn't," he said, going over to a bureau and pulling it open. "Stan said he had a brother, but I had no idea it was you, not until I heard about what happened." He handed me over a sealed envelope. "Up at the hospital."

I nodded and took the envelope. There was nothing on the front. "What is this?"

"Stan's letter."

I held my breath and looked at him. "His *what?*"

"Letter. He wrote it, before he did himself in."

126

I sat there, holding the envelope in my hand. "But...I don't understand. The coroner made no mention of any suicide note...how...?"

"I went up there, after the lad had found him. I knew Stan, knew him well. We were mates. I knew he wouldn't just pop-his-clogs like that without leaving something." He nodded towards the envelope. "And there it is. I haven't read it. I have no intention of reading it. My guess is, it's for you."

I slowly breathed in and out a few times, trying to still my heart. "So...you knew Stan had a brother?"

"Of course. Mentioned you a lot."

Time was becoming suspended, or altered in some curious way. My mind began to unravel for a moment, but then I recovered something of my wits and decided to try a different route. "But...why leave this to me. Not to our dad? Dad kept in touch with him, wrote him a letter every week."

"Oh...yeah, well, I think he mentioned something, but...Dunno. Guess he thought you would be more interested. Just read it, then you'll see. I'm sure it'll bring everything into sharp focus."

"Yes...but he talked about me?"

He bristled a little. "I've just said, haven't I? Look, I know you're a reporter and everything, but you need to stop with all these questions, mate. People will get upset."

"I'm upset, Mr Stoates."

"Well, yeah...of course. Look, me and Stan, you know, we talked a lot. He'd tell me stuff. Told me about you, how he was feeling, that sort of thing."

"And how was he feeling?"

"Depressed. Life was getting him down. I suppose he thought there wasn't much point going on."

"And you're sure this is for me? There's no name on it."

"Read it, mate. All right? Look, I'm trying to help, you know. If you're not interested, then...Just read it, yeah."

"Okay, I will. Thanks for your time, Mr Stoates. You seemed like a good pal to Stan."

"Yeah, well...like I said. We talked."

We shook hands and I left. I wasn't sure if he wanted me to open the letter there and then, but he made no indication that this was his intention, and I much preferred to read it alone. That way I could react to it far more naturally.

I sought out the ornamental gardens once more to read the letter.

'Dear John,
I can't put this any more plainly than this. I've had enough. Life is nothing more than a daily grind and I don't see the point in anything anymore. Give my love to everyone and tell them I'm sorry.
Stan.'

Plain and to the point. A little bit like Stan himself. Except for one rather significant detail. I knew for certain that Stan had not written that note.

THIRTY-ONE

One by one I checked off the points, like a completed shopping list but without the satisfaction of knowing that one item, at least, was worth having.

Stan had never written a letter in his life. In fact I couldn't even remember him writing so much as a 'love' in a Birthday or Christmas card.

Dad never wrote either. But then, he had an excuse. Killed in El Alamein back in nineteen forty-one. Mum, who had never recovered, followed him two years ago, in nineteen sixty-seven. If Stoates and Stan were as close as the plumber had said they were, how come none of this was ever mentioned? Fairly pivotal events I would have said. And as for the salutation at the end of his note – *give my love to everyone.* I was the only family he had!

Stan was a loner. Always had been, standing apart from the group, preferring his own company. But being alone, choosing to be alone, was very different from being *lonely.* Lonely people get depressed. Loners don't; they prefer solitude, it isn't forced upon them. So what was he doing being a member of a sailing club? It just wasn't Stan.

This had all happened because of what he and Max had discovered down in that cellar. But was it important enough to kill for?

Obviously the answer to that was a resounding yes.

Following my hunch, I'd rung the suppliers later on. They were very helpful. Yes, a MGB Roadster had been delivered to the island last July. If I'd like to order one, then it would be best to visit the showroom for a personal meeting. The company was very particular with whom it dealt. And no, they couldn't possibly give me the name of the customer. But a car like that wouldn't be difficult to find on such a small place, would it?

The next stage had been mapped out.

True, it wasn't all that big a place, but it was still big enough. I spent a fruitless afternoon tramping up and down, trying to find any sign of that damned car. The likely conclusion was that it would be in a garage somewhere. But where, well that was anybody's guess.

Returning to the hotel, the manager had another package for me. Not as bulky this time, but just as interesting.

It was a copy of an old newspaper. Attached was a brief note, from Marjory Poole. *'An old edition of the local press. It might help.'* I went back to my room.

The journal was still in its place. I'd tidied-up my room a little and there was no sign of any further disturbance. I laid out the newspaper and read the headline, and the story that went with it:

'MASS GRAVE FOUND

The bodies of almost two hundred prisoners-of-war have been unearthed in fields close to the airport. All of the bodies showed evidence of a single gunshot to the back of the head. It is believed that many of these prisoners were forced to work, building the many pill-boxes and gun-emplacements that litter the island. It is not known why they were killed en-mass. Forensic experts will be visiting the island in the course of the next few days to rule out any recent foul-play.'

Marjory had obviously thought that this had some significance to the mystery. She had seemed standoffish, almost rude in her dealings with me, but now I felt I had misjudged her. Perhaps the use of the word *'garage'* had been a genuine mistake.

I absently flipped through the magazine. It was well produced and there was a good selection of articles and photographs to fill its pages. Nearer the back I came across a small report that I might have missed had it not been for the photograph that accompanied it.

A gleaming MGB Roadster, standing proudly in the harbour, and next to it an even prouder owner. *'Director of Trans-Marine Financiers, Remy St-Claire takes delivery of a beautiful MGB Roadster. Remy said he was looking forward to driving it around our beautiful island home with the top down and the wind in his hair!'*

Less than an hour later I was standing across the street from *Trans-Marine Financiers*. The office was small and unpretentious, a simple sign above the door the only evidence that the business was located where it was. Fortunately for me there was a public house on the other side of the street and I positioned myself in a window seat and watched the comings and goings of the many people who shuffled in and out of that tiny office.

Of course, I had no idea what Remy St-Claire looked like so he might have been any one of the rather dapper looking businessmen who called every now and then. But as I watched I was eventually rewarded with a face I did know.

He came down the street looking like the bull-dog that he was. Without his hat I could clearly see his features. A massive, square head, flattened nose, thick skin around the eyes and cheek. A fighter by his trade but one who was, perhaps, past his prime. Although heavy, he had a paunch and his movements were sluggish. Dangerous, nevertheless. And very capable, as I myself had experienced. He came up to the door and was about to enter, when it opened, as if by itself, and two other men came out.

I pulled in a sharp breath and instinctively drew back from the window.

I recognised them both.

Mumford and Stoates. They greeted the big man as if they were long-lost friends. But then they soon became serious as they huddled together and began to talk rapidly to one another. Mumford suddenly held up his hand and dipped back inside the office. Very soon he returned. And he was not alone.

I smiled slightly to myself. At last I knew what Remy St-Claire looked like.

THIRTY-TWO

My work as a journalist has put in me into some fairly tight spots. Working out of London, I began work reporting on sporting events, but soon became transferred to a team that investigated a much broader range of subjects. Most of my time was spent sitting in parked cars or smoky pubs, either spying on people or trying to get them to talk. I'd written some fairly interesting pieces, but the big break came a few years ago when I was tipped-off about some dodgy dealings going on with a string of bookmakers. My piece won an award for investigative journalism, but I'd never been able to follow it up. One good thing, however, was that it made me acquire some very practical skills. One of the most important was following people without them knowing it.

The four of them were easy to follow; anyone could have done it. A complete beginner, wearing luminous green clothes and a hat with a revolving, flashing light perched on the top. All they seemed interested in was getting to where they wanted to go as quickly as possible.

Despite this, I was naturally cautious, hanging well back, not moving when they moved, remaining in deep shadow or darting into shop doorways. Eventually, as they rounded the top of the hill and left the town centre behind, they all disappeared inside a rather old and grandiose looking house, set inside its own grounds, with a large, wrought-iron gate baring the way.

Another skill I'd acquired is a little less savoury.

Breaking and entering.

It wasn't something I used often. Never really had call to do so. But I did now. And that is what I did.

It didn't long for me to find a back entrance. I was well hidden from the road but I nevertheless sat down on my haunches for a considerable time, just to make sure that no one had seen me scale the wall.

When I was certain that no one was around, I moved over to the smallish window I'd seen and shook my head. People do the silliest of things, they really do. The window was unlocked and I quickly pushed it open and wriggled my way through. I had been fully prepared to break it, but I had no need and I was relieved about that. I'm not a natural criminal, although it may sound like I am sometimes!

I was standing in a sort of storeroom, with large shelves on either side. It was quite dark, but I could easily see the door ahead of me. I tried to open it, half-expecting it to be locked. To my surprise, it wasn't and I very slowly stepped out into the hallway that had now opened up before me.

There was the sound of voices, far off in the distance. I guessed from which direction they were coming and began to make my way down the carpeted corridor.

It was deathly quiet, except for the low drone of the voices. I kept moving, keeping myself close to the far wall. It was long corridor but eventually, it split into two directions. To the right were two doors, opposite one another. To the left, at the end, a single door, slightly ajar.

Without a second thought, I went left, eased the door open a little more, and began to descend the steps that were there.

They ran deep those steps, down to the basement area. At the foot of the stairs, the floor space opened up and again there were two doors. I tried the one to the right, but it was locked. I paused, frowning. If I had been thinking I should have known that this was all too easy. But I wasn't thinking. I was gripped by the thrill of discovery, the expectation that the answers were only a stone's throw away. So I went straight through the left-hand door and down another flight of stairs. Deeper still into the very bowels of the house.

One final door. Large, black with age, a massive central handle. I should have stopped then, turned back, gathered my thoughts, devised some sort of plan of action.

Like the fool that I had become, I plunged on, pressing the heavy door inwards. It groaned as it opened and I gasped.

Approached from the wide stairs at the top of which I was now standing, the room before me opened out into a massive, wide, deeply shadowed space. The floor, covered in chequered tiles, was dominated by a central plinth, shaped in the form of what looked like a two-pronged fork. As my eyes grew accustomed I could make out what the design actually was. Not a fork. A double S. Raised from the floor by at least a metre, this curious symbol was huge, ten metres square. Made from solid black marble, it shimmered in the thick atmosphere of that place, as if it held an invisible power-source from deep within. On each end of the arms there was an elaborate candelabra of intricate and ancient design. Candles burned, the flames flickering, casting weird shapes on the vaulted ceiling. My eyes were drawn upwards, possibly deliberately so. Suspended from this ceiling, forming a sort of canopy, was a massive banner, held at each of its four corners by red chord. The device that was emblazoned upon the banner was instantly recognisable and sent a chill down my spine. A Swastika.

Along the semi-circular walls, set at equal distances apart, were large, heavy wooden doors. At the far end, at each corner, were even heavier wooden doors. There were no other details. No windows, no natural light.

This was a meeting place.

But for what, I had no way of knowing.

With slow, careful steps, I began to walk downwards. Before my foot landed on the chequered floor, a door opened on the far right hand side. I caught my breath as my limbs became petrified. I couldn't move, seized as I was by the cold terror that engulfed me.

It was Stoates, and in his hands was a shotgun. He was grinning, like the ape that he was, and he came towards me with an arrogant confidence, certain of his victory.

I took a step back and sensed rather than saw, that there was also someone behind me. I turned and sure enough, there he was. Mumford, the historian. Standing at the top of the stairs, hands on his hips, head cocked to one side, smiling. It wouldn't have been much of a problem to get past him, I mused, but that was before the big fellow arrived, standing at the historian's shoulder, hefting his huge shoulders as if readying himself for a fight.

"I am very pleased to meet you at last," said a voice. I turned to watch the man I took to be Remy St-Claire come walking, almost strolling, towards me. When he was abreast of Stoates he clapped his hands together in obvious glee, "My name is St-Claire. But then, you already know that. You already know what I do, the name of the corporation I own. You know many things, Mr Hedges, but there are many things that you still do not know. For instance, you do not know that today you are going to die." He looked at his wristwatch, "But you are. In about ten minutes or so. Comforting to know, isn't it?"

I was slowly beginning to regain some composure. St-Claire and Stoates were no more than ten feet away from me, but that shotgun made all the difference. However, a shotgun blast spreads. If there was some way...

"The problem we have," continued St-Claire, "is your friend Max."

"Max?" I'd found my voice. The sound of Max's name had done that.

He smiled, like the smooth operator he was. And he had a voice to match. Assured and confidant. Slow. The words dripped like liquid velvet from his lips. "Yes. You see, he knows a great deal more than you. All *I* need to know, at this juncture, is have you written it all down? Have you submitted your findings? If you have, then it will be most unfortunate for your young friend. At the moment, people just think he's hysterical. No one believes him. But if your paper publishes anything..." He pursed his lips. "That would be a shame."

It was a bluff, I knew it was. They'd lured me here, made it so easy for me to follow them. The open window, the unlocked doors, and now this. Toying with me, prodding me for clues as to what I'd done. If I'd sent off a report, they'd kill Max. That's what St-Claire meant. But what if I hadn't? As indeed, truth be known, I hadn't. There was no doubt that they would kill him anyway, all they really wanted was some insider information so they could prepare for damage limitation.

The sad truth was, however, I didn't really have a story to write at all. A few shreds of disconnected evidence. I had no idea how it all fitted together. And

137

until I did, the story would remain unfinished and unpublished.

But none of that mattered very much at that precise moment. I'd stepped into a horror story, with little chance of escape. I knew that these people were capable of anything that was necessary to shut me up – permanently. All I could do was try and talk. Gain some time. Time to plan.

"So," St-Claire pressed his palms together in that familiar attitude of prayer that Mumford had also used, which seemed to be a deliberate, shared gesture "have you sent it?"

"I may have done."

He gave a little laugh. A sneer then crossed his mouth and his tone grew menacing. "Don't try and be clever. I could kill you now, if you wish...Have you sent your story?"

It was time for my bluff to begin. I had no other choice. "I've filed it, with a colleague of mine. If anything happens to me..." I shrugged. "We can make a deal."

"A deal?" He raised his eyebrows, "I don't think you are in any position to make any kind of deal, Mr Hedges."

"If I'm not back at my desk this time next week, the story goes to the press."

St-Claire nodded his head slowly. "I see. What exactly will be going to press? What is it you've found out?"

"That you murdered Stan. That letter your messenger-boy handed me," it was my turn to smile wryly towards Stoates. "Stupid. Stan's never written a letter in his life. You were no more a friend to Stan than I am to..." I turned to St-Claire, "Well, you!"

138

"Even so, if we are to take your feeble meanderings to their logical conclusion…why would we murder him? What had he done to cause us such concern, such trepidation that we would resort to such methods?" He sniggered again. "This is very thin, Hedges. Nothing of substance, no proof."

"You think not? Stan had found things, things you didn't want known." I pulled myself up. "Like the journal."

It was my trump card. I knew that this was the one thing that would keep me alive, give me some leeway. They couldn't afford to kill me without knowing where the journal was."

St-Claire took a step closer. "You have it, the journal?"

"Oh yes. And I've read it."

"Nonsense!"

I swung round to see Mumford stomping down the steps towards me, looking angry. "I'm afraid it's not nonsense, Mr Mumford. I've read it, translated by Aneeka. The woman you also murdered. And her boyfriend. And Clari. And all for what?"

Mumford was so close I could smell his fear. There was a slight tremor in his voice, the confidence seeping away. "That journal holds incredibly important evidence. Evidence that will tell the whole story of what happened here. I must have it."

"It's got nothing to do with any of that and you know it." I glared into his face, all of my anger beginning to build, replacing my fear, giving me a grain of courage. "That journal reveals what truly happened, all right, but it does a lot more than that." I turned to St-Claire, my smile widening. "It reveals the identity of those involved."

That was the moment.

They all froze, stunned by my words. I heard Mumford gasp, saw St-Claire grow ghostly pale, and sensed Stoate's relaxing his grip on the gun. I didn't know about the other man, but then I didn't need to.

I moved.

Bending my knees, giving myself the required leverage, I did what all of that army training had told me to do. My fist hit Mumford hard in the solar plexus, doubling him, pitching him forward, losing total control. I swung him downwards, taking him by the lapels to flip him towards Stoates, using his own momentum to send him crashing into the much larger man. I knew Stoates was going to be a difficult proposition, perhaps an impossible one. He was big, strong, had probably fought his way through any number of contests in the boxing ring. I couldn't take any chances.

It was a race, because the big man at the top of the stairs was already reacting, coming down the steps like a bull. I stepped forward as Mumford hit Stoates, both of them falling backwards in a heap. I hit St-Claire before the man knew what was happening, and saw him fall down, more in surprise than from the effect of my blow.

I cursed out loud, my knuckles had hit his chin. Stupid thing to do. Never hit them in the face, my tutors had said. Now I knew why.

Ignoring the pain, I bent down to lift up the shotgun that Stoates had dropped, and moved away just as the big man came to the foot of the stairs, his big bear arms spread out to grab me, crush me, kill me. Just as he'd tried in my hotel bathroom.

But now I had the gun. And that put paid to anything he had in mind.

I took another step back, covering all four of them as they either froze or staggered to their feet.

St-Claire was growling. "You fool! Do you think you can get away? Don't you know we'll find you, *stop* you?"

He was rubbing his chin, but it wasn't the pain that was causing him to grimace, it was the idea that I had a chance of getting away, revealing to the world what I now knew to be true.

"Why the girl?" I asked through clenched teeth. My hand hurt like hell, but I wasn't about to let them know that. Besides, my anger was still filling me. Pain was only a sideshow.

"An accident," he grunted. "Unfortunate."

"Is that it? Is that all you've got to say? *Unfortunate?* You're slime, St-Claire. I mean to see you put away for a long time. You and your goons here."

"Like I said, you're a fool. As soon as you leave this place, you're a dead man. Nothing moves here without my say-so. Don't you know that, yet? Hasn't your silly, naïve little mind worked that particular part out?"

"Don't say anything more," said Mumford, stepping up close to the other man. "He doesn't know enough to do anything. You can't link any of us to any of those deaths, Hedges. All you've got is assumption. Nothing more."

"I want those photographs. They were the only thing Stan had, and you killed him for them. He told Max he knew who the commandant was." I pointed the shotgun directly towards St-Claire. "I think I know who he was as well."

There was a stunned silence. I knew, in that brief moment, I'd struck the jackpot. My hunches weren't always so spot-on, nor so immediate.

St-Claire recovered a little. "So...what is this deal you propose?"

I smiled. He hadn't denied a thing. I'd achieved a small victory, but a significant one nonetheless. "This is what I want you to do..."

THIRTY-THREE

Propped up in the corner, it might have been mistaken for an umbrella or a walking stick, or anything at all other than what it was. Who would think to look twice? But it was my security in case any of them came calling.

Max's dad was not in an affable mood, and I understood why. I'd told him as much as I could, which wasn't all that much. Nothing that I could prove anyway. He said it himself when he finally opened his mouth, "This is all conjecture, Mr Hedges."

"So why threaten to kill me?"

"I don't know. Maybe you touched a nerve? But...linking these people to the deaths of so many...Remy St-Claire is a highly respected member of our community here. I deal with him regularly. He is a very successful businessman...not a murderer."

"With all due respect, you haven't been here that long."

"Longer than you. Time enough to get to know those I deal with. People like Remy and Peter Mumford, they're not *gangsters* for heaven's sake! The idea is preposterous."

"So, you don't believe me – any of it?"

"It's not that I don't believe you—"

"It's just that you think I've got things confused."

"Yes. Sorry."

"Let's call Max in, shall we?"

"I don't think that's such a good idea. He's still not fully recovered from the terrible shock he received. I'd rather—"

"It's all right, Dad. I'm fine."

We both turned to see Max standing in the doorway. His expression was cold, flat, eyes not registering very much at all. His father moved to stand up, but Max stopped him with a raised hand. "Honestly, Dad. I'm okay." He nodded to me, then came in and sat down on the couch. Before I even got a chance to speak, he pitched straight in. It wasn't rehearsed, but he'd obviously been thinking about what had happened for a long time. And his explanations were pretty profound. "Dad. What Mr Hedges has been saying is true. Stan and I, when we found those papers, we had no idea what they were, what they meant. But Stan did. And he paid for that with his life. Those photographs were a record of the people who worked here and who were held here as prisoners. And Stan knew some of those faces. One, in particular. The commandant. The officer in charge of this place, the man who gave the orders for prisoners to be experimented upon, tortured, murdered. That man was Remy St-Claire."

"Max, you can't possibly know that!"

"But I can, Dad. I remember the face. It's him. I saw them too. All right, we no longer have them, I gave them to Mumford. But don't you think it's strange that as soon as I pass them over to him, Stan is murdered?"

"Stan wasn't murdered, Max! He committed suicide."

It was my turn to speak. I sat forward, staring at the man intensely, "No he wasn't. I know my brother, know what he was like. And I'd stake my own life on saying that Stan would never have done anything like that."

"But, I'm sorry to say this, that is again only conjecture. The coroner gave his verdict, and he had all the facts. The police were satisfied that there was no foul play. You can't *disprove* any of this."

"And what about Aneeka?"

"A tragic accident. Look, I know you're both upset, but to try and make this into something it isn't, well, it's just nonsense. I'm sorry."

144

"Dad." Max's voice was very calm, very patient. I marvelled at his self-control. "Aneeka had the journal. In that journal was the testimony of a young girl who was held here. Aneeka translated that journal, then sent it to her boyfriend. They killed her because they thought she still had it. When they found out that she didn't..." He looked at me. "You've got it, haven't you?"

I nodded once. "Peter Phelps came to me and asked me to keep the translated journal. The next day, he was dead."

"Yes. But, Mr Hedges, *you* killed him."

I nodded, struggling to keep the feelings of bitterness and guilt from rising up from inside. Nobody needed to remind me of what had happened, how I was responsible. "I know that. But no one has ever asked me, or anyone else for that matter, what Peter was doing up there. Why was he running, what was he running from?"

"Who can say? Maybe he wanted to speak to you again. Could be any number of reasons."

"A coincidence then?"

"Exactly. Just like poor Clari. She just happened to be in the car with Aneeka at that particular moment."

I sensed Max stiffening. But he didn't reveal any weakness in his resolve. "I'll agree with that, Dad. I think Clari's death *was* an accident. But Aneeka's wasn't. They killed her."

He was shaking his head. "No. This is all just speculation, fanciful, off-the-wall stuff; and, I've got to say, utter nonsense. Both of you have been hurt, probably damaged by what's happened, and you're scraping around trying to find a reason, *anything* that will help you make sense of what these terrible events actually were – accidents. They happen, you know. Life is like that."

145

I breathed a heavy sigh. "All right. I was hoping I could convince you, but I see now I can't. And if I can't convince *you...*" I closed my eyes. I didn't finish the sentence, there was no point. The police were going to need a lot more convincing than Max's dad. Without hard proof, there wasn't much I could offer but my theories.

THIRTY-FOUR

It took me a few drinks in a few pubs to find him, but in the end there were only three mechanics on the island, and Paul Leclerc was the one I wanted to meet. Retired from the industry for well over ten years, he still kept his hand in. Literally. When Max and I wandered up to his home, we found him in the garage, underneath the bonnet of a very sick-looking Austin eleven-hundred. When I explained what I wanted, he was at first reluctant. Fifty pounds pressed into his oily palm changed all that. I was past tiptoeing around. Things needed to happen.

Simon Beaumont had a little shop at the top of the street. Wedding photographs, family portraits, that sort of thing. A nice man, quite young, he'd been on the island for just under six months and was finding it hard to make ends meet. The little bit of business I brought his way lightened up his face as though he had been put in one of his own powerful spotlights. I was hoping that when he'd finished I'd be just as pleased.

We were on our hands and knees, Max had the torch. The gorse was thick and nasty, barbs slicing through my hands as if the flesh was tissue paper. Bleeding and sore I was on the verge of giving up, when Max spotted something. It wasn't much, but it gave us a new zeal and fairly soon we found more.

Both of us were sitting in Samantha's kitchen, eating great slabs of cheese on toast.

"It's amazing how a bit of hard cash opens up the possibilities," I said, applying more tomato sauce.

"I hope it's worth it."

147

"Oh, I think so."

"I have to ask this, and it scares me to even think about it."

I paused in my munching, a fork full of toast and cheese poised inches in front of my mouth. "Go on."

"If all this is true, why didn't the police find anything?"

I smiled and Max gave an exasperated sigh. "Sam," he said, putting down his cutlery on his empty plate. "The police are part of this! They have been from the start. That detective...what's his name?"

"Mitchell. Charming man." I chewed down the last piece of toast.

"Sam. We found blood in the gorse bushes, lots of churned up earth. We reckon," he looked towards me and I nodded my encouragement, "that there was some sort of fight there. We found bits of clothing as well. Peter was fighting someone, managed to get away and..." He turned to his toast.

"But, the police...I just can't imagine they'd let all of this happen..."

"What? Even if they weren't involved?" I grinned. "How old would you say he was, that Mitchell bloke?"

Max shrugged, looking over to Samantha for some help. Both faces were blank.

"Forty-five? Give or take a year or two."

"What's that got to do with anything?"

I sat back in my chair, looking from one to the other. "Twenty-six years ago, it was nineteen forty-three. He'd be eighteen."

"And?"

"And..." I put my hands behind my head. "The perfect age for military service. In the German army."

*

148

It was time for the final act in my efforts to cement my thoughts into solid facts. And to have Samantha's support. Max, I knew, was already convinced.

All three of us were sitting around the kitchen table, now cleared of the meal we'd enjoyed. Samantha and Max were standing opposite me and, very theatrically, I produced the envelope, the one Mumford had given me in return for my promise to give him the journal. I had about an hour before we met. Time enough.

One by one I dealt out the photographs, pausing each time, asking the same question, "Recognise him?"

It took me a good twenty minutes to deal the whole wad of photographs onto the tabletop. But by the time I'd finished, there were two sets of photographs. One, the larger, set to the right. And to the left, those ones which had been picked out by Max and Samantha. The ones they recognised. The ones I now knew.

The years had taken their toll, but those men were still recognisable.

The big goon, who had tried to drown me in my own bathtub. Just as big, just as apish.

Stoates, although I doubted if that was his real name. Flashing a great set of teeth.

Mumford. Dressed as an officer, peaked cap bearing the skull badge of the SS. What was *his* original name, I wondered.

Remy St-Claire. Suave, dapper, looking for all the world like a Prussian aristocrat.

And the one that should have surprised me most of all, but didn't. His ferret eyes peering out from below his cap. A junior officer. Detective Sergeant Mitchell.

Samantha had her fists pressed against her mouth, not really understanding what she was seeing. Max, sitting back, a look of complete indifference on his face...or was it a smouldering anger? It was difficult to tell.

And me. These men had all worked here, in that hospital, dolling out death like it was as natural as giving out presents at Christmas. To them, it was something that should be done, and done properly, with feeling. They must have loved their work. From what the journal had said, they certainly seemed to enjoy it. Laughter always accompanied the most grotesque acts. And now, here they all were, living new lives with new identities, right in the very heart of the hell that they had created. How clever was that! They must have thought that they'd got away with it, that their lives were mapped out as one that was full of relaxation and normality. Pillars of society. If only that society knew.

Which was why they wanted me dead. They had no intention of letting me get off the island, that was obvious. How could they? I knew everything. And now, I had the beginnings of the proof.

I'd purposefully neglected to tell either Max or Samantha the deal I'd made. But that wouldn't prevent justice being done.

That was my hope, at least.

THIRTY-FIVE

"Its going to cost you another fifty," said Paul Leclerc when he met me at the harbour.

I gave him a smirk for a reply.

"I had to lie through my teeth," he continued, looking venomous, "if they'd have found out what I was doing, they'd have reported me!"

"Okay," I said, and peeled off three ten-pound notes. "I'll give you thirty – and that's *if* what you've found out is worth it."

"Tampered brakes," he said, looking around shiftily, as if he half-expected someone like Stoates or Mumford to appear out of the shadows. "Will that do?"

"Are you sure?"

He raised an eyebrow, "You asked me, I'm telling you."

I nodded. "Will you swear to it? Sign an affidavit to that effect?"

He sucked in his breath, "*That,*" he said, "will cost you another hundred."

"Deal. But you'll get the rest when you've signed." I gave him twenty more and we went our separate ways.

It was almost time for my meeting with the cast and crew of the deadly charade that was being played out. Firstly, I had to have one more chat with Max. Alone.

The sun was setting when I met him up at the cricket ground. It was an open area, one of the few places I could think where nothing much would happen. There were plenty of houses around and too many curious eyes gazing out across the verdant pitch. Twitching curtains were in abundance.

He came and sat down without a word. Perhaps he already had an idea what was going on. I wondered if his clairvoyance extended into looking into the future.

"Max. I have to give you these." I handed him over a small package. "It's the photos. Not the originals, those I'm giving back to Mumford. They're copies. Very good copies, the best that money can buy. Inside is a sworn statement saying that they are exact copies of the originals. I've also given you a sworn statement by a local car mechanic. It's all above board. I've done this sort of thing before; comes with the job."

"John...I have a terrible feeling that what you're going to do is going to end disastrously."

"Well, you could be right. But I owe it to Stan. I have to know what all of this is about."

"And you think they will tell you?"

"That's the deal. I told them I was going to show you the photographs. That you were going to see that they were worthless, that there wasn't anyone you recognised."

"But that's not true."

"I know that. But that's what I'm going to tell them. In return, they'll tell me who they are."

"Then what? They ask you to pack your bags and leave?"

"Something like that."

He shook his head. "I know I'm only a kid, but that is just a load of old tosh. They'll never stick to their word. You know it. They've killed four people. They're not going to stop. They'll kill you, then me."

"No. Because if they do, the story is going to my newspaper."

"What's to stop you doing that anyway?"

I closed my eyes and looked out to sea for a moment. I could sense Max next to me begin to stiffen. "What part of this deal aren't you telling me?"

"If I publish, you die…"

I let those words sink in. It took a long time.

At last, his voice a little less certain, Max spoke. "So, let's get this straight. You find out what this is all about, then it's back home, riding off into the sunset like some faded gunfighter – job done, onto the next one? Meanwhile, we still have to live on this rock, knowing that there are a bunch of murderers hanging around, living their lives like nothing has happened? Is that it?"

"You're pretty smart, Max."

"I'm not stupid, and if you think I'm going to stand by and let all of this happen, then you've got another think coming!"

"Oh? And what are you going to do, Max? You can't beat them, they've got this place sewn up! Police, banks, businesses, the press…no one will ever stand up and face them because everyone is *owned* by them! They have some sort of hold over virtually everybody on this island. There is nothing anyone can do – this is the best deal we'll ever get. This way we have guarantees, Max! It works both ways: if they harm you, the story goes to the press."

"Banks?"

"What?"

"You said they had everything sewn up…including banks. So, how does that leave my dad?"

"I've no idea. Perhaps he hasn't been approached yet."

"Or maybe his reluctance to believe us…" He stood up and gazed out to sea, his hands deep in his pockets, obviously trying to find some order amongst the chaos that was now his mind. He very slowly turned around and stared straight at me. "I'm sorry, John. I've heard what you said, but I'm not prepared to keep quiet about this. Clari was killed by them," he put up his hand before I spoke, "I know what you're going to say – but accident or not, if they hadn't tampered with those brakes, she'd be alive right now. And Stan...how can you just roll over and let them get away with that?" He closed his eyes, as if trying to find the right words. He found them all right. "You're a coward. But I'm not. I don't care what happens to me." He held up the photographs, still in their package, "I'm going to use this. Go to the mainland, tell the *real* police what's gone on here. I'll force them to make an investigation. And I will get to the truth, despite your pathetic deals!"

And with that, he stomped off, his face reddened by the anger that had rushed to the surface.

I sat back and stretched out my legs. I smiled very slowly.

My plan had worked almost perfectly!

PART
THREE

THIRTY-SIX

My room was cold that night, freezing. I'd woken up, feeling convinced that there was someone lurking in the far corner. But when I flicked on the light, there was nothing there. I sat back, not daring to close my eyes. I hadn't had any dreams or visitations, but John Hedges' words had made me feel so angry that I felt certain that my highly charged state would conjure up all sorts of demons. But there was nothing and I slowly began to relax.

I heard the voices not long afterwards. Quiet, muffled, as if someone were deliberately keeping their voice low. Slowly I slid out from beneath the sheets and crept over to the door, easing it open ever so slightly.

It was my mum and dad and they were talking in very hushed, but very urgent tones.

Not waiting, I made my way down the corridor. I'm not usually all that interested in what my parents had to say, but there was something that John had said that had set off alarm bells in my head. How Remy St-Claire may well have already approached my dad, forced him to join their society. Maybe he hadn't even used force? Dad had been acting a little strangely lately. He always seemed tense, his mind elsewhere, as if he were wrestling with something deep inside. A decision, that's what it had to be. But what sort of decision? So I halted outside the kitchen door and pressed my ear against the wall.

Dad was speaking, proving my thoughts were true when he said, "Nothing's decided, not yet anyway."

"But it'll be for the best! God, when you think of all that money – what it could mean to us. Everything would be so much more easy! Nothing for you to worry about, isn't that what's always held you back?"

"We've got to be careful. It may well make us money, more than we've ever known...but then it could all go disastrously wrong. It's a once-in-a-lifetime opportunity."

"We don't have a choice. We've lived like this for too long, and it's killing both of us. When will you go?"

"As soon as I can. Friday. I'll make a few 'phone calls then take it from there."

"I think it's for the best. Once we have the money in the bank, we can plan things. I don't think there is any reason to include lawyers, do you?"

"I hope not. You know how I feel about all of that. Making money out of people's misery. No, we'll keep it between us. Straight share."

"That's very fair of you. I thought you might, you know..."

"What? Try and punish you? Take my revenge?"

"Something like that."

"Well, I'm not going to. I just want it over, over and done with. Then I can begin to get my life back."

"What about Max?"

"Max will be fine. We'll explain it all to him when everything is sorted. He needn't know anything yet."

I pulled away, not needing to know any more, and went back to my room with a heavy heart.

So, that was it. Dad had obviously been approached and was now almost totally convinced that he should fall in with a group of murderers and deceivers! My dad, whom I always thought of as being fair and just and honest...I couldn't believe it. What had they done to him, what had they said to make him join their ranks?

The answer, of course, was obvious.

They'd threatened to harm me, and probably Mum as well. Was there no limit to their depravity? They were so intent on protecting their true identities that they would go to any length to maintain their new lives.

It was sick. *They* were sick. And now Dad was with them. How would I ever be able to look him straight in the face again? After what they'd done to Clari, how could he?

Sleep didn't come until the very early hours.

School was something of a blur. I hadn't been concentrating and my work was suffering. My teacher sent me to see the Head after I had stood there, at the desk, with my pathetic attempt at mathematics spread out in front of him. He looked up at me, frowning deeply, "What's this?"

I looked down at the page. I'd managed to do one sum. One. I couldn't offer an explanation.

"I've had enough of this," he snapped and marched me down to the Head's office.

He'd shaken his head in stunned silence. Mr Cross. *Cross by name, Cross by...*He was talking loudly, jabbing his finger at me, but I wasn't listening. Like everything else, it was of no consequence. I perked up, for all the wrong reasons however, when he said he'd be calling on my parents that evening. I felt my world was crumbling.

The rest of the day was like standing in a pit of glutinous slime. I couldn't find my footing and I didn't know how much longer I could remain upright before I slipped underneath. I'd lost total control. Everything was going wrong and there was nothing I could do. And the really galling part of this is, no one ever asked me what was wrong! What were those time-honoured words that everyone spouted, *'He's going through a phase.'* Yeah, that was it. *A phase.* Like I was a character in a play or a book or something and soon, in a few pages, I'd be back to normal. It made me sick that nobody was prepared to take the time and simply ask me what was wrong! They just assumed, assumed I was suffering the teenage years. They call it *angst* now. In those days, they called it *a phase.* God, how I hated being a teenager!

Mum and Dad sat and listened to Mr Cross after he'd called at the house after school. He'd telephoned and had insisted that Dad be there too. So Dad had to take time off from work. He was probably seething inside. Both of them sat there, opposite the Head, listening to him rambling on. They didn't speak, which was actually much worse than if they'd screamed and shouted.

Mr Cross was very concerned. I'd been a *top-performing student.* My work had been *exemplary.* But now, I had changed. Was I on medication? Was there a problem with the family? Had anything happened? There was a laugh! If only he knew. But at least he was asking questions, trying to find reasons why I was acting the way I was. I sat with my eyes fixed on the carpet and after he'd gone, Mum just stared and after a long time said, very quietly, "We'll have to do something about this." I caught something in her tone. I looked up sharply and for a fleeting moment, a shadow came over her face. It frightened me and I went to bed feeling very uneasy.

Every waking moment since I returned to the island, all I'd thought about was Clari, Stan and Aneeka. The three people whom I'd grown close to, cared about, missed…all dead. The most painful, of course, had been Clari. No matter what I did, I couldn't shake the thought that I was in some way responsible, that if only I'd stayed and hadn't gone back with my family to sort out the stupid house, all of them would still be alive. I could have done something, *anything.*

They say things happen for the best. Well, I'd need a lot of convincing, especially over all of this! But one thing was certain; if my friends hadn't been taken from me, then John Hedges would never have arrived. And if he hadn't come here, perhaps the truth would have remained hidden for a lot longer.

And now, here I was, with a wad of photographs, and the letters and the journal that Aneeka had translated. I'd read it, of course, almost as soon as John had given it to me. The letters, however, were another matter. Aneeka hadn't started translating those before she...Well, we all know what happened, no point in repeating it. So, later on, with the day behind me, I stretched myself out on my bed and began to look through them, trying to get the gist of what they said. But, of course, that was impossible. My Russian – or was it Polish – was non-existent, so I just lay back with them on my chest and let myself drift off to sleep.

I awoke with a start. It was night. I had been asleep for a long time and I was a little annoyed – why hadn't anyone come in and woken me? Sitting up, I realised how quiet the rest of the house was. It had that empty, lonely feeling when there wasn't anyone around. But then, there was the light. The light from under the crack in my door. A very bright light.

As softly as I could, I went over and slowly eased open the door. I had to wince as the light flooded in, so very, very bright, glaringly so. Almost painful. Blinking my eyes repeatedly, I slowly became accustomed to the stark, sheer white light. And I could begin to make out details, details that shouldn't have been there. This wasn't the hallway of my house. It was a corridor, very wide, clinically white.

I was back in the hospital.

Instinctively, I stepped back, reaching out to swing my bedroom door shut, to close out the scene in front of me. I didn't want this to be happening, I wasn't ready, I was still not strong enough.

My room, however, was no longer my room. It too had undergone a startling transformation. From where I stood I could see it all. A bright, bare room, a tiny bed against the far wall. And upon the bed, huddled up, head down, knees pulled up against her chest defensively, was a girl. Alena.

I knew it was her. I didn't have to see her face. She was whimpering, ever so quietly. Then, gradually, her voice began to break through. Soft, pathetic almost, like a tiny, wounded animal, nothing more than a squeak.

"Dear Mama, how can I find the words to describe what is happening to me? Every day they come, those men, those horrible men, and they laugh and they gloat. Then they drag me, because I can still fight a little, to another room. A larger room, and here they stick their needles into me. I cannot remember what happens then. I just remember their faces, looking down at me, grinning. They enjoy what they do and I hate them for it.

"Yesterday was the worst. I know because when I woke up, there was blood. Then came the pains in my stomach and I had to squash myself up into a ball to try and stop the stabbing daggers that winced through me. But the pain didn't go away and I bled all over the floor. A nurse came in. She swore at me, picked me up by the hair, slapped me across the face, and threw a mop at me, ordering me to clean up my mess. As I did this, I cried, not because of the pain, but because I am

161

ashamed. Ashamed of what I have become. I am nothing but a plaything for these men. They use me, they abuse me, then they throw me back into my room. And I wait, until tomorrow, when it will all begin again.

"I wish I had the means to end my life. To take away the pain. But I have nothing. The room is bare and they check me all the time for anything that I could use to end my own pitiful existence.

"Sometimes, when it is very dark and very cold, I remember our village. Especially how it is in the early summer, with the sunshine playing on the wheat fields. How we used to run alongside the river, laughing, skipping over the wild-flowers, enjoying the freedom, the sheer, simple happiness that comes from contentment. A life wrapped up in the love I shared with my family.

"Where did it all go, Mama? Will it ever come again?"

She'd dictated one of her own letters, there and then, but not in her own, native tongue. By some inexplicable means she had translated her words into English so that I might understand what she had written.

I slid down the wall and sat there, watching her, not knowing what to say. In all honesty, there was nothing *to* say. So I sat and the weariness overcame me and I slept.

THIRTY-8EVEN

Like drunkards, the men stumbled across the dunes. Dressed in ragged, coarse pyjama-like uniforms, hair cropped, they were prisoners. Almost twenty of them, their eyes sunk into their heads, lifeless, watery, without expression, all hope gone. Gone long ago. Uniformed men shouted and cursed at them, some had whips and these they swiped at the prisoners without mercy. Dogs, huge, gnashing teeth, strained on the leash, jaws constantly snapping shut, desperate to bite down on the men, rip their flesh. And all the time the rain trickled down, piling misery upon misery in these, the last few filthy moments of a life corrupted by violence and sadism.

One man fell and lay motionless, too exhausted to move any further. As he lay, his face in the cruel, churned-up earth, an officer stepped forward, already drawing out the P.38 from its holster. He levelled the barrel of the gun against the back of the fallen prisoner's head. A single crack retorted across the barren landscape and the poor man's life was ended in the blink of an eye.

Some of the others looked back, their eyes wide with terror, tongues lolling from dried, parched lips, and they quickened their steps. Others carried on regardless, as if in a dream, heads down, legs pounding, forever forward, forward towards the sea.

They passed through a tunnel, low, stinking of damp and rotting seaweed. In happier times this had been the route from the surrounding scrubland to the beach. Now it was the highway to oblivion.

By the water's edge, the soldiers stood, silhouetted black against the skyline, their rifles and sub-machine guns already waiting, cradled nonchalantly in their hands. They shifted in their stance, pulling back the firing bolts of their weapons, preparing themselves for what was to come.

Many of the prisoners, sensing the inevitable, began to wail in fear. Some fell to their knees, holding their heads, bobbing backwards and forwards, refusing to accept the horror about to engulf them. One or two sprinted off to the left or the right. Those more fatalistic merely stood, breathing hard, taking in the view across the gently lapping sea, one, last, fleeting glance at a world that had turned its back on them.

As the officer strode forward, his pistol still in his hand, he barked out an order. Soldiers brought up their rifles to their shoulders, squinting down the barrels of their guns, drawing a bead on those foolish individuals who had thought to run. Shots rang out, heads disappeared in a great burst of blood, and the fleeing prisoners fell, their already lifeless, limp bodies flipped over like kites caught in a strong breeze.

There were three prisoners on their knees, chanting some ancient prayer that the officer neither recognised nor cared about. Pressing his gun against the back of each head, he fired a single shot into each man's brain. He didn't flinch and his eyes did not show a single flicker of emotion.

He nodded to the soldiers and they herded the remaining prisoners into a tight bunch. The dogs snapped at their heels, the rain streaked across their faces, and they waited without sound for their last few seconds to pass.

The sub-machine guns spewed out bullets, spraying the prisoners with a hail of death, and their bodies jumped and bucked, twisted bundles of bloodied flesh, throwing them down into the sand, knocking some of them back into the sea. Perhaps ten seconds, at the most fifteen, and it was over.

A curious silence settled over the scene. For a moment, even the sea was still, as if sensing that there should be at least the tiniest show of respect for lives snuffed out so mercilessly.

The officer carefully walked through the corpses, checking each one with the toe of his boot. A few moaned and he finished these, again with the customary bullet in the brain. It didn't take long, and he enjoyed his work, a smile always on his lips.

He ordered the soldiers to bundle up the corpses, weighting them with rocks, and when the little boat came around the headland, the soldiers laboured to put the bodies on board. This was the part they had dreaded. The sweat of it, the strain of it. Nothing was as heavy as a lifeless body, nothing so awkward. It took them longer to load up the boat than it had to run those men from the camp and kill them on the sand.

But they did it, and they stood on the beach afterwards, some of them, watching with mouths open, sucking in the air, as the little boat bobbed out into the bay, its hellish cargo making it lie low in the water. When it was far enough out, comrades pitched the bodies overboard, sending them down into the deep, to be devoured by fish, forgotten. Who would know? Who would ever care? What were these prisoners, were they valuable, were they even human? *Untermensch* the soldiers called them. Lower than people. Lower than anything that lived and breathed and moved upon the earth. Filthy foreigners with filthy habits, a disgrace to humanity. They had to be liquidated. Removed from the world, to make it a clean and just place in which to live. For the sake of the future, for the sake of the children. These were the lies that had fed upon the ancient fears of an entire population and had created the Holocaust. Lies that people had believed to be true.

And so those prisoners had died, alone and probably forgotten, on a wind-swept beach in a place that nobody knew. It didn't matter. It was of no consequence. Their lives had been ended with as much consideration as one would give to squashing an insect. Not a tear, not a thought, not a moment of conscience. Nothing.

I opened my eyes. I was still in my room and it was back as it was, as I knew it, Alena gone, my bed empty. The morning was breaking, dawn's fragile light beginning to peek through the window and into my room. I was cold and stiff, still sitting against the wall, and I'd slept like that throughout the night. The dream so vivid and so real that had invaded my sleep was not a nightmare. It was a replaying of something that had actually happened and, because of that, it was beyond terror, beyond understanding. I had witnessed the unspeakable horror of a world that had gone mad, lost its reason, besmirched humanity.

And, despite what I'd seen, the dreadful truth was that this was only a miniscule part of what had gone on throughout Europe in those fearful years of the Second World War. This fact didn't lessen the awfulness of what I'd witnessed, it actually brought it into sharper focus.

Because the men who had done these terrible things still lived, unpunished, and they feasted on the fact that they had won through, against the odds, and triumphed over justice.

I bit my lip and stood up. A new resolve was strengthening every sinew. If they honestly believed that, if they thought for one more second that justice was not about to catch up with them, then they were wrong. Terribly wrong. For it was now up to me to bring them to book.

I'd slipped into the telephone box and dialled the number. I'd thought about this for a long time, considering about my options. The cold, stark truth was that I had very few. There was no choice. Thoughts of writing and posting letters were instantly dismissed. They'd be intercepted and would never be delivered. One of the huge disadvantages of living on an island. Everyone was dependant upon everyone else. Communication with the outside world was only possible if others allowed it. So, no letter. But perhaps even the telephone would prove difficult. I should have known that this would be the case, because as I prepared to drop my money in the slot, dialled the number and waited for the pips, a voice cut in. It was a woman. "I'm sorry," she said, "but we are experiencing problems with outside lines at the moment. Please try again later." Then it went dead.

When I came out there was someone watching me from across the road.

Hurriedly I moved away, not daring to look back.

The solution came quite unexpectedly. It was the annual fly-in. Classic aeroplanes from all over Europe flew into the island for one weekend in the year and everyone had the opportunity to inspect those beautiful and sometimes obscure looking aircraft. I'm not particularly keen on aircraft, but I had a simple, if not desperate, idea. So, shelving my usual reluctance, I got talking to one of the pilots, asked him all about his plane, what it was, how he'd restored it. He spouted his story with all the passion he could muster. Then, I casually dropped into the conversation, the problems we'd been having with telephones and postal services. Could he deliver a letter for me? He didn't hesitate. *Of course*, he'd beamed, *it would be a pleasure.*

I thanked him and pumped his hand. My shadow was there, as always, watching but not so close that he could see what I trying to do, or what I was saying. I made sure that nothing was said to my new friend and at last, at the end of that last day, I watched as he soared off into the crystal clear sky, my letter safely pocketed away in his flying jacket.

Perhaps one thing, at least, was going to work in my favour.

THIRTY-EIGHT

I wandered aimlessly around the front of the old hospital complex, now sympathetically restored into comfortable dwellings. Once I'd walked here with Stan, listened to him jabbering on about gardens to tend, paintwork to touch-up, fences to repair. Now, not even the ghost of his presence was to be found. I pondered on this thought. Aunty Peggy had told me that I was 'gifted', but what was the point in having this gift if I couldn't use it for what I really wanted – to be re-united with my friends? Stan and Clari. Why was it that I could 'see', with such clarity, what had gone on with strangers, and yet of my friends, I knew and experienced nothing. It just didn't seem fair, or right. The more I thought about it, the more depressed I became.

Aunty Peggy hadn't explained it very well, I didn't think. Not satisfactorily anyway. She'd told me that we couldn't control who came through, or anything that was ever said or hinted at. We were the *deliverers of messages*, that was all. Sometimes, if we tried too hard, nothing came through at all. We had to be open-minded, clear-headed, patient, we shouldn't resist. Nothing should be forced. And we had to learn how to interpret the signs, the signals. It was often frustrating and whenever people asked me what I could see, what I could hear, it was difficult to describe. Random images. Pictures. Most of which were only partially revealed. Rarely would I hear sentences of easily decipherable speech. That wasn't how it worked. Lately, however, the things I'd seen had been crystal clear. They were like nothing I had ever experienced before. And in a strange sort of way, that's what made them so terrifying. It was as if I were part of what was going on, experiencing it as if I were actually there.

Without really being conscious of it, lost in my thoughts the way I was, I'd come to Aneeka's house. It was empty, the windows shuttered, a sign stretched across them declaring that the property was 'To Let'. I tried the side door and, not to my surprise, found that it was open. Nobody ever locked their doors on the island. I carried on down the path which led to the garden and, beyond that, to the stables where her horses had been kept.

It was all empty now. Lonely and sad. I had no idea what had happened to those animals, where they had gone, who had taken care of them. Perhaps nobody had. Perhaps...

Not wanting to dwell on what might have become of those beasts, I stopped by one of the stables and peered inside. I took in a deep breath, the sweet, thick smell of hay was still there, filling my nostrils and I closed my eyes and cast my mind back to happier times, when Clari and I had gone round there, cleared-out the horses, laughed and joked, thrown straw at each other.

A gentle footfall made me spin around.

There he was. He'd found himself another hat, almost the same as his lost one, but obviously newer. He stood before me, his great shoulders bunched, his head on one side slightly, a smirk on his fat, ugly face.

"Where's the journal?"

His voice was cold, flat, and immeasurably sinister. Here was a man who was capable of anything. I could sense that, without using my clairvoyance! There was a dull, dismissive look in his cruel eyes, a look which was absent of compassion or humour. A dead look. He took a step closer and I tried to move away, but of course I was right up against the stable door. He had me trapped.

He grinned then. An evil glint of uneven teeth, chipped, some of them blackened stumps. "I'll not ask you again."

"I haven't got any journal," I managed to blurt out. But it didn't sound convincing. I knew that, because his grin broadened into a vicious snarl. Slowly he reached inside his coat and brought out a thin black object. I frowned, not knowing what it was. But then he pressed something on the side of the object and I jumped as a blade suddenly came out with a snap. It was a flick-knife, and he waved it around in front of him, the blade glistening wickedly as it caught the light. He was toying with me, enjoying my fearful reaction, and he was lapping it up.

He took another step towards me.

I scrambled for the stable door. I had no idea what to do, my only thought to get away. But there was nowhere to go. Only the inside of the stable. Desperately, I managed to open the stable door a little and dived inside, but when I went to slam the door shut in his face, he already had his foot jammed inside, preventing me from doing so. I cried out in frustration and staggered back, looking from left to right, hopeful that there might be something, anything with which to fight him off.

But there wasn't.

Only the well-swept floor, the smell, a distant memory of the animals that used to live there. I was truly trapped this time.

He pulled open the door and filled the frame with his bulk. I knew he was grinning, even though I couldn't see his face. He was just a black shape, standing there with the sun behind his back, blocking out most of the light. Slowly, with deliberate menace, he stepped inside the stable.

"You gave it to that pilot, didn't you? That was a stupid thing to do."

"No, I didn't! I swear to you I didn't."

"I saw you. I watched as you handed it over to him, thinking that you were so very clever." He shook the knife with obvious intent, "But you're not clever. It won't do you any good. Not now anyway." His eyes narrowed and I tensed myself.

What happened then was a mystery to me. I cannot explain it. All of my experiences, the dreams, the images, the voices, they'd all been at night, within the confines of my room or my house. Here we were, standing in that stable, then suddenly, unbelievably, without there being any gradual transformation we weren't.

That little confine space had become something else. Instantly. Lights glared out, filling the gloom blindingly. I squinted, pulling my face away. He must have done the same, because as I chanced a look up I could see his arm coming up to shield his eyes. He staggered around, like a man lost in a whirlwind of despair, because now he was sensing something or seeing something and he began to cry out, a high-pitched shrill. And then, as my eyes grew accustomed to the new surroundings, I could see why.

It was Alena. She was there, her right arm raised, her mouth set in a maniacal grin. And in her hand she held a huge hypodermic needle, the blade as big as a knife's. Then I knew it for what it was – it was an evil mockery of the man's own knife.

As for him, he was frozen with fear, unable to react, move or save himself. Alena brandished the hypodermic then plunged it downwards without hesitation. The man squealed like a piglet as the point of the needle pierced through his eye and entered his brain. Then, his great bulk convulsed and he fell backwards, a loose wet rag of a man, all the strength gone from his body as he folded, hitting the ground with a sickening slap and he lay there, a spreading cloud of blood issuing from his head.

Dead.

My eyes were fixed on his corpse. I could barely breathe. It had all happened so quickly that I was not really registering the massiveness of what I'd seen. From somewhere I managed to find the strength to lift up my head and look towards Alena.

She nodded simply, her face having no more expression than if she'd just finished the washing-up, then she began to fade into the background, the lights dimmed and the stable returned.

And then I was alone again, with the body of the man at my feet. The shaking began then, starting from my knees, then creeping upwards to take over my entire body. I had to get out of that dreadful place, run away, flee from the horror of what I'd seen. No dream this time from which to wake. Reality. Immediate and deadly.

THIRTY-NINE

I wanted to find John Hedges, he was the only one on the island who could get me through all of this, the only one who fully understood what was going on. But he was nowhere to be found. I went back to his hotel, but they told me he'd checked out. The airport were evasive and not very forthcoming, and down at the harbour they told me to 'clear off!' Trudging up through the main street of the town, I was at a loss what to do when all of a sudden a little green mini pulled up alongside me and a man, with steely blue eyes and a look that would freeze a polar bear, stepped out and barred my way.

"I want a word with you."

He told me his name was Mitchell and I recognized him as the policeman that John had spoken about. He showed his warrant card nevertheless, without being asked to. I was told to get into the back of the car, which was a bit of an effort even for me, and he took me on a short journey to the far side of the island, and a small dwelling that I had never visited before.

Perhaps I should have been suspicious, perhaps even a little afraid, but the man was a police officer. If anyone could ensure my safety it was him.

How little I knew.

He stopped the car and opened the door for me, giving me a helping hand as I stepped out uncertainly onto the coarse grass where he'd parked.

It was windy up there and a short distance away was the cliff edge. The little building. that nestled amongst an outcrop of rocks, was an old fishermen's cottage, long since deserted. Glass still clung on in the windows, but the main door was rotted and crashed relentlessly against the frame, opening and closing in the sporadic blasts of wind.

Mitchell beckoned me over to join him. He was standing with his hands in his pockets, gazing out towards the sea. Reluctantly I stepped up next to him. He nodded to the rocks below, the sea smashing against them, swirling eddies of froth and foam churning up as nature continued its eternal battle with itself.

"Nasty drop," he said, above the noise. Even though he had to shout and I had to strain to hear his words, the menace in his voice was very obvious. Without thinking I took a step backwards and he turned and grinned. Why did they always grin? "Someone could fall over here and wouldn't be found for...well, months. Maybe not ever. The current is particularly strong around here. A body could be taken out to sea and simply disappear."

I didn't say a word. This is what I'd seen in my dream. The little boat, filled with the murdered bodies, being dumped unceremoniously into the depths. Never to be found. I felt a wave of fear crashing over me now! How could he know about my dream? That was impossible. Or perhaps it was something else. Did he know what had happened to the big man at the stable? Was that what all this was about?

"Autopsy report," he continued, confirming my suspicions, "It said that Rudy fell on his own knife. Curious that. The blade went right through his eye, straight into his brain." He gave a little laugh. "Now how do you think that might have happened?"

"I don't know," I lied, trying to make my voice sound assured.

"Strange that he should be found in a stable. That Polish woman's stable. Do you know anything about *that*?"

I shook my head.

"You see, that's where I get a little confused. Rudy was following you, that much is obvious. I presume he followed you all the way to that stable. Then something happened."

"I told you – I don't know."

"Yeah, but I know that you're lying."

He moved incredibly quickly, completely taking me by surprise, and he had me by the lapels and threw me to the ground with ease, as if I were nothing more than an old disused sack. I tried to scramble to my feet, but he stood over me, legs either side of my body, glaring down at me, the grin gone, his fists bunched, hard as stone.

"What happened?"

I tried to wriggle away, but this only succeeded in forcing him to react in the one way I was dreading. He reached down with his left hand, pulled me up by the throat and then smashed his right fist down into my face. I cried out and fell back to the earth, my cheekbone screaming with pain. I felt sure it was broken.

"Once again – what happened?"

My vision began to blur. But it had nothing to do with the blow. There was something else happening, something which was far bigger than either him, or me. Something bigger than anything I had ever known. The sky began to change all around us, swirling as if stirred by a gigantic spoon, clouds becoming like ribbons, grey and blue all mixing into one. The wind grew stronger, tearing at his jacket, knocking him backwards, away from me. He staggered as if he were being pulled about by some invisible hand. I took my chance, finding the strength to marshal my wits and I rolled over, wiping my hand across my face. There was blood, lots of it, but I was neither interested nor concerned in that. Too much else was happening.

I saw it, like a film. An old newsreel. Black and white, jumping, staccato. I saw men being prodded and poked by bayonets, forced to the lip of the cliff. There were a dozen or so pajama-clad prisoners, all of them moaning, wailing, pleading with their captors to let them return to their camp. But the soldiers weren't listening. The officer was barking his orders and one by one, those bayonets thrust forward, stabbing the prisoners hard in the back, pitching them over into the abyss. I saw them fall, arms flapping pathetically in an attempt to prevent their downward spiral into oblivion. But nothing could stop that. They fell like stones, hitting the rocks far below, their bodies smashing against the jagged points of the vicious outcrops, broken like rag dolls by the force of impact. Then the sea came washing over them in great, relentless waves. I saw the white foam turning red, and I could see each and every one of those poor, wretched men being pushed to their doom. And there was nothing I could do.

The officer gave a great cheer as the last prisoner was sent over the top and the soldiers gathered around in little groups, all of them smiling, some of them lighting up cigarettes. A job well done. Time to relax.

The young officer turned, that grin so recognizable. Those eyes so steely blue.

It was Mitchell. Younger, much younger, but it was him. I could see that clearly.

Then the sky shifted, the colours becoming more intense, darker, much more foreboding. And I was no longer looking into the past. It was the present again and Mitchell was there, standing feet apart, his eyes wild with fear. He had seen it too. He didn't understand, that much was plain from the befuddled look on his face. A face full of strain and disbelief. Fear. Massive, overwhelming fear. But we had no time to register what we had seen. No time to question, or think. From out of the living earth burst forth hands, great claws, which grabbed him by the ankles, toppling him over. He flayed about for a moment, but it was only for a brief moment. Because then the rest of those hideous beings erupted from the ground, like phantoms or ghouls, I don't know which. They were stone grey, faceless, but all-powerful. Two, three, four of them, lifting him to their shoulders. He was screaming now, shouting out at the top of his voice, desperately trying to break free. But they were too strong, their power from another, unknown world where retribution ruled. They swung him high out into the air and I saw his face, just for an instant, and the sheer terror that was written there was awful to behold. Then he was falling, down towards the rocks, his piercing scream lost amongst the crash of the waves. These nameless, faceless ghouls had tossed him out high into the roaring windswept air. I ran forward without a thought and peered down to those evil rocks, following the descent of his still wildly flapping body. I watched him as he hit those unrelenting outcrops, watched as he sort of bounced, rolled over then hit them again, bones breaking, flesh torn, his body limp and destroyed, dashed and broken, the waves taking him without pause, buoying him up for a second, then dragging him down into the murky, unforgiving depths.

He was gone.

FORTY

Sitting alone in the cafeteria, my hands cupped around the hot chocolate before me, I stared sightlessly into the brown, swirling liquid. My thoughts were fixed on the horror I had witnessed. I'd come away, as if in a daze, leaving the little Mini, running until I couldn't run any more, finding myself on the road into town. I held onto a tree until I got my breath back then made it to the nearest place I could find, desperate to have some quiet time and pull myself together.

But it wasn't working.

There were a couple of other teenagers hanging around but they didn't pay me any attention. There wasn't exactly a great deal to do for kids of my age in that place, but I liked it that way. I've never been one for bright lights and pulsating music. Always been a bit of a loner, I suppose. But at times like this, I was desperate for a friend.

When we'd gone back to the mainland and Dad had spent most of his time with solicitors and estate agents, I got the chance to call on my old friend Russell and we shared some good times. But it was such a brief visit that when I came away again I was left feeling once more depressed and even more alone than I had at our first parting.

Then, on returning, the news was given to me and I felt like I was in a daze. I had no idea what had happened whilst I'd been away and to have those revelations hitting me straight between the eyes almost as soon as we got off the plane...well, it was the most devastating moment of my life. I'd never felt so completely and totally alone.

I'd gone and stood next to Clari's grave. It seemed so wrong to me that someone so young, so full of life, could have been taken away like that. And then there was Aneeka and Stan. All gone. I felt betrayed in a way. Angry. At first I hadn't known what to do, stomping around the house, head in my hands, bleating like a goat! For days I was lost. I'd wail and thump my fists into my pillow, unable to find respite through sleep. Their faces would come to me. Not like before, as dreams, but as pictures. Photographs. They were my friends. Leaving Russell behind was one thing, but this, this was like the most awful punishment imaginable! I'd gone away, always thinking I would return and things would just continue as normal. But to find that they were all dead. Killed. It was just all so utterly terrible.

But time is a healer. Everyone says that, and it's true. The initial shock had gone, replaced by numbness. But the sadness, that still remained. Anger too, now modified to become a simmering desire for revenge.

Already two of the men responsible for the murder of my friends had met with the most horrific deaths. I knew it was murder, but I didn't care. They had murdered too, murdered my friends. John's investigations had proven that. They would all be held to account, eventually. That secret society, or organization, or whatever it called itself. Remy St-Claire at its head, able to stoop to any level in order to preserve his precious position in society, to continue his life of luxury and fortune. I felt no remorse, no sense of guilt over what had happened so far. In fact, to be brutally honest, I was buoyed up, elated almost that those men had experienced true terror in their final moments. Justice, I suppose, had been served. And I looked forward to a similar horror being visited upon St-Claire.

Was I really that callous? Had the deaths of those two men had no effect on me? Of course they had, who was I kidding? I'm not some tough-nut who breezes through life with a hearty smile and a quick put-down. I'm not like that. In my quiet moments, alone in my room, I like to act out scenes where I'm the tough guy, sorting out the villains, but the reality is not the same. I'm just ordinary, and I'd been affected deeply by what had happened. I could try and dress it up, brave it out and pretend that I was happy that more lives had been taken, but in my heart-of-hearts I knew that none of this was right. Natural justice, or simply revenge? I was so confused by it all, and it was draining me, making me weak. I felt ill with the whole sordid lot.

I drained my cup and gave a little start as Samantha came in. She was windswept, the weather having really closed in very quickly. Her eyes fastened on me and I could see the relief on her face. She came straight over and plopped down in the seat opposite. Her blonde hair was in streaks across her washed-out face, the blue kagool dripping with rainwater. She was breathing hard and I suspected she'd been searching for me.

"I've been frantic with worry, Max!" she began, looking around the little cafeteria, double-checking that there wasn't anyone there whom she recognized. Satisfied, she leaned forward, "Have you seen John?"

I frowned. "No. Not since...We had a bit of a fall-out, Sam."

"What about?"

I shrugged, "He seems to have come to some sort of a deal with them...Mumford and the others. I couldn't stand the way he's just rolled over. So I got angry, told him what I thought of him."

"I've just had a phone-call. He sounded anxious, his voice nervous, uncertain. Not like him at all."

"You think he's in trouble?"

"I don't know. Then the pips went and that was it. I haven't a clue where he is. Then I went round to yours –

181

Max, there's no one there! It's like the Marie-Celeste! What's going on? Where is everyone?"

I breathed out a long sigh. "My parents, I don't know, something is happening with them. I overheard them talking. I think, in some way, they've got themselves tied up with all of this – Dad's a banker, don't forget, so he'd be a prize catch. He'd have been recruited into their secret society. That's my guess anyway."

"Your parents? No, I can't believe that! "

"Well, I overheard them talking, and I'm pretty much convinced that they've joined up. If you can call it that."

"We have to find them, and John. They could be in danger."

"You think so? But John said he was going to do a deal, a deal that would keep me safe."

"The journal. Did he take that?"

"No, I—" I stopped abruptly. Why would she suddenly mention the journal? Alarm bells went off inside my head. Could she be a part of this? Samantha? Clari's mother? No, that was a stupid idea. I was becoming paranoid. All of those deaths were taking their toll on my reasoning!

"You've got them?" Her eyes were wide with expectation. She seemed too eager somehow. Too intense. Perhaps my suspicions were correct.

"No," I lied, looking away for a brief moment towards the little group of kids in the corner. They were experimenting with their hairstyles, combing through *Brylcreem* and sculpting their locks into the best Tony Curtis they could manage. How I wished I was one of them right at that moment!

"Well, where is it? John hasn't got it."

I narrowed my eyes. Slowly the icy chill that had been tickling at the back of my neck began to spread. I felt my stomach turning to water, the strength leaking out of my limbs. That accursed journal! Everyone was desperate to get their hands on it. Or possibly not everyone...just one man. "Why do you want to know?" I asked, keeping my voice very steady and very calm.

She must have sensed my mood, how I'd changed towards her. But it wasn't difficult! "Are you all right?" she asked with deliberate slowness. "You seem...defensive."

My face again told the story. Was I all right? I'd just seen a policeman thrown over a cliff top by a mass of screaming ghouls that had sprung from the ground. All right? I doubted if I'd ever be *all right* again! But there was more. I didn't trust her. Her desperation had given her away and I wasn't about to tell her anything.

She looked around, like a thief about to take someone else's possessions, then she stood up and went over to the counter, from where I heard her ordering an espresso. It wasn't long before she came back and sat down opposite me, taking tiny sips from her cup.

"I'm going to be perfectly honest," she said at last. "Even though they told me not to say anything...I will."

I was more than a little intrigued. Was this going to be the big confession, the moment when she told me how she'd struck a deal with the bad guys? Just like John. Or was it going to be worse – that she was actually one of them, had been all along? I watched her, hardly daring to breathe.

"They've kidnapped John."

I was stunned. It took a few moments before the news began to sink in. I struggled to find my voice. "They've *what?*"

"Kidnapped him. He made a deal that if they harmed you, he'd reveal everything, publish the lot, send them all to hell if need be. But...if they promised to leave you alone, he wouldn't publish. They seemed to go for it at first, then they had a sudden change of heart for whatever reason. They've kidnapped him and they ordered me to find you." She looked around again, just to make sure for the umpteenth time that no one was listening. Satisfied, she leaned closer. "If you don't give me the journal, they said they will kill him." She held my eyes. "I believe them."

So did I! She didn't have to tell me what they were capable of. I wondered, however, if either Samantha or any of the others knew that two of their membership were already dead?

"Well?"

I sat back, trying to remain calm. "Where are they keeping him?"

"I don't know. They came round to my flat. That Stoates character. Horrible man. And Mr. Mumford. He was far nicer. A lot more gentle. He even apologized for what had happened to Clari. He explained that they had never meant for her to be harmed—"

"And you believe them? How could you?"

Within an instant, she lost her initial bravado and her eyes began to well up. She pressed her face into her hands and sobbed. I looked around. The boys in the corner were looking over, giggling like morons. Only the man behind the counter seemed remotely concerned and he made to come around, a deep frown on his face. I stopped him with a raised hand and quickly went around the table to Samantha and sat down next to her, tentatively putting my arm around her. "Have you any idea where they're holding him?"

She shook her head, her face still buried in her hands. "They just gave me the message which they said I had to pass on to you. They'll meet me at eight tonight near the old mill."

184

"The old...?" I tried to picture the building in my mind, but it meant nothing to me. "I don't know where that is."

"I do." She dragged her hands down. Blowing out a long, juddering breath, she looked totally broken. The transformation was complete. How could I have doubted her? She'd been put under massive pressure by those monsters. To have suffered so much and now this...I gritted my teeth.

"Well...we'll get there early. See if we can use the land to our advantage."

"Max, I hate to say this, but you're a teenager, and I'm a mess...what possible good can we do against that whole gang?"

I smiled, lightly squeezing her arm. "I have friends."

She frowned, not understanding. And how could I convince her? To do that I'd have to tell her everything and with those revelations she might think that I had indeed toppled over into insanity. So I kept quiet and just gave a forced smile. "Just trust me," I said, "Everything is going to be fine."

FORTY-ONE

Home was an empty place when I got back. Not in a literal sense. Cold. Unwelcoming. Mum was in the kitchen, soundlessly preparing the tea. Dad was working late. I went straight to my room and tried my best to think. It was difficult and I soon became restless. I took out the journal and once again read through it, still not making sense of the words but knowing what they meant anyway. This was due to my 'dreams'. When Aunty Peggy had first told me about my so-called 'gift' it had been a shock but somehow it also felt exciting. It made me *different*. Now, however, it was that very difference that was causing me such stress and unhappiness. The burden of being able to 'tune in', as she used to say, was becoming unbearable.

"We can all do it," she had told me, "Anyone, who is prepared, can open up their minds. All it takes is a little bit of belief...and courage."

"Courage?"

"Lots of people are afraid of the unknown. Things they can't see, or prove. For some, everything has to be black and white, absolutely guaranteed. You and I, Max, we deal with the grey bits in-between."

"But we can help people, can't we? Loved ones who are no longer with us, stuff like that. We can help people get through their loss."

"People need hope, Max. Hope in an afterlife, another chance, a better option. Most just want their hurt to stop. But you're right, we can help. But not always. We have no control over what comes through. Sometimes something totally unexpected meanders down the air-waves. That's when we have to be very careful that we don't lose control."

Her words, coming to me from out of the past, had shown themselves to be true. The last few days had proven that. Some of the things I'd witnessed had been horrific, death and murder. All of it inexplicable and none of it my choosing. Now I was about to enter a new phase – I had to do something to help John Hedges. I didn't agree with his deal with those awful people, but now he had been betrayed and he needed my help. The journal was obviously the most important thing to those people, or should I say the revelations that it contained. What I needed was a certified copy, as a guarantee. But how was I supposed to get one, the author having been dead for years and years?

I lay back on my bed, put my hands behind my head, and tried to think of something, anything that would help me get through this mess.

The small room was freezing, like an ice box. Huddled in the corner was the girl, Alena. She had wrapped around her shoulders, in a pathetic attempt to find warmth, a thin, threadbare shawl. She was trembling uncontrollably and when she raised her head, her eyes were black-rimmed and sunken deep into her face. Like a skull. And filthy, streaks of black running in rivulets down her cheeks, across her shoulders, through her stinking, dirty clothes. I could smell the stench. The stench of fear.

The door burst open and two burly men strode in, grabbing her, pulling her to her feet. Another man, an officer, crossed to her. The blade glinted in his hand and he struck.

She screamed.

One long, tormented cry of agony and despair.

I saw her face, arched upwards towards the ceiling, and her eyes locked at something there, something she had seen. She bit down on her lip and the tears rolled down her cheeks, then her eyes closed as the officer drove home the blade, deep into her abdomen, twisting it evilly, slicing through intestines, ending her young life in an instant.

She went limp and they let her drop to the ground, lifeless.

The officer stooped down to wipe his blade on her shawl, then he stood up. And I could see his face.

An officer. A man of bearing and authority.

It was Mumford.

My eyes sprang open. Now I knew it all. In that instant, I knew for certain that they were all guilty. The crimes that they had perpetrated. All of them.

Guilty. Every one.

Mum was still standing over the sink when I wandered into the kitchen. She barely flinched when I came up next to her.

"Where's Dad?"

She shrugged. Not in the mood for talking! I sighed and went over to the fridge and pulled open the door.

Inside, on the middle shelf was a large, ball shape, covered with a cloth. The cloth was quite large, cream coloured, but the juices from whatever it was covering underneath were beginning to seep through the material. Red juices. Red as blood.

Rooted to the spot, my limbs petrified, I stared at that cloth for many long, drawn out moments. I was shaking, my teeth clamped together in an effort to stop myself from shouting out. I knew for certain what it was that was under the cloth.

Dredging up a miniscule amount of courage, I managed to turn to look back at Mum.

She stood at the sink, her eyes wide and bulging, her mouth hanging open, spittle drizzling from the corners, her head titled downwards, looking at me from beneath her brows. And in her hand, a long, sharp carving knife.

A single step in my direction.

In a blur, I gripped the far edge of the kitchen table and, with all my strength, I upturned it, hurling it towards her and I ran, tearing out of the kitchen, down the hallway and to the door. I clawed at the handle and turned to see her coming after me, the knife raised in her fist, the teeth set in the grin of the insane. Possessed by the demons that still dwelled in that place, that still replayed the harrowing episodes of murder and violence that had gone on there, that were now about to be re-enacted once more. Only this time in the present and this time, the victim was to be me!

She was almost upon me as I managed to rip open the door and staggered out into the daylight. I didn't stop this time, I just kept going, knowing that I could outpace her. Head down, I pounded around the far corner and along the little alleyway that led to the courtyard at the back. I had to get to Samantha's. I had to warn her that the power of the hospital was too strong, that any plans we had were doomed to failure. There was nothing we could do.

I raced into the courtyard and almost collided with her as she came through her own front door.

Samantha.

Except, it wasn't her. At least, she was not like any Samantha I knew.

Bedraggled, wild-eyed, an almost green pallor colouring the tightly drawn skin stretched across her face. She looked towards me with ferocious eyes, an intense hatred burning there, and I knew, in an instant, that whatever horrors were over-taking the old hospital complex they had possessed those closest to me. I was trapped between the two of them, my mother and Samantha.

My only chance of escape was to make a run for it, and that meant I had one option left open to me. I quickly darted around Samantha, wrong-footing her, and tore into her house. Both women must have thought that victory was theirs and I heard their laughter as I ran directly towards the back room.

I knew the house well. It was a mirror image of my own. I went straight towards the big window in the back room and pulled it open. Peering down, it was a comparatively short drop to the little pathway that led down between the rocks to the main road. Without pausing, I slipped through the window and dropped down. Soon I was putting distance between myself and the old hospital complex and almost certain death!

The sky was growing darker by this time. If I'd had a watch I would have been more precise, but I didn't and I estimated the time at around eight. Which meant I had to find John. Time was running out. Samantha and I had arranged where to meet up, the old windmill, but it wasn't somewhere I knew particularly well. As I continued to jog down the road I tried to keep the panic within me under control. I had no idea where to go, and I was now completely alone. There was no one left whom I could trust and there was no one to come to my aid. If I didn't get to that windmill in time, they would kill John. I was frantic and I had no time to stop and think. If I hesitated, they'd be on me, those possessed women with those curved, deadly looking knives. I had to keep moving, it was as simple as that.

As I neared the final bend in the road, the headlights of an oncoming car dazzled me for a moment. I shielded my eyes and turned away just as the vehicle pulled up alongside me.

"Max?"

It was Dad! I gaped at him, half expecting him to have become transformed into some horrible beast with great, gnashing teeth. But he was beaming from ear to ear as if he'd just scooped a fortune on the football pools! The relief began to wash over me and for a moment I almost lost balance, so overcome with relief did I feel. I had been convinced that he had been murdered, probably by my mum and that it was his head that I had seen inside the fridge! But, he was here and very much alive. I could have hugged him. Then, almost instantly another thought began to overtake me...if it wasn't his head in the fridge, then whose was it?

"What are you doing out here? Come on, get in. I've got some news to tell you."

But I wasn't going anywhere with anyone. Perhaps Dad knew about the grisly contents of the fridge? Perhaps he didn't. Perhaps he hadn't yet become part of this gruesome play that was being acted out before my very eyes. I didn't know, I didn't care. For the time being, it was essential that I tried to keep my wits about me so I tried not to reveal my inner thoughts. I hadn't forgotten that I'd overheard his little conversation with Mum. He was part of all of this. He had to be. The only thing in my favour was that he didn't know how much *I* knew. I also felt sure that I could use him to my advantage. Especially now. I had the beginnings of a plan.

"I've got to get to the windmill, Dad. It's really important."

"The windmill? Why have you got to go there?"

"I'll tell you on the way – please, just drive me there."

He took a moment to consider my words. Anxiously I kept looking back up the road, half expecting to see my Mum and the crazed Samantha steaming down the tarmac towards me, brandishing knives, screaming like banshees.

"I should really go home – I'm really late and Mum will be worried."

"Trust me, Dad, Mum will *not* be in the least bit bothered! I've spoken to her. She said I could go."

Another moment of sighing and shrugging, and me, hardly daring to breathe, giving up silent prayers that my lies had been swallowed. Then, at last, he motioned for me to get in. As he turned the car around I took one last look up the road and saw, in horror, the two women coming round the bend at a run. I had a sudden, insane urge to wave back at them, but thought better of it.

"Would you like to hear the news?" he said then, barely able to contain his glee, like a little schoolboy unable to keep a secret.

"What news?" I was begging him to put his foot down. What if he saw them in the mirror? What if he stopped and began to ask questions. My heart was in my mouth and I closed my eyes and offered up another prayer.

"This is a bit naughty...but what you said got me to thinking."

"Said? Said about what?" The car was moving faster now. I chanced another look. They'd gone, we'd out-distanced them and Dad hadn't noticed. I sat forward and allowed myself a long sigh of relief. And a little *thank you* for my prayers being answered.

"Cellars." He said suddenly. I snapped my head around and glared at him. "I found one...or two or three, I should say. They're everywhere."

"Cellars? You found three cellars? Whereabouts did you look?"

"Well, that's just it – I just took a stroll and underneath some of the bunkers were these locked rooms. They soon gave way, the doors that is, after a little bit of concerted effort...Max, I found some paintings."

"Paintings?" I didn't know whether to laugh or cry. "What sort of paintings?"

"Oils. In frames. They looked really old. I took them to a dealer and she did a bit of phoning around – Max, they're worth nearly fifty thousand pounds."

"*Fifty thousand...*? Have you sold them?"

"They've gone off to Sotheby's in London. They're up for auction next week. Max, this could mean a new beginning for all of us – no job for me, private school for you, new house, Caribbean cruise...It's going to be fabulous! And it's all down to you!"

So that was it! That overheard conversation had nothing to do with secret societies, murderers and thieves. It was all to do with a discovered treasure that could transform our lives. If it hadn't been for the other developments, I would have joined in with his celebrations. But I had the images of Mum and Samantha still very fresh in my mind's eye. There wasn't much to celebrate about any of that!

He carried on driving, chattering away about what he was going to do with the money, how there might be other things hidden away in the dark recesses of the cellars and subterranean corridors beneath the old hospital. No mention, however, of how the paintings happened to be there, to whom they had originally belonged. I knew, of course, but I didn't dare say. It was part of my plan to keep him in the dark as much as I could. I felt safer that way because even now I wasn't sure how much I could trust him. Soon, I'd know. Meeting up with them all at the windmill, that would give me an insight into the scope of the web they had spun. They'd stolen the paintings, hidden them as a sort of retirement fund, letting them accumulate value. The ill-gotten gains of a selfish, evil war. If Dad could benefit, so much the better. If he were innocent. If he were still my dad! I patted my pocket. The journal was still there, my insurance policy. I wasn't going to reveal its contents to Dad. Not yet anyway. I still didn't know to what extent he was part of all of this. Willing helper, or innocent bystander? I'd soon know.

I settled back in the car seat and tried to put some sense of order into what had been happening.

Whatever had taken over my mum and Samantha seemed to be contained within the hospital. Why hadn't I sensed it? My gift allowed me an insight into the 'other side', but I had no control over what I saw or experienced. I was simply a receiver. That's what Aunty Peggy had called me. I could tune in, but I couldn't choose the programmes! So, what if I had some sort of resistance to evil? What if malignant spirits couldn't work through me? But then, confusedly, I'd witnessed, experienced first hand, some fairly terrifying and, it had to be said, evil goings-on recently, so it couldn't be that. Maybe it was because my mind was elsewhere, concentrating on other things. Like John and what was happening to him. Perhaps that was why Mum's transformation had been so unexpected? I didn't know, I couldn't work it out! I'd have to talk to Aunty Peggy. That was the only way I was going to get any clear understanding out of all of this. A few days more and hopefully I'd get some answers.

I almost chuckled to myself.

A few days more? Who was I kidding? Did I – or John – even have a few days more?

We turned around a tight corner and Dad took the car off the main track up along a broken path towards a piece of deserted moorland. Crowning the slight rise was the black, threatening outline of the old, disused mill. The sails had long-since disappeared, and the solid-looking tower appeared lonely and forlorn in that desolate place. I wondered why it had never been pulled down. But that thought would have to wait, because there, standing in front of the ancient structure, were the shadowy shapes of three figures, one of whom was on his knees.

FORTY-TWO

"What's going on, Max?" Dad was angry now, bringing the car to a halt, and peering through the murky evening gloom towards the figures before him. Most of the time, he was fairly mellow, but when his temper rose up he was like a monster. Right now, I needed him to be calm.

"It's all right," I said, not too convincingly. "this is just something I have to sort out."

He peered through the windscreen again, almost pressing his nose against the cold glass. The car headlamps picked out the three figures quite clearly. "That's John Hedges, the journalist! What is all this? Why is he on his knees?"

"Please, Dad. Just wait here."

I clambered out before he could say another word, and strode towards the trio with what I hoped was something that looked a little bit like confidence. But when I got closer, that all disappeared and I felt suddenly very afraid and totally out of my depth. Which of course, if I had to be honest, I was!

"You're a very brave lad," said Mumford almost as soon as I was within earshot. He was smiling and he took a step towards me. "I also hope that you're a sensible one." He nodded towards the man called Stoates, the man who had brought me up sharp, who had made me realize that this was something far more serious than I could have imagined. He had a gun leveled against John's head.

I could see John Hedges clearly now. He had a very distant look about him, almost as if he had been drugged. His eyes were heavy, his head lolling about and he was on his knees, his hands tied behind his back. There was nothing in his expression that told me how he was feeling, or what had happened to him. Vacant was the best word to describe him.

"Don't worry about Mr. Hedges," said Mumford. "At least not yet. All I'm interested in is the journal." He thrust out his hand, palm up. "Give it to me."

To underline his words, Stoates very slowly eased the hammer of his revolver back. I could hear the distinct and heavy sound of the click as he prepared to fire it, pressing the barrel even harder against the side of John's head. I winced. John, on the other hand, didn't react at all, no doubt still in a daze.

"Not nice," continued Mumford, "seeing a man shot at that range. Quite awful." He smiled. A sickly smile. Without humour, without feeling. Without anything. A little like John at that precise moment, only infinitely more evil. Mumford, after all, wasn't drugged..

Very slowly I reached inside my coat and pulled the out the journal. "I know I can't trust you," I said, "but I hope this is the end of it."

"Well, that's just a risk you're going to have to take. You've done very well, for someone so young. I'm impressed. I think you'll go far, once you get back to school and all of this is forgotten."

"Forgotten? How am I supposed to forget any of this?"

"Oh, I think you'd better try. Because if you don't...well, I don't need to go into details." He stepped up to me and snatched the journal. "Good lad. Now, what happened to Steiner?"

"Who?"

He hit me then, right across the face. I wasn't expecting it and that, far more than the pain, caused me to cry out as I fell down, clutching at my cheek. He looked down at me, taking me by the collar, twisting my shirt tightly around my throat whilst his other hand snatched up the journal. His face filled my vision. "I won't ask you again. What happened to him?"

"You mean the big fellow?"

"You learn fast, Max. Yes, the big fellow. Rudy Steiner. Where is he?"

"I...I don't know. I thought you knew. The policeman, Mitchell. I thought you and he..." He drew his hand back for another blow and I closed my eyes, waiting for the pain.

"Stop it!"

It was my dad's voice. Mumford let me go and stepped back. Dad was suddenly at my side, holding me. I blinked open my eyes. "You said you wouldn't hurt him!"

"I said a lot of things. I want to know where Steiner is."

"He's dead," I spat. It was better and more effective than any blow I could have landed on the local historian and for an instant he was lost for words. Dad helped me to my feet. "That's right," I said, pulling myself free. "He followed me. Wanted the journal. He had a knife...and then...then something happened to him."

"Something happened to him? What exactly do you mean?"

"I don't know. It just...I can't explain it. He killed himself, I think. With his own knife."

"That is preposterous!"

"It's true. Mitchell had all the details. I know he's in on this too, because he told me. He'd had the forensic reports, they said that Steiner, or whatever his name was, had killed himself. But Mitchell didn't believe it. He drove me up to the cliffs on the far north side of the island. There he...he..."

"He what?" Mumford raised his hand again, only this time Dad stepped in and grabbed his wrist.

"I'm warning you."

It was Mumford's turn to wrench himself free of Dad's hold. He nodded towards Stoates and I knew, in that single moment, what was going to happen.

"No!" I screamed, but it was too late. Even as I tried, pathetically, to put myself in front of the line of fire, the big man had already begun to squeeze the trigger.

FORTY-THREE

We all stood there. Except John of course. John, for his part, was still on his knees, still in a daze.

He was still on his knees!

It took me a moment to register the full implication of what was happening. Mumford reacted first, yelling at the top of his voice, "*Kill him!*"

Stoates, a look of total incomprehension on his face, leveled the handgun once again and again squeezed the trigger.

As before there was nothing, just a very thin metallic click. He turned away, spinning the bullet chamber a few times, clearing it of any possible jam. To make doubly sure, he snapped the gun open, re-checked it ,holding the bullets up in the murky light before bringing it back together again with violent impatience. Slowly, methodically, he pressed the gun once more against John's temple, muttered a curse, and squeezed off a single round. But, as before, there was no sharp retort of the bullet as it erupted into John's head. There was nothing except for that click.

Then it happened.

Perhaps I should have been prepared. I had, after all, witnessed all of this before. But nothing that had happened previously was to prepare me for what occurred next. This time I was to be completely overcome with sheer, unimaginable terror.

As Stoates began to work feverishly at the gun once more, the earth around us began to tremble, as if being shaken by some unseen machinery deep below the surface. Mumford, for whatever reason, was almost beside himself with rage, jumping up and down in a sort of weird jig, his face contorted into a mad grimace yelling at the top of his voice. It was Stoates who was the subject of his fury. But Stoates was frozen, the gun in his hand forgotten.

I went over to Dad, who was standing there with his mouth open, unable to come to terms with what was taking place around him. And John, thankfully, was still in a faraway place. The best place. I stood next to them both, and all I could do was watch.

A huge crack appeared around us, the ground parting in a jagged rupture, and from within the gaping hole a swirling smoke oozed out, as thick and as putrid as crude oil. The stench was revolting, causing us all to gag. Except for John, still locked in his apoplexy, we could sense the rising tension and the fear it brought with it. But I feared for John more than any of us. If he were to regain any sense of what was happening, it could tip him over the edge into total madness. Or perhaps that would happen to all of us, I suddenly thought, because now, the great gouts of black smoke began to congeal into some sort of twisted shape, not unlike a gnarled and decayed tree trunk.

But this was no tree. As I watched, without understanding and in total disbelief, the shape began to form itself into something more recognizable, but no less terrifying. From its mid section sprang forward huge legs, bulging with heavy muscles, and from its upper portion, the same happened but this time there appeared arms. Arms so huge and long that it was as if they were of some giant or titan from ancient myths.

Contorting its still developing body, its great arms spread outwards, as if in some awful kind of exultation, its whole, writhing form rocking from side to side. And then, from the top, erupted a great head, mouth wide and gaping, revealing rows of glistening white teeth.

A creature from the very bowels of hell itself.

It roared. And it was like no sound that had been uttered upon this earth since the dawn of time. A forgotten sound, so terrifying, so ancient, that the very grass beneath the creature's feet seemed to shy away in fear.

As I watched it, with a mixture of horror and fascination, I could see that its twisted form was actually made up of many bodies. The bodies of men, their faces peering out sightlessly. Dead men, dressed in the striped pyjamas of prisoners.

Stoates and Mumford ran, as if an unheard order had sparked them into action. They went in different directions, Stoates away to the left, Mumford towards the old mill. For a second, the creature seemed unsure which way to turn. But then, deciding, it took one great bound and out-distanced the hapless Stoates, plucking him from the ground in one of those mighty paws. It brandished him, like a trophy. He cried, high-pitched, pitiful, the scream of a man who had lost his mind. And we watched, unable to help even if we had wished to, as the other hand of the creature took hold of the man's head and ripped it off as if it were nothing more than fruit from an apple tree, to be picked and eaten at will. And eaten he was, first the still writhing body, crammed into the cavernous mouth, then the head. No more than two bites.

It licked its fingers, sampling the delights of its meager snack, then turned to the still fleeing Mumford, who had by now made it to the mill. With a few bounds, it was there, uprooting the building, a mere twig in the ground, and tossing it aside. Suddenly it pulled back its head and roared in sheer frustration and anger and slowly it began to fall back into the earth, the bodies returning to their resting places, hidden beneath the earth. As suddenly as it had begun, it was over. The ground was as it had been only moments before. Flat, unbroken and undisturbed. It was as if none of it had ever happened.

But we all knew it had. And the shattered hunks of fallen masonry from the once erect mill were witness that something momentous had occurred.

I sat down on the grass, breathless, unable to contemplate anything. Except I had spotted something, something I needed and I slowly picked it up and put it into my pocket.

John was still rooted to the spot, on his knees, that blank expression never having changed. Perhaps it was for the best. How might he have reacted if he had experienced that fleeting nightmare? As for Dad, he was standing, but was shaking uncontrollably, his hands clamped to his mouth, his eyes wild, disbelieving. For a moment I thought he was going to faint.

All of us, in our own way, stunned into total, disbelieving silence.

Dad was the first to slowly begin to recover, but even as he did so I could see that he was still very unsteady when he placed his hand on my shoulder and forced a smile. "We'd better get out of here."

I had questions, lots of questions, but they could wait. Right now I was as anxious as he was to get as far away from that place as quickly as possible. For all I knew that thing might come back at any moment.

Together we managed to guide John back to the car. We took our time, and it wasn't easy. the car being so small. But finally we managed it and I got into the passenger seat, John lying down in the back and Dad put the car into gear and drove us down towards the harbour road. No one spoke. The images swirled around in my mind. Pictures of that creature, that impossible creation that we had all witnessed. I was stunned. And what stunned me more than anything was that Dad had seen it too. It had been real, not a dream or another example of my overactive imagination. Dad had stood and watched it all. If he was going through the same thought processes as me, he must have been in a very dark place indeed. Darker, perhaps, because at least I had had some inkling of the sort of things that could happen. I'd had the voices, the images, the deaths of the large man called Steiner, and of Mitchell too. But nothing had prepared me for what had happened to Stoates. It was beyond imagining.

When we reached the harbour approach road, Dad eased the car up against the verge and stopped the engine. It was still quite early, not yet nine, but there was little traffic about. We sat in silence, just gazing out across the bay towards the distant horizon. The water was as still as a millpond.

I looked at John Hedges. He was slumped in the back seat, chin on his chest, fast asleep. It was the best place for him. He hadn't witnessed any of the events that both Dad and I had been through. I thought he could be safely left alone for the moment. Dad, on the other hand, was another matter. He had barely recovered at all. He had his hands on the steering wheel, gripping it as tightly as he could, his knuckles showing white beneath the skin. He was gnawing away at his bottom lip. Eventually he caught my eye and let out a long, bedraggled breath.

"You're coping well," he said.

I shook my head. "No, I'm just a little more used to it."

"How can you be used to *that?*"

"Other things. Similar...in their way."

"I knew that when Aunty Peggy said you had a 'gift' it would bring us nothing but trouble."

I stiffened, feeling angry all of a sudden. I felt as if I had the right. "This is not my fault, Dad! This is the fault of those men you've got yourself involved with!"

His yes narrowed dangerously then. In the dim light of the dashboard his face looked positively evil. "Don't you dare talk to me like that! You know nothing about any of it."

"I know that they are hiding, Dad. Hiding under a mask of respectability. That journal that Mumford wanted, it tells it all. How they tortured and murdered prisoners of war, sent to this place to work as slaves. They were supposed to be put to work, but St-Claire had other ideas."

"Rubbish! You can't possibly know any of that, Max! Your fabled sixth-sense has let you down."

"So what was that we saw tonight, Dad? Was that my imagination? You saw it too, you saw what it did to Stoates. It would have done the same to Mumford if it could. Why not us, eh Dad? Why, after Mumford had got away, did it return to the earth? I bet that if we took a shovel and spade we'd find the buried bodies of those men. And they would be identified as prisoners of war! Right here, in this place we call *home*. And no doubt we would discover that they had been murdered in the same way that all of the others were."

"No...that's not it. Ever since we came here, that damned flat – that room of yours...what you and Stan discovered—"

"Led to his death, Dad. You seem to have forgotten that."

"I haven't forgotten it, Max. None of it. I just think differently from you. I'm not into any of this hocus pocus nonsense. Never have been. It's all suggestion. Suggestion and imagination. What I saw...I don't know, I can't explain it. But I do know there is an explanation, a rational one. One that has got nothing to do with ghosts or voices from the past. It's all nonsense!" He was seething, rejecting even the truth he had seen with his own eyes. I gaped at him, unable to believe that he still wasn't convinced, that he somehow believed it all to be trickery. Was it his way of hanging on to the vestiges of his sanity? He rubbed his face with his hands. "No. There has to be...It's just not *possible.* It's dark, we're confused, frightened. Tricks of the mind. And, if you really want to know the truth, how I feel about all of this, I think if you hadn't started your meddling, none of it would have happened! Stan and that other woman—"

"Aneeka, Dad. Her name was Aneeka."

"Yes. Well...another one who meddled in things she shouldn't. It's all *you,* Max! You're the key to all of this." And with that he slammed the car into gear and headed back to the old hospital.

FORTY-FOUR

We sat John down in the kitchen and Dad poured the still semi-conscious journalist a large whisky whilst I went and got a blanket to drape around his shoulders. Dad went outside for a moment and I sat down opposite John and tried to coax him into taking a sip of the fiery liquid. "John, can you hear me? Please, try and just have a little of this. It'll help."

From somewhere deep within him, I could see that he was beginning to win the battle against a mind that was addled with whatever poison they had injected into him. It must have been so easy for them. Reliving the past, rekindling their old talents.

He reached out a hand and, like a little old man, weak, frail and confused, he lifted up the glass and took a tiny gulp. A sudden bout of coughing seized him and for a moment I thought he would hurl the glass away. But he recovered himself and took another, much deeper mouthful. It had the desired effect and his eyes, becoming brighter, turned to me. "What a mess," he managed and closed his eyes as the alcohol worked through his body and slowly, bit by bit, he came back to something like his old self.

We both started when Dad came back in, breathing hard, looking red-faced and close to erupting. I readied myself for another outburst.

He strode across the room to the Welsh-dresser and pulled open a bottom cupboard door and began to rummage around in there.

"Dad," I began tentatively, "before you took me up to the mill. Mum. Mum and Samantha...they..."

He stood up, his back still towards me and John. He was trying to control himself, I could see that. His head was down, keeping his breathing even. "What about them?"

"I...Dad, they seemed possessed. Mum had a knife and—"

His fist came down like a hammer on the dresser. "Enough! I've had enough of all of this...And I've had enough of your lies!"

"Lies? Dad, I'm not lying. They were wild, Dad. You've got to believe me."

Slowly he turned around to face us. His face wasn't red any more. It was almost deathly white. And in his hand was a gun. "Shut up, Max. You *are* a liar! Where's the journal?"

I sat in stunned silence. This was my Dad and now he had a gun. First my mum, now him. This was becoming too much and I knew I was close to breaking point. John, no doubt sensing this, placed his hand on my arm. A tiny gesture, but a welcome one.

"Put the gun away," he said very quietly.

But Dad was in no mood to listen to reason. He came closer, the gun pointing directly towards me. "Mumford dropped it, when that...that whatever it was came after him. You picked it up, didn't you? You've got it, and I want it."

"*You* want it?" It was John again. "Don't you mean St-Claire wants it?"

Dad's eyes narrowed. "Just pass it over, Max. Then we're all going for another drive."

It all fell into place then. Dad had been upstairs, to the other phone that he had next to his bed. He'd called St-Claire. There was no getting out of this one. Without any more hesitation, I pulled out the creased, rolled-up journal and threw it towards him.

Slowly, his gun never leaving its intended target, me, he stooped down and picked up the journal. He appeared momentarily triumphant, a little smile flitting across his lips. "Mr. St-Claire invited me to join his organization. That's the truth. It's all perfectly legitimate and respectable. It's got nothing to do with prisoners, torture or any of that other nonsense you've been led to believe by this," he waved the journal, "Mr. St-Claire has told me all about it. How a spiteful group of destitute refugees concocted this pack of lies in order to bring him down. They've been blackmailing him. And you've been their very willing partner, Max. And you," he jabbed the gun towards John, who flinched.

"Careful with that damned thing!"

"Both of you, taken in by all of this nonsense."

"It's you who've been taken in, Dad. Not us."

"Really? Well, we'll see about that. I've heard the tapes, Max. I've seen the films. Mr. St-Claire is going to show you quite a lot when we get there. And when you realize what a pair of idiots you've been, you're going to be grovelling at his feet for forgiveness. Now, get your coat on and let's get going."

The drive down to Remy St-Claire's home was done in silence. John was at the wheel and I was next to him. Dad was in the back seat, his gun in his lap. I thought it might have been a bad decision to have John driving. After all, he'd only just recovered from the drugs that had been pumped into him. As it was, everything was fine. Dad barked out the directions, and John followed them. Like an automaton. The night was black and foreboding, not a star in the sky. When we turned into the driveway of St-Claire's home, it was already starting to rain.

A weak light flickered out from one of the rooms upstairs, but other than that the house was in darkness, its shape looming out at us like some prehistoric beast, huge and lumbering. The gravel crunched under the tyres as we swung round in front of the main entrance and almost as soon as we stopped, St-Claire was already coming out of the house, rubbing his hands in expectation of what was to come.

Grinning, he came up to the car and tore open the door. He pulled something out of his coat. It was then that I saw that Dad wasn't the only one who was armed.

"Nice and easy," he said, gesturing with the gun for me to get out.

The wind had grown stronger and whipped his words away, making it difficult for me to hear clearly what he was saying. However, as he waved the gun towards the door, I understood well enough and soon I was stepping outside. St-claire kept his gun trained on me as John came out, pausing only to tip the driver's seat forward in order for Dad to join us. Then St-Claire motioned for us all to move inside the house and I, for one, was thankful to be out of the storm.

John came in behind me. He didn't have a coat and he was already wet-through. I made a face and he merely shrugged.

We were standing in a large, open foyer, a huge, broad staircase before us, rooms opening up on the left and right. Along the walls were hung huge portraits depicting mythical and historical scenes, plenty of people being killed or eaten by wild beasts. Each painting was illuminated by a tiny bulb set beneath it, the glow given off lending them a sinister air. It was all done to heighten the sense of menace. It worked very well.

A door opened over on the far left and Mumford came out. Even in the dimness of that entrance hallway, it was easy to see the terrified look on his face. Like a hunted man, his eyes darted from side to side, no doubt expecting the nightmarish creature that had destroyed Stoates to reappear at any moment.

When he saw everything was comparatively safe, he gave a forced smile.

"Good to see you, Max! Does this mean you've come to your senses at last?"

I didn't answer, I didn't want to.

"Max needs to know the truth," said St-Claire and he gently prodded John in the small of his back with the gun. "Just go through those doors, Mr Hedges. You need to see this too."

John did as he was bid and I fell in behind him. Together we went through the door from which Mumford had emerged.

Over the course of the next hour or so, we were presented with a very well prepared attempt to change our minds about what had been happening over the last few weeks. We were played tapes, mostly of distant voices, curiously distorted as if they were speaking in an echo chamber. These were followed by various film clips – back projections of shadowy figures moving around in hospital wards, girls cowering in corners, soldiers marching. It was all very impressive, designed to convince us that we had been duped to believe that the ghosts or spirits of the dead had in some way encouraged us to expose St-Claire as a war criminal. That in actual fact it was all an elaborate hoax, dreamed up by a group of disaffected and disposed refugees to blackmail and damage St-Claire's good standing.

John appeared to be convinced. Or was it all just simple, but effective, play-acting? He was a difficult man to read.

But what I saw did come as a shock. I could see it in his face. At first he seemed to fight against what he was being told, but the evidence was so compelling, so believable that very soon I could see his whole demeanour changing. From contempt through to grudging acceptance, he swallowed what they fed him.

Or did he? I was so confused, so much had happened, all of it so shocking and sudden, I felt I could no longer trust my own instincts.

Of course, I'm looking back at this now, from a safe distance. When I was there, in that room, bombarded with the whole force of their weaponry, I too – just for a moment – considered that what they said might be true. But that moment didn't last long. I remembered all that they had said to me, the threats, the episode in the stable, Mitchell. How could St-Claire think he could blind me to the realities of what he and his group were about? What I had to do, what I was *determined* to do, was to not let my feelings show. So I sat, wide-eyed, caught in the lights of their oncoming juggernaut of facts and evidence and I made out that I was stunned into acceptance.

Perhaps they believed me.

Or, at least, it was my hope that they did.

As the films came to an end and the reel-to-reel tape machine was switched off, the lights came on to reveal St-Claire standing, hands on hips, head on one side, staring at me like a patient school teacher having just given his most difficult student a lecture on how to live his life.

"It's a lot to take in," he said. The gun was in his waistband, but it still dominated our exchange.

"Perhaps too much," said John. He sat forward, uncrossing his legs, and stared at the floor. "These people you say have done this...where are they now?"

"Some have gone back to their own country, some have been arrested. One or two remain at large. But soon their plan will be seen for what it is, and the authorities will act."

"So why did you go to such great lengths to seize the journal?"

I couldn't but shout out, "And kill Stan, Aneeka and Clari?"

St-Claire bristled at the mention of the names. "Will you never understand? We did not kill them...they were accidents. That is all."

"And Stoates?"

It was the last straw. They couldn't disguise the horror of what had happened, nor could they explain it away as some trick of the light, or, as they strived so hard to show, another trick of photography. That would have been laughable. Indeed, it was all laughable. Even if I hadn't been a medium, if those voices had never spoken to me and Alena had never come to visit me, I still would not have believed St-Claire's words. The real reason he had gone to such great lengths to persuade me to change my mind was obvious. And that reason now spoke.

It was Dad, and his voice was trembling. "Max, this has gone too far. It's out of control. What Mr St-Claire has shown you is the truth. The rest of it isn't. You've got to believe him. Please."

I nodded. Not because I agreed. Far from it. I now understood. St-Claire had gone to all this trouble for Dad's sake. Dad, who loved me and cared for me, was trapped in a net of his own making. He's been initiated into St-Claire's group, but I was the obstacle that was proving to be too difficult to scale. Dad's dilemma was now what to do. About me.

A decision was made right then. Slicing through my disbelief, St-Claire went up to John and whispered in his ear, then they went out. I was left with Dad and

Mumford, both of whom surveyed me with annoyed expressions, making me feel uncomfortable and, bizarrely, a little ashamed. Why wouldn't I accept what St-Claire had said and had shown me? Not even for Dad's sake. A last, futile attempt to bring me on board. And now that it was obvious that none of it had worked, what next I wondered?

No one spoke. I just sat, gazing at the walls, wishing that I was anywhere else but there. The cold, oppressiveness of that room was crushing me, from all sides and I had nowhere to go. I huddled myself up into a tight ball and waited.

After what seemed an age, the door opened again and, still whispering, the two men returned. John seemed troubled and in his hand was a rolled up newspaper. He came over to me, shaking his head. Whilst he stood there, St-Claire motioned to Dad and Mumford to leave with him. Soon I was alone with John.

"I don't know what to make of any of this," he said without preamble. "He's just shown me something which...I don't know. Made me question everything."

"You actually believe all of this pantomime?" I almost gave a little laugh then. I was using Dad's words, or a close mockery of them. The same way he had tried to convince me, I was now doing the same with John. I didn't continue.

"That's just it, Max. I don't think any of it is a performance, of any kind!" He slowly unrolled the newspaper and showed me some reports. He tapped the paper with his forefinger. "This one in particular. About Stan."

"Stan? But I thought you'd read them all? I thought you'd dismissed what they said?"

"So did I. But I missed one. It hints at there being some suspicion over what happened, implicating something like foul play in Stan's death. The first glimmer of someone else casting doubt on the verdict of suicide."

I took the paper and quickly read through it. It was there. A question. Was it suicide? Stan was popular, led a good life, seemed well content. Why would such a man take his own life?

"Well, that proves it then! Stan *was* murdered, and if he was, then..." I bit my lip, memories of Clari threatening to overwhelm me. I pressed my fingers into my eyes.

John's voice was gentle when he spoke again, "It doesn't prove it, Max. It just plants a little seed of doubt, that's all."

"And St-Claire showed you this? Is he trying to commit suicide, for himself and his organisation? This could be what we need, John. To bring him down."

"No, you don't get it, Max. The report doesn't implicate St-Claire at all. In actual fact, it exonerates him. It names another group. The group that St-Claire has talked about."

I sat transfixed, gaping at him. Then I read through it again. There it was. Quite clear. "You...you believe all of it, then?"

"I'm not sure what to believe anymore. But this," he took the newspaper from me and slapped it into the palm of his other hand, "this has certainly got me thinking. I'm going to get in touch with the reporter. It'll mean me leaving for a few days. But I'll be back."

"Can I have another look at it – the report, I mean?"

"Of course!"

He unrolled the newspaper and passed it over to me again.

I opened it up. The report on the cover was only the introduction. There was more, on the inside. A half page given over to the investigation and the photograph of a young girl glaring out at me, dominating my senses as if it were an image of a huge, screaming skull. I was horrified.

It was a photograph of the girl that had come to me in so many of my dreams. It was a photograph of Alena.

FORTY-FIVE

Was I going mad? This was the thought that burrowed through my brain like some virulent parasite. I couldn't resist it. I had no way to stop it. Confusion and self-doubt had taken over and were threatening to overwhelm me. I needed time to think, so I told John that I had to go somewhere – anywhere – just to try and sort my thoughts out into some semblance of reasonable order. He said he would speak to St-Claire whilst I went out into the grounds of the house. But I wasn't to go too far. It was late and dark. He seemed concerned and I was touched that he, even more than my dad, seemed to have my safety uppermost.

Outside the rain had stopped, but the air was chilly and I had to pull my coat closer to me. I found a garden bench to sit on.

Around me the wind trilled through the trees, a strange song being sung by the leaves and branches. Autumn was well advanced and leaves floated down to the ground where they settled, like my thoughts, damp and miserable. I put my face in my hands and broke down into quiet, soulful sobs.

I was alone. No one to help me, no one to guide me.

A voice came to me then. A gentle voice, soft and caring. I recognized it but I did not look up, fearful of what I might see.

"Max, I can feel your pain. Don't despair, I beg you. You've come so far, you've done so much. Trust me Max. Together we can make this right."

The rustling grew louder as the wind built up and suddenly a great clap of thunder boomed across the sky. I jumped, looking up. There was no one there, the disparate voice gone, its owner nowhere to be seen. But her words had given me something to cling on to. And they were words of truth. Not the lies and confusion that St-Claire had used to twist my reason, my belief.

Alena. It was her.

And she had given me a new resolve.

For a few moments I had been consumed with self-doubt. I had begun to actually question my senses. Everything I'd witnessed and suffered, all those images, all those moments of terror. I had actually begun, just for a short and awful time, to consider that it might all have been a massive fabrication. A hoax. A trick to ensnare me, to bring me on the side of political agitators, hell bent on destroying a distinguished and honourable man. A pillar of society. Remy St-Claire.

How could I have been such an idiot? Aunty Peg had taught me to be open-minded, accepting of things beyond our own understanding. To receive, not reject. And I had. I believed. Now I had to have the strength to continue to believe. But I had to be careful. I was entering very dangerous territory indeed.

They were still there when I eased open the door and stepped back into the house. John, still looking a little troubled. Dad, standing some way behind, arms folded, serious. St-Claire and Mumford, as they always were, stern and unmoving. But the biggest shock was to see Mum and Samantha. I gasped and went to go out again. Dad rushed forward quickly, arms out, eyes pleading. "It's all right, Max! You mustn't be frightened."

But I was. I'd seen my mother in our kitchen, transformed into something evil and twisted. She wasn't my mother any longer. And neither was Samantha. Both of them strangers to me. Fearful strangers.

"Max. It's not what you think."

"Yes it is," I managed to say, dredging up a smidgen of courage. "I know, Dad. I know."

"What do you know?" It was St-Claire. All the bluff and deceit gone, he crossed the room, his mouth set in a grim line of anger. "Tell me what you *think* you know, Max. We're all ears."

I looked across to John. He said nothing. He didn't have to. It was like I'd said, I was alone.

St-Claire was standing over me, tall and straight, his eyes brim-full of hatred and anger. He was tapping his foot impatiently, so I gave him what he knew was in my heart. "You're a liar," I spat, my words coming out at a rush, "You may have convinced John, but you haven't convinced me! I know what I've seen and nothing is going to take that away from me. Not you, or your threats, or your control of everything and everyone around you. I know what you did, the terrible things that went on in the hospital and everywhere else on this island. And I'm going to bring you down."

His hands shot out and he gripped me around the throat. I gagged, clawing at his fingers, but it was useless, he was far too strong and he lifted me up and pushed me back against the door, the handle jabbing into my back. I tried to scream, but nothing came out. I was off the ground, and I kicked out desperately but hopelessly.

"You've handed over the journal, Max. That was good. Now, you'll sign a declaration in which it clearly states that it was a fake, a consequence of a breakdown you've suffered, brought on by the tragic deaths of your friends. You'll sign it and John Hedges will witness it. If you don't, or if you dare to whisper a word of any of this to anyone, then..." He let me go and I fell to the ground in a heap, gratefully gulping in the air, holding my throat where his iron-grip had almost cut off my life.

219

He stepped back and when I'd recovered a little, I looked up at him through tear-filled eyes. I was quaking inside, but my courage was undiminished. I had hardened myself to it all and I snarled, "Never!"

A little smile began to play at the corners of his mouth. I wondered why but I soon received my answer. He motioned to Mumford with a single nod and the historian returned to the back room. St-Claire's smile grew. "You really are a fool, Max. A silly little boy." He knelt down next to me, his voice so low that only I could hear. "If you don't sign, Max, she'll die."

I frowned. What was he threatening me with now? The life of my mother, Samantha? Was this his final play? Didn't he realize that such threats didn't mean anything to me, that I'd—

The door to the back room opened and Mumford came out. Next to him, her hands tied together in front of her, was the one person I thought I'd never see again. The one person who had given me the reason to reveal St-Claire for what he was, to pursue him to the grave if needed.

It was Clari.

My head was whirling. I squeezed my eyes shut, unable to believe what I was seeing. This couldn't be happening. I had been pitched into some impossible, nightmare world, a world controlled by St-Claire and his cronies. I had to escape, run away to the real world where life was ordered and normal and...I opened my eyes and she was still there.

"Max," she said. Mumford deftly untied the cord around her wrists and she ran forward. I half stood and caught her in my arms and we stayed like that for long, wonderful minutes. She was real. I could smell her, feel her. Solid. Alive.

Samantha was suddenly next to us, taking her by the shoulders, turning her around. The tears were tumbling down her face. "Oh Clari," she managed, then she crumpled and the three of us stood in the midst of the car-wreck that had become our lives.

The hot tea tasted good as we sat around the large dining table. None of us spoke, all of us stunned by the enormity of what had happened. Samantha seemed the most affected. Her hands were trembling, as if she were going through some invisible struggle within herself. "I'm sorry," she said at long last, her voice tiny and afraid. "I don't know what happened to me...Some spell or suggestion. Hypnotism."

"Hypnotism?" I shook my head. "You wanted to kill me."

"No, Max!" blurted out Clari, clutching at her mother's arm. "No. Mum would never do that."

"He's right, darling. St-Claire came to see me. He was so kind, so polite. We sat down in our front room and that was the last thing I remember – until you came through that door. That shattered the trance." She looked at me. "I'm so sorry, Max."

I tried to make some sense of all of this. "But...even if that is true...what about Clari? You were in that car, with Aneeka."

"No." She reached forward, taking one of my hands in both of hers. Her eyes were warm and wide. "That was another girl. They swapped me. I was in the crash, that much is true. Aneeka took the corner far too fast, panicked and pressed down on the brakes. She screamed because there was nothing there. No brakes at all. We went off the road, hit a bank then spilled over into a ditch, rolling over onto our backs. That was the last thing I remember until I woke up here, in this

221

house. They looked after me, fed me, but kept me here. I was their prisoner." She let my hand go and sat back in her chair.

"Monsters."

Samantha embraced her daughter for about the fiftieth time.

Monsters was the perfect description for all of them.

"What do we do now?" I asked.

Samantha sighed deeply. "What can we do? We're all going to have to sign the statement, Max. Then, hopefully, we can rebuild our lives."

"You think it will be that easy?"

She looked across to her daughter and smiled. "It'll be *easier.*"

And that was it. The painful truth was that we had no other option. They'd won.

FORTY-SIX

The little boat skipped and bobbed across the surface of the water, occasionally pitching quite alarmingly as a sudden swell hit the side. Clari and I were outside on the deck, despite the cold. Samantha was inside the little cabin. I could see her through the porthole, looking decidedly green. Mrs. Mubbs, the captain's wife, was sitting next to us with a large metal bowl clamped next to her. It was an unsettling experience that, waiting for her to be sick.

I've always had a resistance against seasickness. Clari too seemed unaffected by the constant rolling of the waves, until we turned into the little harbour at Dilette and she hurled all over the deck. Mr. Mubbs, perched up in the steering cabin, shouted out his annoyance, but I hastily reached for mop and bucket and swept it all away. That seemed to quieten him down a little.

The harbour was very quiet, just a few locals milling about. Even in the summer, Dilette was not the most bustling of places, in the late autumn it was positively comatose. I helped Samantha off the boat and together we made sure that Clari didn't stumble. She looked ghastly, but as we walked along the little jetty she seemed to perk up a little.

I heard a voice. A voice I knew very well.

Aunty Peggy.

There she was, lemon yellow raincoat, enormous handbag, coiffured blonde hair, waving madly towards us. I couldn't help but yelp with glee when I saw her and I ran up to her, hugging her so hard that she gasped.

223

"It's lovely to see you again," she said, holding me by the shoulders as she stepped back to look at me. "You've grown. And who have we here?"

Samantha and Clari sauntered up and soon Aunty Peggy was pumping their hands as if they were long lost friends.

We all went to a small café not far from the harbour and there we had breakfast, baguettes and coffee. The conversation was light and cheery, a little like the weather, and all in all everyone got on well. Until, that is, Aunty Peggy decided to bring the talk around to what had been happening back home.

She pulled out a large manila envelope from her bag and smoothed it out on the table top. "I've read this," she said quietly.

I could sense Samantha and Clari shuffling uneasily in their seats. I explained, "It's the journal. The one I gave St-Claire is a copy."

"A copy?" Samantha's face reddened, "Are you mad? When he finds out—"

"He won't find out," said Aunty Peggy, "Max had help. Didn't you, Max?"

I gave a single nod. "He'll never suspect."

She carried on, "We have enough evidence here to send him to prison forever. Together with the photographs and the other documentation."

"But St-Claire has everything," blurted out Samantha. She was becoming exasperated. "Max, I thought we were putting all of this behind us?"

"We can't Mum." It was Clari, and she now gripped her mother's forearm, calming her. "We owe it to the people who were murdered. We can't just turn our backs on them."

I smiled with relief. Clari. My ally. I could have kissed her!

"Your daughter's right," said Aunty Peggy, "What St-Claire has got is only a sample. Max has uncovered more documents. A lot more."

I smiled thinly, "I found another cellar. There are lots of them. Dad found one too."

"Your dad?" Samantha shook her head. "But surely he's given all of his findings to St-Claire?"

"No. What he found were paintings. Stolen, by the Nazis. He sold them. Right now he's waiting for the money to come through. It will set him – us – up for life."

"But...but he's one of them."

Aunty Peggy leaned forward. "No. He may appear that way, but believe me, I know my own brother. When the dust has settled, he'll understand. I've been making a few investigations of my own. I think I've got a fairly good idea about what's been happening and, perhaps more importantly, what's going to happen. You see, I'm a medium too. Max has a wonderful gift, inspired if you like. But the one thing he hasn't got," she winked at me, "is experience. I have that in spades!"

The little town appeared to be asleep as we strolled through the streets and made our way up to the headland. We sat down and looked out across the bay towards the shimmering Channel. It was a beautiful day and it matched our mood. For the first time since leaving England, I felt positive.

Later, Samantha and Clari went off to do some shopping which gave me the chance to speak to Aunty Peggy alone. We had much in common and what we needed to talk about may well have caused the two others some alarm.

"Your father's in grave danger," said my aunt almost as soon as the others disappeared around a corner. "This Remy St-Claire has extraordinary powers and we have to be very wary when we go up against him." She took me by the arm and together we went into a little café, dark, nondescript. We found a quiet corner and she ordered some drinks.

"What about Mum?" I said, sipping at another hot chocolate. Irresistible. I eyed her over the rim of the large bowl as I softly blew over it to cool it down. I'd already told aunty Peggy about what had happened in the kitchen and I still wasn't completely convinced that she believed me.

My aunty looked troubled. "I don't know." As if reading my worries, she smiled slightly, "I believe you, Max. Don't worry. She's always been a curious woman. Ever since your real mother died, with your dad the way he was..." For a moment she looked away, remembering the woman I never knew. She'd passed when I was too young to remember. But aunty Peggy had known her since the early days, and she'd loved her. That much was clear. She pursed her lips and carried on. "Your step-mum, she...she seems to have some control over your dad. Always has had. I don't know what it is, but there we are. And now, this...There's always been something, an aura, a mystery. We never got on."

"Is that why you hardly ever came round to the house?"

"Mostly." She glanced away, her cheeks reddening slightly. "I shouldn't be talking this way. She's brought you up, after all."

"She's always been good to me. And to Dad, as far as I know. I've hardly ever heard them say a bad word to one another. Until recently."

"No, well...that's not always such a good thing." She took in a deep breath and obviously wanted to change the subject. I wasn't going to argue. "I'll need to come back with you, visit the hospital. If, as I suspect, there is a presence there, I should be able to make contact with it. Discover its purpose."

"But Mum won't be happy – and she'll tell St-Claire."

"Well, that's something I'm going to have to prepare for. I can't pussy-foot around! Sooner or later, St-Claire and I are going to clash...or shouldn't I be calling him Standartenführer Paul Heinlein? After all, that is his name."

"Stan...What's a Stan-dart-er-whatever it is?"

"An officer's rank, in the SS. Max, do you know anything about the Second World War? What happened?"

"Only what we did in school. The Blitz, the Home Front, rationing. What's that got to do with all of this?"

She looked around, suddenly becoming cautious. But there was only one little old man over in the opposite corner, stooping over a newspaper. "The War was far more than that. It was a clash of ideologies, a struggle for the very survival of everything we knew. And in the process millions lost their lives. Millions." She looked out of the window as if the words that she was speaking were somehow painful to her, ripping up memories that she would have perhaps preferred to have kept hidden. "Hitler's twisted lies meant that anyone he felt was different, inferior, or who didn't fit in with his maligned sense of racial purity had to be destroyed. The Final Solution they called it. The Nazis. A man called Heydrich put the whole thing in motion and so condemned six million Jews to death – murdered. Millions of other people, Slavs, Gypsies, anyone deemed as *Untermensch* , beneath humanity, lowest of the low, were also put to death. Many went to death camps in Eastern Europe, countless others were simply rounded up and shot, gassed, executed. Others were worked until they dropped. Literally. And it was these people, forced to work in the most inhuman conditions, that Paul Heinlein was involved with.

"He rose through the ranks, joining Hitler's SS in nineteen thirty seven as a junior officer. He fought in Poland, earning himself a Knight's Cross, one of the highest awards for bravery in Germany. A soldier first and foremost, he was then wounded as Hitler turned his attentions towards France. He was invalided out of the armed wing of the SS, the Waffen-SS, and was transferred to commandant duties. From that moment on, he became something less than human himself; a sad, twisted irony in many ways. He believed he was working to destroy those whom the Nazis believed to be the destroyers of the world! But it was actually the other way round. It wasn't those he was murdering who were twisted and corrupt it was he, and all those others who followed Hitler's words. They were the evil ones, the ones who should have been destroyed!" Again she paused, taking a moment to try and compose herself, but I could see she was finding it difficult. "And now, years later, he lives in the height of luxury, without fear, want or need. It's a monumental injustice and I have to put it right."

At that time, little of what she said made much sense to me. All that talk about executions and racial purity washed over me, but one or two things did hit home. The idea that St-Claire had overseen the murder of prisoners was, for me, a heinous crime that had to be revealed to the authorities. But Alena, who had suffered so much, seemed intent on pursuing another course, one that transcended time itself, one that would lead ultimately to St-Claire's death. I was the key to that and I had little doubt that the inevitable confrontation, when it came, would be most frightening and terrifyingly deadly!

When we met up later with Clari and her mother, the mood was much lighter than it had been for quite some time. I think we all sensed that things were moving to a conclusion and that soon, very soon, all of it would be over. None of us, of course, had any idea what the final outcome would be, but Aunty Peggy's boundless optimism had worn off on us all, and we returned to the boat feeling chirpy and light-hearted.

All of that, of course, was to change when we returned to the island and the tragic news that hit us like a sledgehammer between the eyes.

John Hedges was dead.

FORTY-SEVEN

I'd opened up his briefcase and read through his journal. *His* journal. It was all in there, how he'd discovered what St-Claire had done, the tampering of the brakes, the threats. I'd never even thought of reading it before, at least not whilst he was still around. Now, with his death, everything had changed. I sat on my bed, leafing through the pages, not daring to believe he was gone. And I couldn't help thinking that, if it hadn't been for me, he would still be alive. Like Stan. Aneeka. It was like a vicious circle or a carousel of wickedness, and I was at the centre, driving it all onwards. So many people I was responsible for. Responsible for killing.

Aunty Peggy had moved into Christy's room. Mum, who had returned to her former self and who had never mentioned anything about threatening me with a kitchen knife, gave Aunty Peggy a frosty reception. But Dad insisted. Where else could she go, at a time like this? Although he wasn't part of our family, John's death had thrown everyone into a dark mood. Being together was going to bring some sort of comfort.

They'd asked me to formally identify the body, the authorities had. Dad had kicked up a right stink about that and so Samantha had stepped forward. She was terribly upset when she came out of the little mortuary room underneath the police station. Dad and I took her for a drink and we just sat at a tiny table and didn't speak a single word. What possible words could there be? John was dead, and that was that.

Except it wasn't, of course.

It began that night.

John, apparently, had been found face down in a ditch just beneath the main road that led to the old hospital complex. The circumstances of his death were

230

obscure. Head trauma they said. But what did that mean? The police didn't appear in the least bit interested, at least not until the plain-clothes man came over from the mainland. He was young, very serious looking, and didn't seem convinced by what he was being told. He made some enquiries, took copious notes and then, totally out of the blue, he was recalled. Aunty Peggy was livid, saying it was all a conspiracy. Dad just smiled that patient smile of his.

I was in my room and it was late. I'd just finished John's journal and was looking out of my window, gazing across the darkened courtyard. I could see the lights flickering in Clari's house and I had to smile, knowing that she was here, safe and sound. A great weight had been lifted from me, despite John's death. Perhaps it was time to close the book on this sorry tale? All it had done was bring misery to everyone involved. And was any of it worth it? What had John's investigations accomplished? Perhaps life really was unfair, unjust? I closed my eyes tight shut. John wouldn't appreciate me thinking such thoughts. He had plans, schemes, things he had to do. He'd duped St-Claire, I felt certain. Lulled him into a false sense of security. I knew, deep within me, that John would never give up on his brother, would never cease uncovering the dirt that would bring the murderers to justice. It may have *seemed* that he had taken in all of St-Claire's lies, but I knew very well that he hadn't. It was a tiny consolation, given the circumstances.

My eyes sprang open. I could see the reflection of my room in the darkened glass of the window and my breath froze in my throat. Behind me, standing still and silent, was John. He was staring straight at me, eyes cold, lifeless, but nevertheless there.

"Don't give up, Max. You're so close. Keep looking, keep searching, and justice will be served."

Even as his words floated across the room, the vision began to blur and suddenly it was gone. I span round, blinking wildly. Had it been an illusion, brought on by my heightened sense of loss?

The door creaked open and Aunty Peggy stepped over the threshold. Her eyes were red-rimmed, as if she had been crying. Slowly she came over to me and held me close. "Oh, Max," she said in a soft, kind voice, "We have to be strong. Both of us."

"You sensed him?" I asked, hardly daring to breathe.

"I sensed him," she said, "I heard his words, Max. You're no longer alone. I'm here, to reassure you that you're not going mad. You must trust in your senses, what is being said to you." She stepped back, looking deep into my eyes. "I've seen things, Max. This very night. In my room. Alena. She showed me what they did here, how they injected those poor souls with poison, then timed them to see how long it took them to die. Searching for the most efficient way to kill. The cheapest. Monsters. Monsters who have to pay for their crimes."

"You *saw* all of that?"

A single nod, then she wiped her eyes with the back of her hand. "And more. Much, much more. I could never have believed that human beings could be capable of inflicting so much torment upon others. It's...it's just unbelievable."

"But it really happened. Didn't it?"

"Yes. It shames me to say it, but what happened here was only a tiny portion of what went on in other places through occupied Europe."

"Then we've got to go on, we've got to gather the evidence, bring St-Claire to justice."

"Yes. John would have wanted us to."

"And Stan. And Aneeka. We've come too far, Aunty Peg."

"It's going to be very dangerous, for both of us. Once they realize that you've reneged on your signed promise, they won't be best pleased."

"I don't care. They've shown they don't give a damn about any promises. I'm certain they murdered John. As a guarantee."

"We'll need proof."

"We'll get it, Aunty Peg. I don't know how, and I don't know where, but we'll get it."

She smiled, hugged me once more, then got up and left me alone, quietly closing the door behind her. I stared at that door, half-expecting Dad or Mum to come blasting through, haranguing me for being up so late and talking to Aunty Peggy. But nothing happened and I blew out a long sigh.

Flopping down on my bed, I tried to bring my thoughts into much sharper focus. Proof, I'd said. We needed proof. How was I going to find any? Where could I start to look for the evidence that would make the authorities sit up and take notice? I had no way of knowing if that detective from the mainland would ever come back, but I knew for sure that if I could find one thing, a single lead that would point the police in the direction of St-Claire, then perhaps justice could begin to be served. But what was I supposed to do? A few weeks from being fifteen, what possible use was I going to be?

I lay down on my bed and gazed up at the ceiling, sketching out images within the cracks of the plaster. I'd always done this, using my imagination to conjure up faces and shapes. This time was no different. One particular corner was proving to be very productive.

I sat bolt-upright, not daring to believe what I had seen.

Proof. Or, at least, the chance to discover something so irrefutable that it would mean the end of everything that St-Claire had attempted to do.

FORTY-EIGHT

It was cold down there, cold and damp. In the distance I could hear the constant plop of water as it dripped from the ceiling. A man-made tunnel, burrowed out of the living rock, wound its way from beneath the hospital towards…well, towards what, exactly, I had no idea. The sketch map I'd seen on the ceiling was simply that. A sketch. It didn't tell me what it was I was going to find, or how far I had to go. But so far I'd followed its route and it was proving amazingly accurate. As soon as I'd seen it, I'd copied it down on some paper, scurried over to Aunty Peggy's room, and told her what had happened. An hour later, with everyone else tucked up in bed, we'd come down here. Through the kitchen and out into the courtyard and across to where Stan's workroom had been. Next to it, an old, forgotten service door, seemingly for the electricity cables that served the houses. But not so. It was nothing of the sort. It was a disguised entrance to yet another underground labyrinth. It wasn't any wonder that Stan had never found it. What lay there was a mangled jumble of blackened coils, ancient, disused electrical cables that once serviced the entire hospital complex. But the sketch map pointed directly to a hidden entrance behind the tangled mass. All I had to do was push them aside. It wasn't easy and Aunty Peggy had to hold them back as I managed to squeeze through between them. Nobody would have guessed that there was a door beyond. A deliberate attempt to keep unwanted visitors out. And it would have worked, if it hadn't been for my helpers beyond the grave. Because I knew it had been Alena who had sketched out that map amongst the cracks on my ceiling. My silent friend. My guide.

Suddenly, I could feel it. It wasn't a door, it was a hatchway, beneath my feet. I stooped down and tried the handle and it moved easily. Without another thought, I readied myself, took a breath, and pulled it open. Shining my torch into the inky blackness I could see the first few steps plunging down into the depths. But the beam couldn't go far enough. I gulped as Aunty Peggy came panting up beside me. It was a long way down!

She squeezed my shoulder and I looked up at her. She gave a little nod of encouragement and I began the descent.

It was slow progress, the steps being covered in slime. One wrong move and I could have easily slipped and fell. I didn't want to think about that too much, the thought of my head cracking against that concrete made my stomach churn. But then, quite suddenly, the steps finished and a tunnel disappeared into the gloom ahead. That was what we were following. In the clammy, freezing cold. Me first, with the torch, and Aunty Peggy, with another torch, a few steps behind, huddled up in her raincoat, the only sound coming from the chattering of her teeth. It was the perfect accompaniment to the drips.

The tunnel gently curled round to the left after about a hundred or so strides, all the time gradually dropping deeper into the earth. A few more yards and there it was, a door. I stopped before it, breathing hard. Aunty Peggy, more impatient than me, reached past me and tried the handle. Both of us gasped.

It was unlocked.

A large room, tables opposite each other. Typewriters. Filing cabinets in the far corner, stubbed-out cigarettes in ashtrays. A large map of Europe on the wall, yellowed with age. A framed portrait of Hitler.

Everything was covered with a fine film of dust but otherwise it was all perfectly preserved, much as it would have looked when people worked there. My torch picked out the details quite clearly and, just as a precaution, I trained the beam into the far corners in case a demon sat there, gnawing on the bones of its victims.

But there wasn't anything. Only the room with the memories of the decisions that must have been made there, memories that still clung all around it, as dreadful and as lethal as cancer. I shivered.

Aunty Peggy, as resolute as ever, went over to the cabinets and pulled open the heavy drawers. They were stuffed with old files, damp but otherwise untouched. She rifled through them. "There are hundreds here, Max. Records of everyone who passed through this place. Names, ages, where they came from. Each with a photograph." She turned to face me and I had to quickly lower the torch so I didn't dazzle her. "I think we might have hit the jackpot."

It was much the same type of evidence that Stan and I had found all that time ago, except there was much more. I stood at my auntie's shoulder and read the names, looked at the face of those poor, unfortunates. But all that this proved was that there had been a camp there, and everyone knew that anyway. The history had already been written. That wasn't the issue. What we needed was something that would link St-Claire to all of it. And not just his autographed photograph either.

There was another door, which led into yet another office. Much the same as the first, but without such large filing cabinets. Then another door and yet another corridor. More rooms, to the left and the right. Smaller, each with a desk, a telephone. One even had a hat-stand. Then, as the tunnel began to slope upwards, a larger office. This one with a window. It was blackened, earth and various bits of rubbish piled up against it, but a window that once would have been the source of comforting, natural light. An officer must have worked in here. An important one.

The desk was huge and when I went around to the other side, and I sat in the plush chair, I could imagine being there, in this place of authority, calmly giving out my orders. It was not a sobering thought.

I picked through the drawers. There were three. I opened each one in turn, the first being empty apart from a pencil, the second holding some paper with narrow, neat handwriting traced across it, and the third...the contents of the third caught my breath.

Photographs. Bound together in a thick wad by a double elastic band. Photograph after photograph of men – prisoners of war - being tortured, black and white images almost faded with age and damp. The top ones were stuck together in clumps, others, covered with a film of white powder. They were rotting away, this record of what had happened. We had only just discovered them in time. A few more years and there would be nothing left but a pile of crumbling, faded paper.

Near the bottom of the pile, the photographs were in better condition. I could see faces, bodies. Men being held down, syringes, electric cattle-prods. Men in white coats. Officers, soldiers.

I stopped, holding one of the photographs closer to my face as I shone my torch upon the surface. It was of a man, a prisoner, being held down by some soldiers whilst an officer...

Breathing hard, Aunty Peggy came in at a rush. "We've got names, Max. Names of the men who served here. And guess what. You won't believe it."

"It gives Remy St-Claire's name?"

"Yes. Standartenfuhrer Paul Heinlein, Commandant."

I held up the photograph I'd found. Aunty Peggy shone her light onto it. "And this," I said through gritted teeth, "clinches it."

She quickly crossed the room and snatched the picture out of my hand. As she looked, she began to smile.

"We have him," she said, slapping the photograph down on the desktop. I looked down at it once more, just to confirm that what I saw was real. It was Remy St-Claire, in the act of slicing through the jugular vein of one of his victims, his face turned towards the cameras, grinning like the fiend that he was. He must have been so certain that no one would ever find out, that he was safe and secure, the truth of his wicked deeds remaining hidden forever. The arrogance of the man was breath-taking.

But not now. Justice had at last caught up with him and his world was about to come tumbling down.

"We have him," I echoed.

We returned the way we came. For a moment, we considered carrying on down the tunnel, traveling on until we found its alternative entrance. But it was late and we had been gone for a long time. The hours had shot passed and soon it would be almost time to get up. I had a handful of photographs and Aunty Peggy had a pile of folders. It was a start, enough to force the authorities to begin a proper investigation. This time there would be nothing Remy St-Claire could do about it.

It was raining when we stepped back into the courtyard, next to Stan's workroom. There were no lights burning but we switched off our torches nevertheless. If anyone was watching, we didn't want them noticing too much. Pulling up my collar, I began to move over towards my house, Aunty Peggy close behind, no doubt grateful for her coat.

The lights came on then. Not from the houses, not from street lamps, but from the two cars that were parked ahead of us, pointing towards us, full beams glaring through the night, picking out the streaking drizzle as if it were slivers of silver.

I brought up my arm to block out the glare. Then Aunty Peggy screamed and I realized, too late, that there were people there. Men, big, burly men, manhandling her towards the nearest car.

A face I knew only too well loomed out from the blackness. Remy St-Claire. "You couldn't leave it, could you? You had to carry on."

"You killed John." I tried to sound tough. I wasn't feeling tough. He must have known it, because he grinned.

"Prove that, can you?"

"Not yet. But I will. I've got enough evidence to see you deported and hanged."

"You've learned a lot, Max. Deported? That's a new one. Where to, pray tell?"

"Israel. They'll try you there, find you guilty, and hang you for what you did."

"My, my, we are quite the little super-action hero, aren't we. Quite the little detective." He snapped his fingers, though I doubt that in that rain anyone would have heard him. But they would have seen the gesture and two men came out of the gloom, one of them grabbing me by the arm whilst the other snatched the

240

photographs and passed them over to St-Claire. Still smiling, he slipped them inside his coat and motioned with his head, "Put him in the car. It's time we ended all of this, Max. Once and for all."

FORTY-NINE

The rain was relentless, coming down like a single sheet, making driving at speed virtually impossible. I was sitting in the back with the large men either side of me. Another man was driving and St-Claire was next to him. The full beam was on, but it merely bounced back against the windshield, reflected by the torrential downpour that drummed upon the roof of the car like a forty piece percussion band.

Aunty Peggy was close behind in the second car. She must have been in a similar position to me. Terrified. I had no idea what was going to happen to either of us, but one thing I did know and that was whatever St-Claire had planned for us it was not going to be pleasant.

The car sluiced around a corner. It was going fast, too fast, and I could feel the tyres losing their grip. Suddenly, we were in an uncontrollable skid. I cowered back in my seat. St-Claire was screaming orders to the driver, but it was useless because all control was gone and we were in a sort of wild twirl, like a mad dance, around and around, the headlights picking up Aunty Peggy's car every time we swirled passed.

Abruptly, we came to a halt. The driver was gasping for breath. "I don't know what happened!" he yelled, but St-Claire was having none of it.

"You idiot!" You could have had us killed! Do you know how close to the edge we are?" He snapped his head around, "Go and tell Mumford that we have to go slower. This road is a death trap."

The big goon on my right grunted and opened the door and stepped out. He gave a sudden squeal of fear as he pitched out into open space. For one horrible moment he tried to grab onto the handle of the door, to prevent the inevitable, but he was already falling out into the night. The car had come to a halt right on the very lip of the track and there was nothing to our right except an abyss. I leaned over, peering down, and I caught a glimpse of a swiftly receding white face, eyes wide in terror, mouth gaping open in a soundless scream. His arms flapped helplessly as the night swallowed him whole.

He was gone. St-Claire was right, the road *was* dangerous. The sheer drop ended amongst the jagged rocks far below. I had images of Mitchell, the policeman, and his broken body being taken out to sea. I squeezed my eyes shut. It was happening again.

I reached over and tugged the door closed.

"Nobody move," hissed St-Claire, not giving a moment's thought for the poor man who had fallen to his death. He very carefully opened his own door and stepped out into the rain.

I strained around to watch him running back towards the other car. As I did so I caught the look on the other goon's face. He was white with terror. "Let me go," I said quietly, "before something else happens."

"What are you talking about?" It was the driver, looking back at me from the front seat.

"This wasn't something that just happened," I explained, "It was planned! You've got to let me go, then get yourselves out of here as quickly as you can. Before it's too late."

"So you can run off to the police?"

"No. So you can continue with the rest of your lives."

He chuckled to himself, dismissing me for some foolish little child who didn't have a clue about anything, and turned back to look through the windscreen. His voice suddenly cracked as he yelped, "Oh my God..."

Stretching over the front seat, I looked out into the night and I saw it too. A great swirling vortex, twisting around and around, sweeping up everything in its path, its ferocity and power terrifying. And, it was coming straight towards us.

As I looked, transfixed, I noticed something else. Within the spiral, I could see faces. Strangely elongated, stretched impossibly thin, mouths opening and closing, wailing incessantly. It was this macabre chant that was creating the dreadful noise all around us, not the storm at all. it was the song of those who had been tortured and murdered. The lament of their still-suffering souls. And all the while it was growing in intensity as it crept relentlessly towards us.

I clambered out, over the big man next to me who was frozen in terror, and managed to scramble out into the open. Without pausing I ran, head down, pumping my arms, battling to get distance between myself and the car. It was incredibly difficult; I could feel myself being sucked backwards, dragged towards the maelstrom that was bearing down upon the hapless men still sat inside the vehicle I had just left. I stumbled and fell, and took the chance to bury my face into the earth as the scream of the vortex grew in volume. It was almost upon me.

A hand was on my shoulder, pulling me to my feet. I had no choice but to allow myself to be dragged away, and I looked back for a moment to see the car being lifted up by the swirling storm as if it were a mere toy. The vehicle disappeared, swallowed up by the thousand screaming faces that now enveloped it. And coming from deep within the violent rage, I could distinctly hear the screams of the two men, pitiful and terrible, as they, along with everything else, were consumed by the whirlwind.

It stopped suddenly then, as abruptly as it had begun and I found myself sitting on the wet earth, St-Claire beside me, his breath ragged and laboured. The rain had ceased and a curious calm settled over us. There was no evidence that the car had ever existed; where it had stood there was now only the damp ground. All was still.

St-Claire climbed to his feet and looked back towards the other, remaining vehicle. Mumford and the driver were getting out, both of them shaken, faces ashen. I watched them approach, like drunken men, their legs barely able to support them any longer. And beyond them, in the back seat, I could just make out Aunty Peggy. She must have seen what had happened. Would she have an answer, I wondered. An explanation?

As I stared, the ground beneath the remaining vehicle suddenly split open, pulled apart, torn in two as if it were nothing more than thin, tissue paper, and the car disappeared into the abyss within the blink of an eye. A startled face pressed against the side window, an open mouth, nails clawing at the glass. Too late Peggy realized it was hopeless and for a brief moment our eyes locked onto each other. Her fear glared out at me, her despair, her disbelief. I made to run forward, to try and do something, anything. But it was useless. Aunty Peggy and the car slipped beneath the crumbling earth and rock, swallowed up. Consumed. A great groan followed as the gash closed up, rock grinding across rock, and I stood and looked and felt the anger and sadness welling up from deep within me. I lifted up my head and screamed as loud as I could.

I was in the open, my face in my hands, rain water dripping from the overhanging branches of the tree under which I was sheltering, the water trickling steadily down the back of my neck. But I was beyond caring and I barely felt it.

Aunty Peggy. I could still her face, those eyes of hers...God, that image had burned itself into my very soul. What was I supposed to do now, without the one person who could have helped me make sense of everything, who had the strength, the knowledge to see it through to the bitter end?

Mumford stood over me. I knew it was him, his stupid little feet, like a small boy's, coming into my line of vision. I didn't look up.

"The car's at the bottom."

"What?" I craned my neck to look at him, his face all blurred through my tears. "What car?"

"The one your aunty was in. It's at the bottom of the hill. Except..." he looked around, ran a hand across his eyes, shivered. "I don't know what's going on. Things have happened that I can't explain, don't really believe...But, the car is there and it's perfectly fine. It starts. Everything. It's just...*insane.*"

"And Aunty Peggy? Did you find her?"

"No."

The single word hit me like a fist full in the face. I winced and sat up. "Nothing? Not a sign?"

"Not a sign."

St-Claire breezed over, his mouth set in a cruel, thin line. "We're going," he snapped, and picked me up by the collar. His face was very close to mine. "Your auntie's gone walkabout. But no matter, she'll turn up. Now, in the car."

FIFTY

Mumford drove the car, tight-lipped. In the back, I sat huddled up with St-Claire next to me. He was gazing out into the night, eyes narrow, all of his attention on the rain that had begun again, no doubt trying to come to terms with what we had all seen. The shock had been immense, but there was something inside me, a tiny glimmer, like a guiding beacon telling me that there was a hope, a chance that justice would still prevail. I had nothing to confirm it, but I felt assured that Aunty Peggy was all right.

After an age, with the car rumbling through the night, St-Claire shuffled around and I could see the whites of his eyes blazing bright. "I won't try and understand any of this," he began. "I know it all hinges on you. You have some power, some method to conjure up these…*demons*…and for now I'm content to return you to your home. For a guarantee, I'll be keeping your mother with me.'

I sat back, blowing out my breath, not able to put up much of a fight. There wasn't a lot I could do anyway. I wasn't about to try and convince St-Claire that in actual fact none of those so-called demons had anything to do with me. I had no power over anything. But if he knew that, then perhaps he wouldn't be willing to let me go. By so doing, he was giving me that chance, however slender. At that moment, I didn't know how much of a chance. If I had, I probably would have jumped up and down with glee.

The sound of the rain beating against the walls and the windows was deafening. I don't think I'd ever experienced rain like it for sheer intensity. I was sitting in the kitchen, still trembling over what had happened.

Dad was pouring me a cup of tea, seemingly unconcerned about my mother not being there.

"That'll do you good," he said, setting the steaming cup down in front of me. I'd told him what had happened, as best I could, and he'd listened, stony-faced. He didn't register any emotion, just clicked his tongue now and again, muttering, "She'll be all right, I'm sure of it." I wasn't sure whether he meant Aunty Peggy or Mum. When I told him what St-Claire had said, that he was going to hold Mum as hostage, there was nothing. No reaction, not even a blink. It was almost as if he knew, that he had half-expected it. It was all very strange.

Streaks of ash-grey dawn were beginning to smudge across the sky. The rain was still coming down, dampening my mood still further. I was looking at it through the window, having turned around, not daring to speak any more, wondering what the day would bring, when the telephone rang. Dad answered it quickly, not in the least bit surprised.

"Good," he said simply after a few seconds, and replaced the receiver very carefully on its cradle. He was chewing his lip when he turned to me. "Max. I think it's about time I told you some things." He sat down opposite me, twirling his teacup around and around, almost as if he were trying to hypnotise himself with the motion. "Okay. Remember those paintings I found? Down in the cellar, the ones I sold to an art dealer in London?"

"Aren't you worried about Peggy, or Mum, or any of them? Dad, I've just seen Aunty Peggy fall into—"

"Just one thing at a time, eh? You said Aunty Peggy was all right. So, let's not worry too much, okay? She's a game old bird and I know she can handle herself in a scrap. So...The paintings, the ones I found?"

I looked at the table top, averting my eyes, keeping my voice flat. "I remember the paintings, but I didn't know you'd sold them."

"Oh. Well, I did. And it's given me a lot...sorry, given *us* a lot of money. So much that I don't have to carry on working. It was like I said. It's actually happened. I'm going to retire, Max. Give up my job. Start again." He ran a hand through his hair, ignoring my startled, gaping expression. I couldn't believe what he was telling me, but I couldn't find any words to stop him I was so astonished. "The thing is...I don't know how to say this...Look, I'll just come out with it, okay? Then, when I'm done, you can ask me what you like. Your mum – hell, Max, she's *not* your mum! You know that anyway. But there's always been a tension, something not quite right. She's always had a hold over me, Max. I don't know whether you sensed it, or knew it, or what. Christy did, more than you, I think. Christy's never really got on well with...Penny...Oh god..." he picked up his teacup and stared into it before he finished off the contents in one swallow. "The thing is, things haven't been too good, even before we came here. I've suspected...I *believed* she was seeing someone else. She denied it, of course, but since coming here, well I've become convinced...She's not the woman I married. Perhaps she never was..." He suddenly stood up and went over to the window. The rain still beat down very loudly. I had to strain to hear his voice, now that he had his back to me. Perhaps he found it easier to talk like that, not having to look at my face, catch my stupefied expression. "Simply put, Max, we're splitting up. Now I've got the means, I'll give her a cash settlement, we'll go our separate ways, divorce eventually." He shrugged. "It's a bit of a mess, but I think it's for the best. She doesn't love me, I know that. She never really has. I was a means to an end, a meal-ticket as the Americans say. Whoever this other guy is…well, he's the one she wants, not me. Anyway…" He turned around and forced a grim smile. His eyes were wet. I didn't know what to do or say. Was I supposed to stand up and go over to him, give him a hug? Were there any words that would help him, comfort him? And if there were, what were they? I had no idea. So I just sat there, feeling awkward and totally useless. Funnily enough, I didn't feel in the least bit upset. And it had nothing to do with the fact that Mum had wanted to harm me that time, right here in the kitchen…No, it wasn't that. It was the fact that she wasn't my real mum, never had been, never would be. My mum was dead. No one could ever replace her.

"…interestingly, when they said that, I wasn't shocked. I think that I already knew."

I panicked. Dad had been talking, but my thoughts had been elsewhere. I looked and shook my head. "Said what? Who?"

"Haven't you been listening?" He was angry, but only for an instant. It soon passed. "All right, I know this has been a shock. I should have told you, given you some clue…Christy knows. I spoke to her, on the 'phone. I'm sorry. She took it well, half expected it I think. But the way things have been here, I didn't want to heap more pressure on you. So I held back. It hasn't been an easy decision, Max. And what with everything that's been going on…But when they caught up with me at the airport, it all sort of fell into place."

"Who, Dad? Who caught up with you? What are you talking about?"

"The Mossad, Max. They'd been keeping us under surveillance for weeks."

"The Mossad? Who the devil are they?"

He came over to me and placed a hand on my shoulder. It felt very heavy. "Israeli Secret Service," he said as if it was the most natural thing in the world to say, a little like, 'would you like jam on your toast?' I just gawped at him. He nodded grimly. "They went with me all the way to the gallery. Said they wanted to make sure I got there safely. Then they escorted me back here. They want to talk to you, Max." He motioned with his chin towards the 'phone. "That was them. They'll be here in about five minutes."

He seemed pleasant enough, the one who called himself Rami. Young, very fit-looking, nice even tan. He could have been a footballer, or a middleweight boxer perhaps. But very softly spoken, polite, patient, not overbearing or arrogant. Not judgemental at all. And I disliked him intensely.

There was a menace about him. Although he smiled a lot and his voice was smooth and kind, I could see in his eyes a latent viciousness, like a wild cat, coiled, ready to strike. One moment quiet, the next...

He pressed me about the things that had happened, the unexplained, the incredulous. Not once did he interrupt, he simply sat, watching me, no emotion, just a quiet acceptance. When I finally stopped talking, he sat back and seemed to be lost in thought. Then, with a sudden flurry, he jumped to his feet, smiled and then went out, pausing only to beckon to Dad to follow him.

The other man had remained silent throughout, arms folded, standing in the corner, brooding almost, a little disturbing. But now he too went and I was alone.

What these men wanted or what they planned to do I simply had no idea. There had been no clue in anything that had been said, or in their manner, nothing. All-in-all I felt crushed. I'd had a hope that these men would bring instant closure to the whole sorry mess. They were, after all, the secret service.

The secret service! That was a laugh. A joke. But an ironic one, given how many secrets there were in that place.

I wasn't finding it easy to smile.

FIFTY-ONE

I awoke with a start as a sudden, violent gust of wind threw the window open, sending it crashing back against the wall with a loud bang. The weather outside was foul, the storm had really set in now. I got out of bed and managed to push the window closed and stood there for a moment, catching my breath. My dreams had been filled with images of Alena, Peggy and, disturbingly, my mum. My real mum. With my mind in tatters it was obvious I was going to have disturbed sleep, but I hadn't dreamt of Mum for years. And now, here she was, coming into my thoughts. Not in a threatening way, but warm and tender. Comforting. Reassuring.

Something flashed across my eyes. I blinked, forcing my eyes to focus through the blur of wind and rain outside, but I couldn't see any details out there, it was all a swirling mess of lashing rain. I shook my head. A dog, perhaps.

The man from the Mossad, Rami, had questioned me relentlessly. He already knew a great deal, but the new information I gave seemed to send him into a kind of delirium. The other man, the bigger one, had followed my directions and gone down into the tunnels behind Stan's old workroom. He'd brought back another bundle of evidence, lifted from those filing cabinets. Now Rami's smile broadened ever-wider as he sifted through the photographs Aunty Peggy and I had uncovered. He was keen to be taken to the cellar himself and I promised him I would do so, the following day. He'd let me go and get ready for school then. A whole day of relentless lessons and jabbering teachers crawled by and when I came out of the gate, he was there. Together with his partner. It was going to be like this, he said, until St-Claire was 'brought to justice'. I noted he didn't say

253

'arrested', but I made no comment. To be honest, I couldn't care less. I just wanted it to end.

The lights were on over at Clari's. I made a mental note to go and call on her in the morning, walk to school with her despite the rain. We could share an umbrella, try and recapture some of the innocence and fun that we used to have before—

There it was again. A shape, black, bulky, rushing across my line of sight, then disappearing into the limit of my peripheral vision. Too quick to discern whether it was human or animal. My heartbeat began to quicken as I felt the first tiny tendrils of fear playing with my skin. I couldn't understand why I was feeling such a growing sense of alarm; perhaps it was my gift of extrasensory perception? I wasn't going to play around with any of this, so I abruptly closed the curtains and turned to go back to my lovely warm and cosy bed.

It stood there, its body towering upwards towards the ceiling, forcing it to stoop forward slightly, great head atop of bunched, bulging shoulders of raw power. The room was filled with its stench, a putrid vileness that was so thick and overwhelming that I gagged, spluttering into my hand as I staggered backwards, disbelief mixing with the massive fear that was taking me in its grip.

"My time...is short." Its voice was a great booming throb, filling the room with its rumbling resonance. It made me fall to my knees, mouth chattering, eyes streaming with tears. I was in hell itself. "Human," it continued, its voice neither threatening nor angry, just very, very terrible. "You have tried to violate me. And that...has vexed me." Its eyes, like putrid pools of green bile, bore into me. I was beginning to tremble uncontrollably. "Cease your meddling, or everything you know, everything you hold dear, will be...destroyed."

The door burst open and I couldn't believe what I saw. Not what. Who. Who I saw. Peggy.

Aunty Peggy!

She stood in the doorway, her hair being whipped around her face by a wind I hadn't even noticed, and she wore that same raincoat she always managed to pull on, tied tight at the waist. She strode into the room, raising up her hand in what I thought was some pathetic gesture aimed at forcing the hideous creature back to wherever it had sprung from. But I was wrong. In her hand was a small glass phial, which she now began to slowly unscrew. The creature gave an annoyed growl and turned its head in her direction.

"Foul, unwanted wretch!" It was Aunty Peggy who was shouting, not the creature. She began to throw the contents of the phial towards the monstrous being, "Begone!" The creature squealed as the water hits its flesh. She continued moving forward, every few words she spoke punctuated with another splash of the phial, "In the name of the Son...the Father...and the Holy Spirit I command you...Begone!"

The creature seemed to grow larger, impossible though that was, its great arms rearing upwards and outwards and it writhed in agony as the liquid seared through its thick, green-tinged skin. It screamed, twisted its body away, then began to fall back into the far corner where it began to dwindle and diminish in size, becoming smaller and smaller, until it was nothing more than a blackened, indistinct smudge on the floor. Then, it vanished completely.

Aunty Peggy was next to me before I could take another breath, lifting me up off my feet, hugging me long and hard.

I was trembling and the many questions I had were caught in my throat. I couldn't speak.

255

So I stood there, feeling the warmth of her, knowing that she was alive and well and that now everything was going to be all right again.

FIFTY-TWO

I spent almost two hours with Aunty Peggy. During that time she made me face up to some things. Why was I not prepared to accept what was happening, why did I resist, what was the point in refusing to accept the inevitability of what I had seen? She made me question my own questions and slowly she brought me round to a new idea, a new focus. I shouldn't resist any longer, I should simply let it all just happen.

It was a difficult lesson. But the revelations she had told me, about what I had seen, what was happening, they brought a new feeling of terror to my heart. This was something beyond anything I could have believed possible.

Later I went with Clari across the cliff tops and we followed one of the coastal paths that led down to the bay. It had finally stopped raining and the sun was trying desperately to show its face from behind the heavy clouds that still populated the leaden sky. We sat on the damp sand, which was a strange feeling. The sand, sea and sky were all grey. I felt so depressed I could have cried. But Clari forced me to smile. How could I not when sitting next to her? And in time I managed to laugh and soon the light brightened, blue crossed the sky and my mood began to slowly change.

A good day, filling me with a new determination. I was sick of being the victim, of letting things happen to me, things that were beyond my control. It was time to take the lead.

Of course, it was easy thinking these brave thoughts when I was sitting alone with Clari. She had that affect on me, made me feel good about myself, strong, brave. But later, when I was eating my tea, with my dad stirring his spoon around and around in his soup, the whole sorry business overwhelmed me and I felt sick to my stomach. I couldn't eat. It was silly to try. Dad seemed to understand and he remained silent as he gathered up the plates and dropped them into the sink with a great clatter.

"Where's Mum?"

It was the only thing I could think of to say. Anything, to break the silence.

"How should I know?" He stomped over to the fridge, suddenly angry, and pulled it open, stared inside for a moment, then slammed the door shut, pressing his forehead against the cold, white surface. "I thought I could do this," he muttered, "but I don't know what to do any more...I thought I'd be strong, put her out of my mind...but...now that she's gone, I feel so *alone*..."

A new, much more awful silence fell over us and all of a sudden Dad began to cry, very softly.

I decided to leave him alone and, as quietly as I could, I slipped out of the kitchen and made my way towards my room. On the way, I passed Aunty Peggy, sitting on her bed, deep in the pages of a book. She hadn't said much since she took me to one side and forced me to look deep within myself. I still had questions, especially about that thing that had come into my room, but I hadn't, as yet, drummed up the courage to ask her very much. I needed explanations and perhaps now was a good time, with the rest of my family seemingly breaking up all around me?

She looked up as I put my head around the door. She smiled. "Hello," she said. "How's Dad?"

I frowned. How did she know so much?

She shrugged, "I sense a lot, Max." She patted a space on the bed next to her, "Come and sit down and I'll try and make things a bit clearer."

"I was doing okay," I said quietly, "but Dad...he's taking things hard. Even he said so. Where is Mum, Aunty Peg?" I flopped down next to her.

She squeezed my knee. "Your Step-Mum is with someone else, Max. Dad pushed her, and she went. I suppose she was always going to go, but I'm not sure if he expected it to happen as quickly as it has." She slowly closed the book she had been reading. I glanced at the title and felt a jolt inside me, like a tiny electric shock. *Necromancy and the Art of Devil-Worship.* What sort of a book was that? She didn't notice my reaction, or if she did, she didn't say anything. "You were told that you were moving here for your Dad's job. That's right, isn't it?"

"Yes." I rubbed my face. A chill had settled between us. "I get the feeling you're going to tell me something I don't really want to know."

"Perhaps. But I think it's something you *should* know."

"I'll tell him."

We both looked up then. It was Dad, leaning against the door well, his eyes red-rimmed, face drawn.

"Are you sure?"

"I think I should. It's only right he hears it from me."

Aunty Peggy nodded and Dad came over and looked down at me. He seemed like a defeated man. The money, in the end, didn't really mean anything at all. "I got a transfer here, Max. I requested it. Not because I wanted a change of scene, or because of promotion...in actual fact, it was a *demotion.* Did me no end of harm, in career terms. Burned all my bridges, that's how the saying goes. My area manager thought I was a fool. And perhaps I was – perhaps I am. Well, whatever I am, I brought us all over here because..." He pulled in a shuddering breath, "Penny's boyfriend lives here, you

259

see. I made the decision to leave so she could be closer to him."

"You...but why would you do that?"

"To try and keep us together, as a family. I thought that if I gave her this chance to be with...*him*...she would somehow..." He squeezed his eyes shut. "Anyway, it's all gone wrong. But...at least I've got the money."

"But who is he, Dad? The man she's been...you know...carrying on with?"

He opened his eyes and they held my stare for a very long time before he finally said, "Remy St-Claire."

Peggy slapped down the photograph and jabbed at it with her finger. "See the eagle on his arm?" I nodded. "Sign of the SS. It's not the death's head, as so many think. That's for the *Totenkopf.* Heinlein wasn't with them. He was with *Das Reich.* Earned his Knight's Cross with them. But when he came here, after being wounded, he was no longer with any of those units. He'd been transferred. But not only that. He'd changed, become something far worse. Far more sinister. It has often been said that Himmler, head of the SS, was deeply involved in devil worship. Whether that is true or not, I'm not so sure, but certainly the excesses of the Nazi regime attracted men – and women – from the most depraved and rejected elements of society. Criminals, perverts, sadists. Amongst them, unfortunately, there were also those who practiced the dark arts. Heinlein was one such man."

"Dark arts? You mean... that book I saw you reading? Necromany. Devil worship. It sounds..."

"Far-fetched? Unbelievable? Unreal? Well, it probably is...but not for Heinlein. Not for those who have fallen under his spell. Heinlein had always delved in the black arts, always been deeply curious. Early in nineteen thirty-seven he had visited North Africa, on a diplomatic mission with the Italians. He visited Libya, Ethiopia, then travelled across to the Middle East and Persia. He became involved in some sort of secret society and it was whilst he was there that he became fascinated with ancient Mesopotamian texts. He studied them, immersed himself in their mythology. It was then that he came under the power of the creature you saw."

"Creature. But...If I understand all of this, what you're saying is, that the creature I saw was conjured up by *him*? Why? To do all of these terrible things? Murder all those people?"

"No. Those people weren't killed by that creature, or any other. They were murdered by other human beings. Heinlein already had a propensity for violence. But what he discovered in Persia only gave it more focus. More *reason*. You see, Heinlein was a Nazi through and through. He idolized Adolf Hitler, and everything he stood for. But he wanted far more than that. He wanted eternal life. And for that he was willing to give the ultimate sacrifice."

I frowned and shook my head, not at all clear what she was saying. I was becoming more confused. "Eternal life? But that's impossible. No one can live forever."

"You don't think so?" She stood up and walked over to the table that stood on the far side of the room. She picked up the heavy volume I had seen her reading before. She lifted it up as she spoke, "This book was written almost two hundred years ago. It is one of the most authentic and celebrated works about necromancy. The conjuring up of demons. The ancient Sumerians had a whole host of demons that they knew and worshipped and wrote about. This book is full of them." She opened it up and slowly came towards me. "Heinlein sold his soul to one of these demons. In return, he was granted eternal life – or as close as anyone can get. The demon will call in his debt one day, but not whilst there is the chance to feed upon the souls of the living. And Heinlein brought it plenty of fresh souls...and is still doing so."

"But you said Heinlein only discovered all of this when he went to the Middle East. That book was written two hundred years ago, Heinlein couldn't have written it."

"No. But then, I never said that he did." She turned the book around, opening it and I gazed upon an illustration of the author of the book. His features were the same as they were when I'd last laid eyes on him. "Now do you understand?"

I could hardly tear my eyes away from that face, but I managed a very slow and very subdued, "Yes. I understand completely."

FIFTY-THREE

We met at Samantha's house. Clari and me, Aunty Peggy, Samantha and Dad. We all huddled together in the lounge, around a large table that Samantha and Dad had dragged in from the dining room. We were in the lounge because Aunty Peggy said it was '*the most active*'. It was a cold night and the atmosphere in the room turned the air to ice. The steam trailed out of our mouths and noses. But no one seemed to mind. All eyes were on Peggy as she prepared herself for the beginning of the séance.

An expectant hush fell over every one of us. I kept my eyes on Aunty Peggy, who was sitting bolt upright, eyes closed, breathing heavily. She began to mumble incoherently and was gently rocking herself from side to side. I'd seen this before, years ago, when she'd first introduced me to the mysteries of contacting those who had crossed to the other side. Aunty Peggy and I had become close in our shared 'gift' and she had guided me in how to channel energies, concentrate my mind, focus on the things that most people missed or weren't even aware of.

But this wasn't quite the same.

Aunty Peggy was growing more and more agitated. I didn't like it, but I knew I shouldn't break the circle. We were all holding hands, leaning forward, the room dark, filled with the growing sound emanating from Peggy's throat. But it wasn't my auntie's voice. It had changed, becoming younger, more troubled.

Suddenly she slammed herself into her chair as if someone had violently yanked her backwards. Her eyes sprang open and she began to speak.

"It is dangerous here. So much has happened, so much is still...to happen...We have waited for you,

Max…waited so long…And now we can taste…" Peggy fell forward, but only for a moment. She pulled herself up again, and this time her eyes burned with a weird kind of luminosity, almost green. Verdant. "Max…" The voice was different. Low, deep and rumbling. The atmosphere was different. Menacing. Every one could feel it. I was holding onto Clari and Samantha and both of them squeezed my hands. "You play with me, Max. You and your friends…" Aunty Peggy arched her back and let out such a wail of sheer desperation it was as if she had been struck by something, causing her immense pain. *"Vile deceiver! Begone from this place!"*

She fell forward again, her head cracking against the tabletop and this time she remained still. We exchanged looks, none of us knowing what to do. Should we go to her aid, should we wait? All eyes were on me. I'd been here before, surely I knew what the procedure was? But I didn't. I'd never experienced a clairvoyant actually collapsing before. All I could offer was a shrug, looking suitably pathetic.

The room then began to take on a distinctly sickly yellow glow. It started to emanate in the far corner and gradually wound its way up the walls until almost the entire area was lit up as if it were on fire. But there were no flames, only a very distinct smell of sulphur. I'd come across this in school, during chemistry lessons. It was thick and strong and we all gagged, coughing hoarsely, clutching at our throats, breaking the circle, but not the sense of panic that was overtaking us.

It came up from the floor, a contorted, twisted shape, heavy and bulky, a writhing mass, bristling with sharp spikes that sprouted from its body. The head was bolted onto the shoulders, there being no neck. And its head was swathed in putrid, thick worm like coils that glistened with a thick covering of white drool.

The creature – the demon – had returned.

Dad reacted first, quickly getting to his feet and moving Peggy away from the table. Soon Samantha and Clari were stumbling out of the room, shrieking loudly, whilst I stood alone, facing the vile thing before me as it towered upwards, brushing the ceiling with the top of its head. It looked down at me, smiling that horrible smile.

"Max!" shouted Dad, as he reached the door, Samantha helping him take Aunty Peggy out into the hallway. "Come on, get away from it!"

I slowly shook my head. "I can't. It wants me, no one else."

It cackled then, a deep, throaty noise, a sound of total contempt. "Don't flatter yourself, human. Your destruction will allow me greater access to more nourishment, nothing more."

"Nourishment?" It was strange. I felt no fear of this thing anymore. Not now that I knew what it was. "Is that what you call it? The murder of innocent lives? To feed your insane lust for souls."

"You know nothing of me. Nothing. Do not think that because you have begun to understand a little about me that you *know* me. I am older than anything that lives upon this earth, older than life itself. I was here before the dawn of mankind and I shall still be here when that foolish race has gone. This is my domain and nothing you can do can defeat me."

"And yet you need St-Claire."

It suddenly let forth a roar of total anger, "I need no one, human!" it screamed. "He is but a pawn in my game. I can discard him without a thought."

"So why don't you."

It leaned forward, its virulent eyes focusing on me with such intensity that I felt it was looking into my very

265

soul. I felt gripped by its power, its pulsating evil coursing through my veins, entering into the very heart of my soul. I shuddered. Its lips curled back, "Perhaps I will...and replace him with a more worthy servant."

Without a pause, its arm snaked forward and its long, reptilian fingers touched me. A bolt of pain shot through me, as if I had been electrocuted, and I felt myself spiraling backwards, my limbs losing all feeling, all control. I whirled, like a drunken dancer, my arms desperately wafting around me, trying to stop myself from collapsing. But it was all swirling around in front my eyes, the room, the creature, and the voices. Voices from a long, long way away, yelling my name, desperate voices. Quiet voices. Blackness engulfing me now, all the fight and all the strength slipping away from me. I didn't care anymore. I just let myself be taken to wherever I was going to go.

FIFTY-FOUR

As my eyes grew more accustomed to my surroundings, I realized that I was back in the inner sanctum of St-Claire's perverted mind. I was lying on my back, on the cold, hard metal of the gigantic SS runes that dominated the massive room. I sat up and looked around. The candles burned in their stands, but that was the only light. And, I was alone. I wondered about this, becoming more and more concerned about what it was that was being planned for me. The creature had sent me into unconsciousness with a mere flick of its fingertips. No doubt, it had then transported me to this place. But what of everyone else? I rubbed my face and went to stand up. But that was as far as I got. My legs were manacled to the slab of metal that I had been placed on.

I let out an exasperated cry and fell back, staring up at the immense, vaulted ceiling. It reminded me of those great, incredible medieval cathedrals that Dad had taken me to see just before we moved from England. York Minster, Salisbury, Canterbury. But whereas those awesome, magnificent building were a celebration of God, this was something dark and sinister. A gross travesty. The stones of this edifice had not been hewn with love and devotion, but with hatred and subjugation. It was a mockery, intended as such, and I turned my face away in disgust.

The great entrance door whispered open and I heard the steady tread of feet descending the stone steps. Craning my neck, I saw him coming towards me with deliberate slowness.

He stood, feet straddled wide, torso bare, bathed with a film of sweat that glistened on his chest and down his arms. His lips were pulled back and he glowered at me. He had become a thing possessed, an evil entity lost to a world of darkness and despair.

Remy St-Claire.

Without further ado, he reached over, revealing a large, old key and he unlocked the chains and pulled them away. They clattered onto the ground, the sound ringing throughout the cavernous room, like a death knell. I sat up, rubbing my ankles, and glared at his face.

"So, Max. Little Max. How far you've come in your quest for the truth." He circled past me, his eyes never leaving mine and I could see the maniacal glint simmering within them. "Does it please you that you have learned so much?"

"Nothing pleases me, not now."

"Nothing? Can that really be true? What about Clari, your father, your precious aunt Peggy?" He laughed. "They will all soon be in my power. Oh yes, didn't you know? Whilst you lie here, they are being held by my will, dear, dear Max, in a state of limbo. They cannot escape, not without my command. Your tragedy is that you thoroughly underestimated me. You thought that by revealing my past you could somehow...what were those words of yours? Oh yes, *bring me to justice.*" He shook his head. "Pathetic. I am under the protection of a power so immense, so infinitesimal that there is nothing, *nothing in this world* that can harm me."

"You murdered all those people. No matter how much you try, no matter what you do, you won't escape."

"As I said. *Pathetic.* You still play the great crusader, don't you? What makes you think that you can possibly overcome me? Your friends in the newspapers, your agents from Mossad?" He caught my gasp of surprise. "Oh dear, didn't you know? Are you so naive? But then, yes, I suppose you are. You never really have had any understanding of my resourcefulness. In a way, your death will bring me only a tiny amount of satisfaction. You are nothing to me. As insignificant as an insect. And I will crush you with as much thought as I would give an ant under my foot."

Raising up his head he bellowed loud the name of the monster he had summoned.

Instantly the flames that had previously been gently flickering from the candles, erupted into a violent spurt of fire, the ground shook, and from within the centre of the pentagram that had been drawn upon the ground, a swirling, spiralling plume of smoke writhed upwards. Within it could be seen a gyrating figure, small at first, but gradually growing until it became more pronounced, its shape more defined.

St-Claire was laughing, beside himself with glee. The thing blossomed into its true size and its great, verdant eyes blazed down at me with such deep loathing that I had to look away, fearful that its gaze alone would destroy me.

I knew then that my moments on this earth were numbered.

St-Claire, who had stepped aside whilst the creature had materialised, now came forward again. He had become a fawning, grovelling wretch in the presence of this thing and whereas I lay rooted to the spot, barely able to breathe, he sort-of skipped around the beast, bobbing his head, wringing his hands constantly. "Oh, my master," he gibbered, "this is he. The one who has brought us so much pain, so much torment."

"The pain shall now be his," the thing grumbled, its voice bubbling deep from within its throat.

It took a step towards me. As its foot stomped down on the ground, the whole room shuddered with the sheer power it. I shied away, instinctively bringing up my arms in a pathetic attempt to ward off any blow it might have delivered.

But no blow came.

A stillness settled over us all. A strange, almost peaceful quiet. The atmosphere had changed discernibly.

I dared to peek over my arm. The creature had stopped, its great head swivelling around to a point behind my left shoulder. St-Claire too was looking in that direction. But he too had changed. From fawning, to terrified and all within a single instant. He took unsteady steps backwards, mouth hanging open, muttering incoherently, his arms now coming up to shield himself from whatever it was that had loomed up behind me.

I rolled over, bringing my feet to the ground and stood up.

It was Alena.

But she wasn't alone.

Behind her was amassed an army of poor, pitiless souls, the victims of St-Claire's excesses. There were so many of them; hundreds perhaps. They began to move forward as one.

"Get away Max," came Alena's voice, as crystal clear as a bright and beautiful morning in summer. Clean, without threat. But immensely powerful. I could sense it and without pausing, I ran over to the far side and watched, horror-struck, as the horde of victims suddenly charged forward, their voices raised in a clarion of anger and hate. They closed with the creature, swarming over it like an army of ants would assault a stricken animal that had wandered into their path. It bellowed and lashed out, its mighty arms thrashing around, trying to swipe away the many attackers that now assailed it. But it was engulfed by their sheer number and it fell back, its great mouth gaping open, screaming as that great writhing mass of humanity, black and twisting, began to rip out great hunks from the creature's living flesh. Gouts of green, virulent blood gushed out from its many wounds and as it battled in vain, I could see its strength ebbing away as its assailants overcame it completely.

Alena came forward, holding in her hands a small, plain looking earthen pot. She waited, until the battle was over. Then she strode through her fellow-prisoners, stooping down to find the piece of the creature that she sought. She held it up, like a trophy, raising it towards the ceiling and on her face was the sweet look of victory. She held its heart, shredded yet still recognisable, and then she dropped it, without ceremony, into the earthenware pot and closed the lid. She turned around and I saw her smile.

"Our time is at an end, Max. Go, do what you must. Serve justice in your world, as we have in ours."

And then, as if none of it had ever happened, I was standing alone in that dreadful place. The candles still flickered and the vaulted ceiling still hung like a gaping cavern above my head, but the malignancy had gone. This was nothing but an empty room now. The giant SS runes lay where they always had, but were now nothing more than a terrible memento of a heinous and hideous regime.

Alone.

It hit me like a punch in the stomach.

I was alone – and St-Claire had fled for his very life!

FIFTY-FIVE

Running, like something possessed, out into the street and on, down the road, never stopping, running all the way.

I had no idea which way to go, all I knew was I had to try and get back to the hospital. Something was telling me, something detached, something distant, telling me to go there. To find them. All of them. I didn't question. I just kept running.

The hills took their toll. I've never been a good runner, even when I was younger. I just didn't have the physical make-up I suppose. Too many chocolate bars, too much lemonade. Whatever, I found the going becoming too much and my breath was growing increasingly difficult to control. Also the stitch in my side was like a knife twisting through my flesh and I had to stop, stumbling forward, bent double, barely able to put one foot in front of the other. But time was not on my side. I knew I had to get there, that every second was precious.

Sweat dripped into my eyes and I fell onto my knees. Cursing everything, everything that lived in this world, I just sat there, doubled-up, pulling in the air, wincing at the pain in my side, knowing I had to go on but no longer with any strength to force myself onwards.

A car drew up alongside me. I knew who it was before I heard his voice. "Get in, you idiot!" Then his strong hands grabbed me and lifted me inside.

The car picked up speed as I flopped down in the back seat. Rami handed me a handkerchief and I dragged it over my face, soaking up the sweat.

"You didn't have to kill yourself," he said, already busying himself with the black gun in his hands. He was working through its mechanism, checking the bullets. "We've had you under surveillance the whole time. You should have waited."

"St-Claire," I managed to say with a huge effort. "Where...where is he?"

"We lost him." I gasped again, giving a little yelp of despair, "But don't worry – we've have Mumford under surveillance too. We suspect St-Claire will go to him. Make good their preparations."

"But...but the others. Dad, Clari—"

"Don't worry. It's all under control. You just sit there and get your breath back."

I didn't argue and I decided there and then that this advice was the best I'd had for a long time, so I laid my head back against the seat and closed my eyes. There was simply nothing else left to do.

The bounce of the car as it ploughed over the rutted track brought me back to consciousness with a jolt. I looked out through the side window. We were close to the airport, but the night was drawing in rapidly. Night flights were rare, except in emergencies. So, whatever the plan was, we didn't have much time to catch a plane.

Rami was staring at me, "Better?"

"A little. What are we doing here?"

"Mumford has a private plane. We're going to intercept it."

The car took a suicidal-like turn to the right, sliding through the mud, apparently out of control. I hung on, but my fears were ungrounded. The driver knew exactly what he was doing and already he had dipped the headlights and was bringing the vehicle to a halt.

Rami was opening the door, keeping low as he stepped out into the approaching night. He turned, his face white. "You keep close," then he was gone, disappearing into the gloom.

I didn't wait and soon I was doing what I do least well – running. Again!

We were in the open. Way over to the right I could see a few dotted lights of the airport buildings. The runway lights were out, the last flight having flown. I kept my eyes firmly fixed on Rami as he continued to jog forward. As we hit the tarmac I could hear it. A low, droning sound. Unmistakably, the sound of an aeroplane.

There were voices too. Voices raised in anger. As we got closer I could see who it was. Mumford, standing outside the plane, talking animatedly with another man, in uniform. Customs. It had to be.

The other car came across the grass then, bucketing over the uneven ground, its lights creating a weird dance-like effect in the darkness. It pulled up sharply and the door was pushed open. It was St-Claire, and he was not a happy man. Then I froze.

He pulled open the rear door and reached inside. When he stepped back, he was holding Clari tightly by the arm.

So, even now, at this twelfth hour, he was still looking for guarantees.

Rami must have felt I was about to cry out, because he quickly turned and clamped his hand over my mouth, using the gun like an index finger in his other hand, pressing it against his lips. *Keep quiet.*

I knelt down. We were out in the open, but because of the night, which was now complete, we could not be seen. However, the headlights from St-Claire's car picked out everything else. I watched as he dragged Clari towards the plane. Mumford gave a sort of little dance, perhaps in surprise, perhaps in anger, I couldn't tell. Reacting, the Customs officer turned, no doubt about to confront this new development in what he probably suspected was an illegal transaction of some sort, and St-Claire hit him. Hit him hard, across the throat, and the man keeled over instantly, hitting the ground with a dull thud. He didn't move again.

This gave Clari a chance and she pulled free. She began to run off and St-Claire turned, and I could see it, quite clearly, black and ugly looking.

In his hand was a pistol.

He brought it up, aiming it at the fleeing back of Clari. Guarantee or not, St-Claire was not about to let her live.

But neither was I about to let this happen! I'd seen too much death, whether from the past or from a distance. Too many people had lost their lives because of me and it had to stop. So I ran, head down, charging like a bull and I hit Clari in the midriff, knocking her over into the dirt with a near-perfect rugby tackle just as St-Claire's gun barked, the bullet shooting over our heads, missing us both by inches.

She was winded and frightened, but unharmed. Snarling I got up and saw St-Claire gesturing to Mumford to get into the plane. But then St-Claire stopped, his whole body going stiff and he dropped to his knees. I couldn't understand what had happened, but then Rami crossed my field of vision and I knew. He'd shot St-Claire, but the sound of the gun had been muffled by the roar of the aeroplane engines.

Rami ignored St-Claire and ran straight passed him as he sat there on his knees, looking perplexed, and grappled with Mumford, who was half-in, half-out of the cockpit. It was only a tiny, two or three seater and there wasn't much space but the Israeli had the advantage and had Mumford around the neck. With a great yank they both now fell back, hitting the earth hard.

Mumford was on top and Rami, although winded, tried desperately to get him into some sort of wrestling hold. I watched mesmerised as Mumford struggled free and got to his feet. He swung round, lashed out with his foot, and kicked Rami across the jaw with a sickening crack. Then he bent down to pick up something from the ground, just as the second Mossad agent came lumbering up, as big as a bear. But what Mumford had picked up was Rami's gun and he fired it again and again at the charging man, peppering him with bullets. The big Israeli bucked and jerked and his legs buckled under him and I knew he was dead even before his bulk smacked into the earth.

Standing there for a moment, breathing hard, Mumford now turned to St-Claire and began to help him to his feet. Rami's bullet must have only wounded St-Claire and now he was being helped towards the plane and freedom!

It was more than I could bear. Leaving Clari whimpering in the grass, I strode across the ground to where the two men were struggling over to the plane and began to try and climb over the wing. Rami was beginning to come round, but I wasn't really interested in that. I had my eyes fixed on one thing, and one thing alone.

St-Claire's gun.

I'd seen him drop it as Rami's bullet had hit him. And now my hand closed around its cold hardness and I brought it up, amazed at how heavy it was.

Mumford's face was turned to mine. He had his arm around St-Claire, who seemed to be in some sort of daze. The shock of being shot must have been immense and his body was like a dead weight. Mumford was

276

paused in the act of lifting his friend into the cockpit, and his teeth were clenched as he screamed above the aeroplane engine, "This isn't over, Max. We'll meet again. I promise you!"

Then he turned again with his burden and began to lift St-Claire further into the plane.

I strode forward, a blind fury urging me on, and I reached out a hand and grabbed St-Claire by the seat of his pants and pulled him backwards. There was no resistance from him and his almost lifeless body flopped down onto the wing and he rolled over into the ground below. Mumford roared with frustration and span round, the gun still in his hand. We stood there, the two of us, with our guns pointing at each other. If only Mumford knew that he now held all the cards. I'd never fired a gun in my life before, had no knowledge of what to do or how to do it. But I was bluffing it out and I must have been making a good go of it because Mumford didn't shoot. He just stood up there, with one foot in the cockpit, glaring down at me, with St-Claire at my feet, groaning incoherently.

It was a stand-off. Or so I hoped.

Mumford grinned then. "Go ahead, Max. Shoot. Because I'm getting out of here. Right now."

I wanted to, believe you me. I wanted to see my bullets hammering into his body, see him die the way the other Mossad man had died. I wanted that so much. I could see it in my mind's eye. And perhaps it was for that reason, more than my inability to fire the damned thing, that in the end I simply couldn't do it. I just didn't have the courage, let alone the ability. There was something stopping me. A belief, perhaps, that this wasn't the way it should end. That justice couldn't be served by the killing of someone with a gun. It had to be done properly, legally. Mumford had to be forced to go through that process himself. A bullet was too quick. Whatever it was that prevented me from squeezing that trigger, Mumford could see that I wasn't going to fire that gun. And he was smiling, smiling in triumph. Because he had no such qualms. Nothing in his physiology was going to prevent him from killing me. So he aimed his gun unerringly and squeezed the trigger.

We both gasped when nothing happened.

His gun was empty. It must have been.

In disgust, he hurled the weapon at me but I easily ducked out of the way and watched him as he slithered into the cockpit not waiting any longer. St-Claire lying next to me, was forgotten. Mumford's only thought now was for his own survival.

In the distance I could hear the faint whine of a police siren but I didn't turn to watch them approach. My eyes were locked on Mumford as he began to taxi the little aeroplane out onto the tarmac. For one insane moment I had the fanciful idea that I could chase after him, leap up onto the wing and rip open the cockpit and pull him out. But I knew this could never happen. I'd watched too many films. And they'd all involved a hero. I was not a hero. I knew it, and Mumford knew it, and as he turned the plane around to begin his takeoff, the headlights from St-Claire's car picked him out, sitting there, looking at me. Then he did something which will be forever seared into my brain. He raised his thumb.

I spat my disgust and watched as the plane accelerated out across the runway, gathering speed along the way, its tailgate rapidly diminishing into the night. Then it was gone, lifting up into the black and starless sky, the drone of its engine swiftly decreasing as it banked away to the left towards France and freedom.

FIFTY-SIX

Rami was on his feet, bent double, holding his face, obviously in considerable distress. He looked up at me, held up his hand. The gun. I went over to him, as if in a dream, and handed it over, just as the two police cars came into view, lights flashing, sirens blaring. As they came to a halt and doors were opened, the runway lights came on, illuminating everything as if we were on centre stage at some major music festival.

It was all too late, of course. Mumford had gone.

St-Claire had got to his feet and already Rami had him by the arm. The first policeman was at my shoulder.

"We'll need statements," he said unnecessarily.

I turned around and saw, to my immense relief, Samantha embracing Clari, and Dad with Aunty Peggy, coming towards me. Perhaps there was some good to come out of all of this after all.

Over the course of the next few days I learned quite a few things about St-Claire and his web of intrigue. He had effectively tied up most of the island, controlling every facet of life there. Not many were unaffected by him. Or, should I say, the ancient demon that he had been in league with. Of course, I didn't mention any of that to the police. They would probably have packed me off to a lunatic asylum if I had! But there was no need. Peggy and I had all the evidence. Photographs, official documents, records. There was just too much. St-Claire, or Paul Heinlein as he was now being called once again, had nowhere left to go. His world, like the demon that had controlled him, had crumbled into dust.

But that wasn't the end of it.

And I should have realized. But stupidly, very stupidly, I believed that it was all over.

I remember the night we all sat round the dining table. Dad had really gone to town and had produced a fantastic meal for us all. Samantha was most impressed and couldn't help smiling throughout the entire feast. Clari and I, sitting opposite each other, exchanged knowing glances. Her mum and my dad. It was all too embarrassing, and I tried my best not to dwell on the thought for too long!

Aunty Peggy, bless her, took her food in her room. She seemed pensive, troubled by something that she wouldn't explain. Anyway, whatever the reason, she left us to enjoy ourselves. And we did. Until the front door burst open.

I'd forgotten she'd had a key.

We all looked up as Mum came through the dining room door. She stood there, hair in a wild mess, eyes bulging, mouth hanging open, looking as she had looked that terrible day when she'd threatened me with the knife.

Dad stood up. He was closest to her and was putting his hand up, preparing to say something, when she just charged him and swatted him with the back of her hand. It was a blow of such force that he was hurled backwards, his feet actually leaving the ground, sending him across the perfectly laid-out table in a maelstrom of crockery, glass and cutlery.

Samantha screamed and went to him, ignoring the mess, taking up his head in her hands.

He was completely unconscious.

I stood up, placing myself in front of Clari in a pathetic attempt to protect her.

"Do you know what you've done," my step-mum hissed, her hands clenching and unclenching as she wrestled to control her rage. "Have you any idea?"

"You're mad," I said. Not the best thing to have said at a moment like that, but I couldn't think of anything else.

She screamed then, like a wild animal, took me by the lapels and threw me across the room as though I was nothing more than an old rag-doll.

I hit the far corner at speed, my shoulder taking the full brunt of the collision as I smashed against the wall. I yelped in pain and curled up, eyes squeezed shut, knowing that something very bad had happened to my arm.

The pain was immense. I'd never known anything like it. Then the feeling of nausea came over me like a huge wave and I knew I was going to be sick.

But I didn't have time. She was on me, that mad harridan, pulling me to my feet, pressing her face close to mine. Suddenly the pain and the sickness were forgotten. She had me by the throat and she was squeezing hard.

"They've taken him! That slime of a friend of yours. Tonight. I could have had a chance, we had plans. *Plans!* But he took him. Broke into the jail, took him out. Took him away." He pulled me closer, so close I could see the coffee stains on her teeth. "Kidnapped. A man like that. Taken to Israel. Jerusalem." She closed her eyes and the tears began to come then, rolling down her face. "*Jerusalem!* " He shook me. "They're going to try him, execute him! And it was you – you who has done this! If you hadn't meddled in things that were of no concern to you, we'd still be together. But you had to be the self-righteous one, the one with a purpose, the one with the sense of justice." She smiled. A terrible, snarl like flash of teeth. "Well, now it's my turn for justice!"

She slammed me hard against the wall, still with her left hand gripped tightly around my throat. I could feel myself growing faint as it became almost impossible to take even the slightest breath. She was strangling me and as I grabbed uselessly at her wrist, her other arm came up. She held a knife. Its blade was long and thin and deadly. I closed my eyes, nothing going through my head, no time to panic or think or pray. Nothing.

I heard the smash, like a thunder clap and my eyes sprang open as her grip was released and I slid down the wall to the floor.

Great shards of glass were everywhere.

My step-mother was reeling around the room, fingers clawing at her head, the blood gushing out from between them. Clari was screaming and Samantha was standing there, the remnants of the huge, heavy, lead-crystal fruit bowl that she had used to bring down over my step-mum's head with such devastating effect, still in her hands.

Aunty Peggy flew into the room then and instantly took in the entire situation. She put her palm into my step-mum's chest and pushed her back against the wall, only feet away from me. They locked eyes and Aunty Peggy began to utter some weird, unrecognisable chant.

The language was obscure, like nothing I had ever heard. But whatever it was, it seemed to have the desired effect, because suddenly my step-mum was going limp and she crumpled to the floor and remained still, her eyes staring sightlessly into nothing.

I was forgotten for the moment as Aunty Peggy went over to Dad. But he was all right and was already coming round as she lifted him up to a sitting position. Next to them, Samantha was comforting Clari, both of them sitting down next to the wreckage that had been our celebratory meal. It was as if the room had been hit by a bomb.

Turning to look at me, Aunty Peggy forced a smile. "We're going to need an ambulance."

I nodded, the pain in my arm was returning and I was unable to move it. It burned with an intensity that I had never experienced before. "Is it true?" I managed to ask.

"Is what true?"

"What she said?" I nodded at the lifeless body of my step-mother. "About St-Claire being taken off to Israel?"

Aunty Peggy closed her eyes and for a moment I thought she had drifted off into unconsciousness. But she hadn't. She was merely looking into things that no one else could see. "Yes. I have images. Vague images. But what she said is true. That man, that Rami person, he took St-Claire. There was a boat waiting out in the bay, to take them to France. It was all planned, probably from the very beginning."

"But what will happen to him?"

"Do you care?"

I looked across at my step-mum. Did I care? Did I care about anything any more? I'd become anaesthetized to the whole sorry mess. I snapped my head around. "No. But I am curious."

"They'll hang him. Justice will be served. At long last."

"But it won't," I said quietly. Because I knew that it wasn't over. And never would be. Certainly not there, not then.

"What has happened here, Max, has been a huge cathartic event. A cleansing of all our souls. You have been the key to everything. Your gift, Max, meant that you could connect with the souls of the lost, the ones who had suffered and had gone unavenged. But all of that is over now. We've won – *you've* won."

283

"No, Aunty Peg. What about Mumford? What about him?"

She pulled in a breath. "Mumford is many things, Max. One of his many names is Ranulph Wrangel. The author of that book on necromancy, he has been alive for at least three hundred years, as far as I know, perhaps more. No earthly power can harm him, as long as he has the protection of the demon. He sold his soul, long ago and has served his master well."

I winced as I struggled to my feet. My arm throbbed constantly. "But...that thing. They killed it, Alena and all of those others. I saw it, I saw it torn to pieces."

"You saw one of them. There are others. They lurk in the darkest shadows, the untouched and unlooked for places in this world. And Wrangel, or Mumford, or whatever other name he wishes to use, is already speeding off to consort with them. We will meet with him again, Max. When, I cannot say, but we will meet, whether it be in my lifetime, or yours. But there will be a reckoning. Of that I am certain."

FIFTY-SEVEN

The years have gone by but the memories are still as vivid as they have always been. It is almost as if it all happened yesterday.

I'm older now, of course. But not much wiser. I always suspected that the day would come when I would confront Mumford, or Wrengal. And now, I feel it is all very close.

I've kept myself ready for this time. Studies and training of the mind. That is how I have passed the years. Everything in preparation. Despite the fact that I have moved on, lived a life, become reasonably successful in the real world, always it has stayed with me. Those words of Aunty Peggy's, *the darkest shadows, the untouched and unlooked for places in this world,* they have been my constant companion.

Aunty Peggy passed away some fifteen years ago. Dad, a year later. He never did find a piece of happiness with Samantha, or anyone else for that matter. He lived alone, with his books and his various hobbies. I often visited him. An empty man, with so much to tell, he never once talked about how dreadful his life had been. How unfulfilled. When he died I cried for days. And I still do.

Clari moved away with her mother a few months after the court hearings and I have never heard from her since. That was a dreadful time, those court sessions. Harrowing. We had to relive it all, but not tell it all. Who would believe us? Demonic possession, ghosts from the past? We'd all be certified. So we just told the essential facts. And, of course, it all matched up. The case was closed, if not solved. How could it be solved when really none of it had anything to do with the physical world?

St-Claire was hanged, for crimes against humanity. I read it in the newspapers. It barely received a mention, just a tiny little piece on page six. No photograph, no mention of the things he had done. But I knew. And, perhaps, that was all that mattered.

Thoughts of John Hedges often come to me. He did so much to bring all of what had happened out into the open. His great plan may have failed, but in the end a kind of justice had been served. At least, I hope it has. I've often thought that I'd like to go back to the island, if only to visit the graves of Stan and Aneeka. Perhaps stand a while and look out across the bay and silently remember the passing of so many. But I never have. Someone once said you should never go back. I think those are wise words. They should all be left in peace, those souls of the departed. But in the final analysis, it isn't going to be me who makes the decision. Perhaps something, as yet unknown, will draw me back.

Although thoughts of re-visiting the island is something that I would have liked to have shelved, the repercussions of what happened there are still very real and they play on my mind constantly. And now, with the years having tumbled by, I have learned that other things have happened there, that other lives have been blighted and are being blighted. The dark spectre has once again risen to cover everything with its vile, perverse malevolence.

I've sensed it, you see. I still have the gift. The choice, as I said, has been made for me.

And now, at last, the final confrontation is at hand.

THE END.

AUTHORS' NOTE:

Whilst this is a work of fiction the following characters mentioned were actual people:

Adolph Hitler, head of the German-Nazi state during the Second World War.

Heinrich Himmler, head of the S.S. and Gestapo.

Reinhard Heydrich, head of the state security service, the SD, and chief architect, together with Adolph Eichmann, of the 'Final Solution', the extermination of the Jews